D0057648

Praise for the novels of Barbara Freethy

Silent Run

"Hooked me from the start and kept me turning the pages through all the twists and turns. *Silent Run* is romantic suspense at its best." —JoAnn Ross

"Barbara Freethy writes romantic suspense that delivers on all counts—a terrific love story, and suspense that begins to build on the first page and doesn't let up until the last. I could not turn the pages fast enough." —Mariah Stewart

Played

"An exciting page-turner. . . . This top-notch author delivers top-notch thrills."
—*Romantic Times* (4½ stars)

"Reading this story was almost like going on one of those spooky rides as a kid: You expect something to happen, you think you know where it will occur, and then something jumps out at you from an unexpected area." —*Mystery News*

Taken

"Terrific and twisty intrigue makes this novel choice reading. . . . An amazingly gripping, fascinating mystery!" —*Romantic Times* (4½ stars)

"Another crowd-pleasing page-turner in the first of a tricky romantic suspense series."
—*Publishers Weekly*

"Romance sizzles between the wary protagonists in this riveting page-turner." —*Library Journal*

continued . . .

Summer Secrets

"Barbara Freethy writes with bright assurance, exploring the bonds of sisterhood and the excitement of blue-water sailing. *Summer Secrets* is a lovely novel."   —Luanne Rice

"Freethy skillfully keeps the reader on the hook, and her tantalizing and believable tale has it all—romance, adventure, and mystery."   —*Booklist* (starred review)

"An intriguing, multithreaded plot, this is an emotionally involving story . . . sure to please Freethy's growing fan base. . . . Like Kristin Hannah's novels, [it] neatly bridges the gap between romance and traditional women's fiction."   —*Library Journal*

Further praise for Barbara Freethy

"In the tradition of LaVyrle Spencer, gifted author Barbara Freethy creates an irresistible tale of family secrets, riveting adventure, and heart-touching romance."   —Susan Wiggs

"A fresh and exciting voice in women's romantic fiction."   —Susan Elizabeth Phillips

"Superlative."   —Debbie Macomber

"If there is one author who knows how to deliver vivid stories that tug on your emotions, it's Barbara Freethy."   —*Romantic Times*

Other Novels by Barbara Freethy

silent RUN

Barbara Freethy

AN ONYX BOOK

ONYX
Published by New American Library, a division of
Penguin Group (USA) Inc., 375 Hudson Street,
New York, New York 10014, USA
Penguin Group (Canada), 90 Eglinton Avenue East, Suite 700, Toronto,
Ontario M4P 2Y3, Canada (a division of Pearson Penguin Canada Inc.)
Penguin Books Ltd., 80 Strand, London WC2R 0RL, England
Penguin Ireland, 25 St. Stephen's Green, Dublin 2,
Ireland (a division of Penguin Books Ltd.)
Penguin Group (Australia), 250 Camberwell Road, Camberwell, Victoria
3124, Australia (a division of Pearson Australia Group Pty. Ltd.)
Penguin Books India Pvt. Ltd., 11 Community Centre, Panchsheel Park,
New Delhi – 110 017, India
Penguin Group (NZ), 67 Apollo Drive, Rosedale, North Shore 0632,
New Zealand (a division of Pearson New Zealand Ltd.)
Penguin Books (South Africa) (Pty.) Ltd., 24 Sturdee Avenue,
Rosebank, Johannesburg 2196, South Africa

Penguin Books Ltd., Registered Offices:
80 Strand, London WC2R 0RL, England

First published by Onyx, an imprint of New American Library,
a division of Penguin Group (USA) Inc.

First Printing, March 2008
10 9 8 7 6 5 4 3 2 1

ACKNOWLEDGMENTS

Many thanks go to Andrea Cirillo and Annelise Robey at the Jane Rotrosen Literary Agency for always providing such great support and inspiration. I also appreciate the many hours of brainstorming, lunches, chocolate, and Starbucks coffee shared with Candice Hern, Carol Grace, Bella Andre, Monica McCarty, Tracy Grant, Jami Alden, Anne Hearn, Kate Moore, Lynn Hanna, Barbara McMahon, and Diana Dempsey. I couldn't have done it without them. Also thanks to the Fog City Divas, who help keep me up to date on everything happening in the world of books, at www.fogcitydivas.com.

silent
RUN

Prologue

Large raindrops streamed against her windshield as she sped along the dark, narrow highway north of Los Angeles She'd been traveling for over an hour along the wild and beautiful Pacific coastline. She'd passed the busy beach cities of Venice and Santa Monica, the celebrity-studded hills of Malibu and Santa Barbara. Thank God it was a big state. She could start over again, find a safe place to stay, but she had to get there first.

The pair of headlights in her rearview mirror drew closer with each passing mile. Her nerves began to tighten, and goose bumps rose along her arms and the back of her neck. She'd been running too long not to recognize danger. But where had the car come from? She'd been so sure that no one had followed her out of LA. After sixty miles of constantly checking her rearview mirror she'd begun to relax, but now the fear came rushing back.

It was too dark to see the car behind her, but there

was something about the speed with which it was approaching that made her nervous. She pressed her foot down harder on the gas, clinging to the wheel as gale-force winds blowing in off the ocean rocketed through the car, making the driving even more treacherous.

A few miles later the road veered inland. She looked for a place to exit. Finally she saw a sign for an upcoming turnoff heading into the Santa Ynez Mountains. Maybe with a few twists and turns she could lose the car on her tail, and if her imagination were simply playing tricks on her, the car behind her would just continue down the road.

The exit came up fast. She took the turn on two wheels. Five minutes later the pair of headlights was once again directly behind her. There was no mistake: He was coming after her.

She had to get away from him. Adrenaline raced through her bloodstream, giving her courage and strength. She was so tired of running for her life, but she couldn't quit now. She'd probably made a huge mistake leaving the main highway. There was no traffic on this two-lane road. If he caught her now there would be no one to come to her rescue.

The gap between their cars lessened. He was so close she could see the silhouette of a man in her rearview mirror. He was bearing down on her.

She took the next turn too sharply, her tires sliding on the slick, wet pavement.

Sudden lights coming from the opposite direction blinded her. She hit the brakes hard. The car skidded out of control. She flew across the road, crashed through a wooden barrier, and hurtled down a steep embankment. Rocks splintered the windshield as she threw up her hands in protest and prayer.

When the impact finally came it was crushing, the pain intense. It was too much. All she wanted to do was to sink into oblivion. It was over. She was finished.

But some voice deep inside her screamed at her to stay awake, because if she wasn't dead yet, she soon would be.

Chapter One

The blackness in her mind began to lessen. There was a light behind her eyelids that beckoned and called to her. She was afraid to answer that call, terrified to open her eyes. Maybe it was the white light people talked about, the one to follow when you were dead. But she wasn't dead, was she?

It was just a nightmare, she told herself. She was dreaming; she'd wake up in a minute. But something was wrong. Her bed didn't feel right. The mattress was hard beneath her back. There were odd bells going off in her head. She smelled antiseptic and chlorine bleach. A siren wailed in the distance. Someone was talking to her, a man.

Her stomach clenched with inexplicable fear as she felt a strong hand on her shoulder. Her eyes flew open, and she blinked rapidly, the scene before her confusing.

She wasn't home in her bedroom, as she'd expected. A man in a long white coat stood next to the bed. He appeared to be in his fifties, with salt-and-pepper hair, dark eyes, and a serious expression. He held a clipboard in one hand. A stethoscope hung around his neck, and a pair of glasses rested on his long, narrow nose. Next to him stood a short, plump brunette dressed in blue scrubs, offering a compassionate, encouraging smile that seemed to match the name on her name tag, Rosie.

What was going on? Where was she?

"You're awake," the doctor said, a brisk note in his voice, a gleam of satisfaction in his eyes. "That's good. We were getting concerned about you. You've been unconscious for hours."

Unconscious? She gazed down the length of her body, suddenly aware of the thin blue gown, the hospital identification band on her wrist, the IV strapped to her left arm. And pain—there was pain . . . in her head, her right wrist, and her knees. Her right cheek throbbed. She raised a hand to her temple and was surprised to encounter a bandage. What on earth had happened to her?

"You were in an automobile accident last night," the doctor told her. "You have some injuries, but you're going to be all right. You're at St. Mary's Hospital just outside of Los Olivos in Santa Barbara County. I'm Dr. Carmichael. Do you understand what I'm saying?"

She shook her head, his brisk words jumbling up in her brain, making little to no sense. "Am I dreaming?" she whispered.

"You're not dreaming, but you do have a head

injury. It's not unusual to be confused," the doctor replied. He offered her a small, practiced smile that was edged with impatience. "Now, do you feel up to a few questions? Why don't we start with your name?"

She opened her mouth to reply, thinking that was an easy question, until nothing came to mind. Her brain was blank. What was her name? She had to have one. Everyone did. What on earth was wrong with her? She gave a helpless shake of her head. "I'm . . . I'm not sure," she murmured, shocked by the realization.

The doctor frowned, his gaze narrowing on her face. "You don't remember your name? What about your address, or where you're from?"

She bit down on her bottom lip, straining to think of the right answers. Numbers danced in her head, but no streets, no cities, no states. A wave of terror rushed through her. She had to be dreaming—lost in a nightmare. She wanted to run, to scream, to wake herself up, but she couldn't do any of those things.

"You don't know, do you?" the nurse interjected.

"I . . . I should know. Why don't I know? What's wrong with me? Why can't I remember my name, where I'm from? What's going on?" Her voice rose with each desperate question.

"Your brain suffered a traumatic injury," Dr. Carmichael explained. "It may take some time for you to feel completely back to normal. It's probably nothing to worry about. You just need to rest, let the swelling go down."

His words were meant to be reassuring, but anxiety ran like fire through her veins. She struggled to remember something about herself. Glancing down at her hands, she saw the light pink, somewhat chipped polish on her fingernails and wondered how it could be that her own fingers didn't look familiar to her. She wore no rings, no jewelry, not even a watch. Her skin was pale, her arms thin. But she had no idea what her face looked like.

"A mirror," she said abruptly. "Could someone get me a mirror?"

Dr. Carmichael and Rosie exchanged a brief glance, and then he nodded to the nurse, who quickly left the room. "You need to try to stay calm," he said as he jotted something down on his clipboard. "Getting upset won't do you any good."

"I don't know my name. I don't know what I look like." Hysteria bubbled in her throat, and panic made her want to jump out of bed and run . . . but to where, she had no idea. She tried to breathe through the rush of adrenaline. If this were a nightmare, eventually she'd wake up. If it wasn't . . . well, then she'd have to figure out what to do next. In the meantime she had to calm down. She had to think.

The doctor said she'd had an accident. Like the car crash in her dream? Was it possible that had been real and not a dream?

Glancing toward the clock, she saw that it was seven thirty. At least she knew how to read the time. "Is it night or morning?" Her gaze traveled to the window, but the heavy blue curtain was drawn, making it impossible for her to see outside.

"It's morning," the doctor replied. "You were brought in around nine o'clock last night."

Almost ten hours ago. So much time had passed. "Do you know what happened to me?"

"I'm afraid I don't know the details, but from what I understand, you were in a serious car accident."

Before she could ask another question, the nurse returned to the room and handed her a small compact mirror.

She opened the compact with shaky fingers, almost afraid of what she would see. She stared at her face for a long minute. Her eyes were light blue, framed by thick black lashes. Her hair was a dull dark brown, long, tangled, and curly, dropping past her shoulders. There were dark circles under her eyes, as well as purple bruises that were accentuated by the pallor of her skin. A white bandage was taped across her temple. Multiple tiny cuts covered her cheekbones. Her face was thin, drawn. She looked like a ghost. Even her eyes were haunted by shadows.

"Oh, God," she whispered, feeling as if she were looking at a complete stranger. Who was she?

"The cuts will heal," the nurse said. "Don't worry. You'll have your pretty face back before you know it."

It wasn't the bruises on her face that filled her heart with terror; it was the fact that she didn't recognize anything about herself. She felt absolutely no connection to the woman in the mirror. She slammed the compact shut, afraid to look any longer. Her pulse raced, and her heart beat in triple time as the reality of her situation sank in. She felt completely vulnerable, and she wanted to run and hide until she figured everything out. She would have jumped out of bed if Dr. Carmichael hadn't put his hand on her shoulder, perhaps sensing her desperation.

"You're going to be all right," he said firmly, meeting her gaze. "The answers will come. Don't push too hard. Just rest and let your body recuperate from the trauma."

"What if the answers don't come?" she whispered. "What if I'm like this forever?"

He frowned, unable to hide the concern in his eyes. "Let's take it one step at a time. There's a deputy from the sheriff's office down the hall. He'd like to speak to you."

A police officer wanted to talk to her? That didn't sound good. She swallowed back another lump of fear. "Why? Why does he want to talk to me?"

"Something to do with your accident. I'll let him know you're awake."

As the doctor left the room, Rosie stepped forward. "Can I get you anything—water, juice, an extra blanket? The mornings are still so cold. I can't wait until April. I don't know about you, but I'm tired of the rain. I'm ready for the sun to come out."

That meant it was March, the end of a long, cold winter, spring on the nearby horizon. Images ran through her mind of windy afternoons, flowers beginning to bloom, someone flying a kite, a beautiful red-and-gold kite that tangled in the branches of a tall tree. The laughter of a young girl filled her head—was it her laughter or someone else's? She saw two other girls and a boy running across the grass. She wanted to catch up to them, but they were too far away, and then they were gone, leaving her with nothing but a disturbing sense of loss and a thick curtain of blackness in her head.

Why couldn't she remember? Why had her brain locked her out of her own life?

"What day is it?" she asked, determined to gather as many details as she possibly could.

"It's Thursday, March twenty-second," Rosie replied with another sympathetic smile.

"Thursday," she murmured, feeling relieved to have a new fact to file away, even if it was something as inconsequential as the day of the week.

"Try not to worry. You'll be back to normal before you know it," Rosie added.

"I don't even know what normal is. Where are my things?" she asked abruptly, looking for more answers. Maybe if she had something of her own to hold in her hand, everything would come back to her.

Rosie tipped her head toward a neat pile of clothes on a nearby chair. "That's what you were wearing when they brought you in. You didn't have a purse with you, nor were you wearing any jewelry."

"Could you hand me my clothes, please?"

"Sure. They're a bit bloodied," Rosie said as she gathered up the clothes and laid them on the bed. "I'll check on you in a while. Just push the call button if you need anything."

She stared at the pair of blue jeans, which were ripped at the knees, the light blue camisole top, the navy sweater, and the gray jacket dotted with dark spots of blood or dirt, she wasn't sure which. Glancing across the room she saw a pair of Nike tennis shoes on the floor. They looked worn-out, as if she'd done a lot of running in them.

Another memory flashed in her brain. She could almost feel herself running, the wind in her hair, her heart pounding, the breath tight in her chest. But she wasn't out for a jog. She wasn't dressed right. She was wearing a heavy coat, a dress, and high stiletto heels. She tried to hang on to the image floating vaguely in her head, but it disappeared as quickly as it had come. She supposed she should feel grateful she'd remembered something, but the teasing bit only frustrated her more.

She dug her hands into the pockets of her jeans and jacket, searching for some clue as to who she was, but there was nothing there. She was about to put the jacket aside when she noticed an odd lump in the inner back lining. She ran her fingers across the material, surprised to find a flap covering a hidden zipper. She pulled on the zipper and felt inside, shocked when she pulled out a wad of twenty-dollar bills. There had to be at least fifteen hundred dollars. Why on earth had she stashed so much cash in her jacket? Obviously she'd taken great care to hide it, as someone would have had to examine the jacket carefully in order to find the money. Whoever had undressed her had not discovered the cash.

A knock came at her door, and she hurriedly stuffed the money back into her jacket and set it on the end of her bed just seconds before a uniformed police officer entered the room. Her pulse jumped at the sight of him, and it wasn't with relief but with fear. Her instincts were screaming at her to be cautious, that he could be trouble.

The officer was on the stocky side, with a military haircut, and appeared to be in his mid-forties. His forehead was lined, his skin a ruddy red and weather-beaten, his gaze extremely serious.

"I'm Tom Manning," he said briskly. "I'm a deputy with the county sheriff's department. I'm investigating your car accident."

"Okay," she said warily. "I should tell you that I don't remember what happened. In fact, I don't remember anything about myself."

"Yeah, the doc says you have some kind of amnesia."

His words were filled with suspicion, and skepticism ran through his dark eyes. Why was he suspicious? What reason could she possibly have for pretending not to remember? Had something bad occurred during the accident? Had she done something wrong? Had someone else been hurt? Her stomach turned over at the thought.

"Can you tell me what happened?" she said, almost afraid to ask.

"Your car went off the side of the road in the Santa Ynez Mountains, not far from San Marcos Pass. You plunged down a steep embankment and landed in a ravine about two hundred yards from the road. Fortunately you ran into a tree."

"Fortunately?" she echoed.

"Otherwise you would have ended up in a boulder-filled, high-running creek," he told her. "The front end of your Honda Civic was smashed, and the windshield was shattered."

Which explained the cuts and bruises on her face.

"You're a very lucky woman," the deputy added.

"Who found me?" she asked.

"A witness saw your car go over the side and called nine-one-one. Does any of this sound familiar?"

The part about going off the side of the road sounded a lot like the dream she'd been having. "I'm not sure."

"Were you alone in the car?"

His question surprised her. "I think so." She thought back to her dream. Had she been alone in the car? She didn't remember anyone else. "If I wasn't alone, wouldn't that other person be here at the hospital?" she asked.

"The back door of your car was open. There was a child's car seat strapped in the middle of the backseat, a bottle half-filled with milk, and this shoe." Officer Manning held up a clear plastic bag through which she could see a shoe so small it would fit into the palm of her hand. Her heart began to race. She had the sudden urge to call for a time-out, to make him leave before he said something else, something terrifying, something to do with that shoe. "Oh, God. Stop. I can't do this."

"I'm sorry, but I need to know. Do you have a baby?" he asked. "Was your child with you in the car?"

Chapter Two

His questions slammed into her, stealing the breath from her chest. An image flashed through her mind . . . pudgy legs, tiny little toes kicking her hand away as she tried to slip the shoe on her child's foot and fasten the bright pink Velcro straps.

Her daughter. Her baby!

A deep, intense, agonizing pain swept through her. She didn't know anything else, but she knew with complete and utter certainty that she had a little girl. She closed her eyes, desperate to see her daughter's face, to know her baby's name, but the blackness in her brain refused to lift. Her past remained just out of sight.

"Miss?"

She opened her eyes and saw Officer Manning staring back at her with a grim expression. "I have a little girl," she said, hearing the wonder in her own voice.

His gaze narrowed. "Was your child in the car, then? Did you just remember something?"

"I-I know I have a daughter," she stammered. "In my head I could see myself putting on that shoe. But I have no idea if she was with me."

"What's her name?"

She bit down on her bottom lip as the truth hit her hard. "I don't know." *Good God!* What kind of mother couldn't remember her own baby's name? "I have to get up. I have to find her." She sat up straight, intent on getting out of bed, but the officer barred her way.

"Easy, now. From what I understand you're in no condition to go anywhere," he said. "And where would you go—if you don't remember anything?"

His sharp, challenging gaze settled on hers. He was right. She didn't know where to go. But she couldn't just sit in this bed when her child could be in trouble.

"Why don't you tell me what you can remember?" Officer Manning suggested. "Even if it's just flashes of memory. Bits and pieces can make up a whole picture."

She closed her eyes again and took a deep breath. There was nothing but an empty void in her head, darkness so overwhelming she was afraid that it would swallow her up. Opening her eyes, she grabbed the railing of her bed, feeling the need to hang on to something solid. A wave of dizziness sent the room spinning around and around. She blinked several times, trying to focus on the badge on the deputy's chest.

She flashed on another image.

A man pulled a badge out of his inside suit pocket. She was shocked to learn he wasn't who he'd said he was. He'd lied to her. Now she was in trouble. And it wasn't just his badge that told her that; it was his smug expression, the look in his eyes that said he had her right where he wanted her, cornered and scared and very, very alone.

"Miss, are you all right? Should I call for the nurse?"

The deputy's voice brought her back to reality. She looked up at him, wondering if he was really there to help her, or if he had a hidden agenda. Was he the faceless man from her memory? Or just who he'd said he was—the officer investigating her car accident? How could she know? She glanced at the closed door behind him, wondering if there was anyone on the other side who would come to her aid.

The deputy's eyes narrowed as the silence between them lengthened. He wouldn't have offered to call for the nurse if he were worried about being discovered in her room. And the doctor had obviously already met him. She was being paranoid. "I'm all right," she said belatedly.

"What did you remember?"

"Nothing," she said quickly, wondering why her first instinct was to lie. But she didn't have time to analyze that now. The deputy was waiting. "I can't remember anything about my daughter or myself. I wish to God I could."

"So do I," the deputy said heavily.

She heard the deep note of concern in his voice. "What aren't you telling me?" she asked.

He stared back at her for a long moment, then said, "We found the child's shoe a few yards from the car. It's possible it flew out during the crash, since the back door was jammed open. Or . . ."

"Or what?" she asked as he paused a moment too long. A terrible fear swept through her. "Or what?" she repeated.

"Depending on your daughter's age, it's possible that she got out of the seat and wandered away. That's why I'd like to verify whether or not she was in the car with you at the time of the accident."

"Oh, my God!"

"Take it easy," the deputy said quickly. "We have a search party in the canyon right now. Everything that can be done is being done. What I need from you is as much information as I can possibly get about your daughter."

She wanted to scream in frustration. Of course he needed answers, but she had none to offer. Knowing that her child was missing, maybe alone in the wilderness . . . she couldn't stand it—the fear was overwhelming.

"Do you remember being in the car after you went off the road?" Manning asked.

"What?" she asked, her panic making it difficult to think.

"The car. Do you remember being in the car after you crashed? If you were conscious at all, you might have spoken to your child. You might have heard her cry."

She thought for a long moment. "I don't think so. But wait, wouldn't the person who saw my car go off the side of the road know if my baby was there?"

The deputy shook his head. "Your car was in a deep canyon. It was pitch-black last night and storming. Your vehicle couldn't be seen from the road. If the witness hadn't actually observed your car cross the center line and go through the guardrail, it could have been days before anyone found you. As it was, a good fifteen minutes passed before the paramedics arrived, and another ten to fifteen before they managed to get down that steep hill to your car. I don't know how old your daughter is, but I have a couple of kids, and I'd say that shoe looks like it would fit a one- to two-year-old. It's unlikely a child of that age could unlatch the car seat and exit the car."

"But not impossible," she said.

"Not impossible," he acknowledged. "Are you sure you can't remember anything about that night, nothing? It's very important."

"I know it's important. Dammit!" She drew in a sharp breath, battling a rush of hysteria. She had to think, to focus on what she did know. "Okay, right before I woke up here in this bed, I thought I was dreaming about crashing my car, but it must have been real. I must have been reliving what happened." She took a moment, retracing what little she could remember. "There were headlights in my rearview mirror, and I felt as if I were afraid, as if someone were following me. I remember needing to go faster, to get away."

"I don't suppose you saw a license plate or noticed the make of the automobile?"

"It was dark. All I saw were lights. What about the witness? Did he see anything?"

"He said there was a car behind you, but it continued down the highway after your vehicle went over the side. He didn't see the license plate."

"The car behind me must have run me off the road. Otherwise he would have stopped."

"Not necessarily. It was a hell of a storm last night, and not everyone stops when there's an accident. Some people don't like to get involved. At any rate, we've broadcast a description of you and your vehicle throughout the county. You also made the evening news, on the local stations, anyway. We took a photograph of you, since you didn't have any identification. Hopefully someone will recognize you and tell us everything we need to know."

His words should have made her feel better, but they didn't. On some basic level she sensed that having her picture on the news was not a good thing. She'd been running from someone. What if that person saw her? What if that person came to the hospital?

"I'll be back later." Officer Manning took out his card and set it on the table next to the bed. "If you remember anything in the meantime, call me."

As the deputy left the room, she forced herself to breathe in and out. Her first instinct was to get out of bed and go to the accident scene, but she felt dizzy, and her head was throbbing with pain. She knew the most logical thing to do was stay put and concentrate on figuring out who she was and what had happened just before her accident. Unfortunately she couldn't seem to will the details into her brain. She couldn't recall her child's face, but she could feel the love branded into her heart.

Putting a hand to her abdomen, she knew that she'd felt tiny kicks and flutters in her womb. She'd heard her baby's first squeal of life. She'd held her daughter in her arms, arms that now ached with a deep feeling of loss. A sense of helplessness engulfed her. Why couldn't she remember if her child was with her in the car?

Tears of fear and frustration spilled over, dripping down her cheeks. But crying didn't make her feel better; it made her feel weak. She grabbed a tissue from the box and wiped her face. Taking several deep breaths, she lay back against the pillows and closed her eyes. She offered up a desperate, pleading prayer for her daughter's safety. While she couldn't see her child's face, in her head she could hear the terrifying cries of a baby who wanted her mother.

His shadow was coming closer. She could hear him talking, his words edged with lightness and humor, as if there were nothing wrong. Don't trust him, the voice inside her head whispered. He looks harmless, with his good looks, his winning personality. Everyone else thinks he's a prince, but you know better. You've seen behind the smile and the mask that he wears. And you know he can kill. You've seen him do just that. Run! Faster!

She woke with a start, body sweating, pulse pounding, breath coming ragged and rough. It took her a minute to realize where she was—the hospital. She was alone this time, no doctor, no nurse, no policeman, and, more important, no dark, menacing shadows. The curtains had been opened, and she could see the sun outside her window. The storm had passed. The nightmare was over. Or was it?

She tried to remember her name, her address, her birthday. Nothing. She closed her eyes again, attempting to conjure up a face in her mind, a father, a mother, a boyfriend, a sister, or a friend . . . She had to have someone in her life, didn't she? Someone who knew her? Someone who'd lived with her? Loved her?

The questions ran around in her brain, one after another. It was shocking to know nothing. Why wasn't her memory coming back? The doctor said she just needed rest. And she had slept. Her recent nightmare attested to that.

Was there an answer in her dreams? She always seemed to be running—from a man. Who was he? And why was he after her?

Dammit! Why couldn't she unlock her own brain? She hit her hands against the mattress. The movement created a wave of pain that ran through her body, reminding her that her head was not her only injury.

Opening her eyes, she wiggled her toes and moved her legs, relieved that every joint and muscle seemed to be working, some a bit more painfully than others, but at least she wasn't paralyzed.

Glancing at the clock, she saw it was after two. She'd been asleep for hours. A lunch tray rested on the table by her bed, but she wasn't at all hungry. What she needed was information and reassurance. She reached for the deputy's business card, but before she could pick up the phone, Deputy Manning entered the room.

"I was just about to call you," she said.

"I hope that means you have your memory back."

"Unfortunately not. Did you find my baby?"

"No. We've been out in the canyon all day with search dogs and experienced personnel, and there's no sign of a child. Our forensic experts believe the back door of the car opened on impact. Other than the shoe that was located outside the automobile, we found no other evidence, no footprints, no articles of clothing, nothing to indicate that a child or anyone else wandered away from the car. We'll get a tow truck out there to retrieve your vehicle, but there's not much left of it."

"I guess that's good . . . that you found nothing." She wasn't really sure whether it was good or not. Her daughter was still missing. As she gazed into the deputy's eyes, she saw a gleam of skepticism.

"What?" she asked. "Why are you looking at me like you think I'm hiding something?"

"I'm just putting facts together, ma'am, facts that don't add up. There's a lot about your accident that puzzles me. We found absolutely no identification in your car, no purse, no wallet, no registration, nothing." He let that sink in and then continued. "Now, I've never known a woman to take a road trip without some sort of bag."

"It does seem odd," she murmured.

"When we ran the plates on your Honda, we learned that the car is registered to a Margaret Bradley. Upon further investigation, it was discovered that Ms. Bradley died in a convalescent hospital two months ago at the age of eighty-two. She resided in Los Angeles County, Venice Beach, to be exact. She had no known relatives."

Margaret Bradley? She ran the name through her brain, but it meant nothing to her. "The name isn't familiar."

"And you don't know how you happened to be driving her car about a hundred miles north of LA?"

"No." She paused, not liking the tone in his voice or the frown on his face. "What are you implying? Do you think I stole the car?"

"I hope not."

"Well, I'm sure I didn't," she said quickly.

"Hard to be sure of anything when you don't know who you are."

Was she the kind of person who could steal a car? It seemed unlikely, but how could she know?

"If you're in trouble, if you're mixed up in something, it's not too late to set things right," the deputy said, his gaze hard and direct.

"I don't know if I'm in trouble. I don't know who I am. I wish to God someone could tell me."

"I can tell you who you are. I can tell you *exactly* who you are," a man said from the doorway.

Chapter Three

Her heart sped up as a tall man wearing faded blue jeans, a gray knit shirt, and a black leather jacket strode into the room with a purpose that couldn't be denied. Broad-shouldered, narrow-hipped, he moved like an athlete intent on reaching the goal line, no matter who got in his way. His dark brown hair, wavy and windswept, brushed the collar of his jacket, and as he drew closer she saw his eyes—a fierce, fiery green filled with accusation and something that looked like hatred. She sat up straight, feeling the instinctive need to protect herself.

Who was this man? And why was every nerve in her body going on full alert?

"Who are you?" she asked warily.

"What do you mean, who am I? You know who I am, *Sarah*. It hasn't been that long since we've seen each other." His gaze burned into hers. "Did you really think changing your hair color would stop me from recognizing you? If you wanted a disguise, you should have covered up those beautiful, lying blue eyes of yours."

She swallowed hard, trying to make sense of his words. "Is that my name? Sarah?"

His gaze sharpened, darkened. His lips drew into a tight line, and his hands clenched in fists at his sides. "Of course that's your name. What the hell is going on? Why are you acting like you don't know me? And where is Caitlyn?" He turned to Officer Manning. "Where's my daughter?"

"I don't know," Manning replied. "The paramedics reported only one person in the car after the accident—this woman you're calling Sarah."

"What do you mean, Caitlyn wasn't in the car?" He turned back to her. "What have you done with my daughter?"

He gripped the bed railing, his knuckles turning white. She had the feeling it took all of his self-control not to put his hands on her neck and squeeze the answers out of her.

"I have a head injury," she said. "I don't remember anything. I don't know who you are, or who I am, and most important, I don't know where my baby is."

"What the hell are you talking about? What is she talking about?" he demanded of Manning.

"According to the doctor, she has amnesia."

"No fucking way," he replied.

"It's true," she said, but her words didn't begin to dim the utter disbelief in his eyes. At least she had a few facts to work with now—her own name,

Sarah. And this man had confirmed that she had a child. "Caitlyn," she murmured. "Is that my baby's name?"

"Of course that's her name. And she's not *your* baby. She's *our* baby," he said grimly. "You had no right to take her away from me, to keep her for so long without a word. Now you're pretending not to remember anything? This is absurd." He turned back to Manning. "Where is my child?"

"That's what we're trying to figure out. Why don't you back up and tell me who you are and who she is?" Manning replied.

"I'm Jake Sanders. She's Sarah Tucker," he said impatiently. "We have a daughter, Caitlyn." His voice roughened with emotion, and he sent her another harsh glare. "You don't remember Caitlyn? What kind of a mother doesn't remember her own child?"

The accusation ripped her heart apart. She closed her eyes against the pain and the sense that he was right. She must be a bad mother, a very bad mother.

"Look at me," he said forcefully. "Look at her."

His words demanded that she open her eyes.

He pulled out his wallet and held up a photo.

"This is Caitlyn. This is the child you took from me." He shoved the photo into her hand.

Her heart stopped as she stared at the picture. The little girl had a halo of gold curls on her head and a pink bow attached with a bobby pin just above her ear. She had an upturned nose and eyes that were a light blue, almost gray, eyes that mirrored her own. This baby, this little angel, was her daughter. She pressed the photo against her heart, feeling a wave of agonizing fear. Something was wrong—terribly wrong. She knew it deep down inside.

"Where is she?" Jake demanded. "Tell me where she is, Goddammit. You can't just keep her from me."

Officer Manning placed a warning hand on Jake's arm. "Take it easy."

Jake shrugged it off. "I have a right to know where my child is."

"Yes, you do, but tell me, do you have a legal relationship with Ms. Tucker? Are you married?"

"No, but we were talking about it, making plans," Jake said with an impatient wave of his hand. "We lived together for almost two years in an apartment in San Francisco. But just because we weren't married doesn't mean I don't have rights as a father. I talked to my lawyer. I talked to the police in San Francisco. They all agreed that Sarah couldn't just steal my child from me. But they couldn't do anything until we found her."

"How did you find me?" she interrupted. "How did you know I was here in this hospital?"

"Dylan. He's been helping me look for you, and he has contacts in this area. Last night one of his police buddies sent him your picture and details on the accident. He recognized you immediately."

"Who's Dylan?" she asked.

"My brother. He's a journalist, you know that. Why are you acting like you don't?"

"I'm not acting. Isn't San Francisco a long way from here? How did you get here so fast?" she asked.

"It's a five-hour drive, but I made it in four. I was afraid you'd disappear before I arrived."

"When did you last see Sarah and your child?" Manning interjected.

"Seven months, two weeks, and three days ago," Jake said flatly. "I was on a business trip when Sarah disappeared with Caitlyn."

"I left you? Why?" she asked.

His hard gaze met hers. "Your note said, 'This isn't going to work. Don't try to find me. Sarah.' That was it. That's all I got. Haven't heard a word from you since. You disappeared off the face of the earth."

She thought about his statement. It didn't make sense. She'd supposedly been in love with this man. She had lived with him, been intimate with him, and had a baby with him—why would she leave behind such a coldhearted note?

"Why would I do that?"

"Hell if I know." He planted his hands on his hips. "You tell me, Sarah. You tell me how you decided to walk out the door one day and never come back. You tell me how you could throw away everything we had without any explanation."

"I . . . I can't."

"Or won't," he challenged.

"I don't remember you."

He drew in a quick, sharp breath at her words. He claimed to hate her, but her words appeared to hurt him. Her gaze traveled down his lean, muscular body, searching for some intimate connection. He said they'd made love, created a child together. Wouldn't she remember laying her head against his solid chest, wrapping her arm around his waist, her fingers playing with the snaps on his jeans, his long legs pressing her down against the bed?

A sudden wave of heat spread through her body, warming her from the inside out. Was she remembering or was she imagining?

When she lifted her gaze to his, she saw a myriad of emotions flash through his green eyes, uncertainty, desire, anger.... His feelings for her were obviously complicated.

"You will remember me," he promised. "Before we're done, you're going to explain exactly why you destroyed our lives. But right now I just want Caitlyn. You want to be free of me, fine, but you don't get to keep my daughter away from me. She's mine as much as she's yours, and you should have known, better than anyone, how I would feel about losing my baby."

She didn't know what to say. She didn't know how to feel. He was accusing her of stealing their child. Why would she have done such a thing? Was she a horrible person? Was she ruthless, conniving, and manipulating, the way he implied?

Or did she have a good reason for leaving him and taking her baby with her?

Her dream flashed back, the warning voice—*He looks harmless, with his good looks, his winning personality. Everyone else thinks he's a prince, but you know better. You've seen behind the smile and the mask that he wears.*

Had this man hurt her? Hurt their child? Was that why she'd run from him?

She saw Officer Manning studying Jake Sanders with the same suspicious gaze with which he'd originally regarded her. Was he wondering the same thing? Did she have a good reason for wanting to take her daughter away from her father?

"Can you prove it?" she challenged. "Do you have pictures of us together—you, me, and Caitlyn? Do you have a copy of Caitlyn's birth certificate, naming you as the father?"

His gaze narrowed. "I have a copy of the birth certificate with my name on it, but not with me. I can get it."

"What about pictures of us together?"

He pulled out his wallet again and handed her another small photograph. "We had this taken in one of those carnival photo booths—before Caitlyn was born."

She stared down at the black-and-white photo of the two of them. Jake sat behind her, his arms wrapped around her waist. She leaned against him, a broad smile on her face, a laugh on her lips. She looked much younger, far more animated and relaxed than the woman whose face she'd seen in the mirror a few hours earlier. Jake also had a carefree sparkle in his eyes and a sexy grin on his lips. "We look . . . happy," she said.

"We were happy, until you ruined everything."

His voice was rough with emotion, and as their gazes met she felt the stirring of something deep and painful, a powerful connection between them. Love? Hate? She didn't know, but she couldn't look away. Neither could he.

Manning faded into the background. It was just the two of them locked in a silent battle that she didn't begin to understand but could feel down to the tips of her toes.

"Why did you have to take away every single detail of Caitlyn's existence, Sarah?" Jake asked her, still holding her gaze. "You stripped her bedroom. And ours. You took everything—the photographs, the toys, all the things we'd bought together. Caitlyn's crib, her blankets, and the rocking chair I'd made for you. It was as if you wanted me to believe neither one of you had ever been there. Why?" He shook his head in bewilderment. "Did it make it easier for you to leave once you'd destroyed the home we'd made together? Did you think I could forget you? Did you think I could ever forgive you?"

Sarah bit down on her bottom lip, tasting blood, almost relieved to have a physical pain to go with the emotional ache in her heart. Why had she done the things he accused her of doing? He must have hurt her or Caitlyn. It was the only thing that made sense. What kind of woman erased her very existence from a person's life?

Only a woman who was afraid of something or someone. Only a woman who was desperate to disappear without a trace.

He had to be the reason for her fear. Otherwise she would have turned to him instead of running away. "You did something," she said. "I don't know what, but you must have done something."

"I never gave you a reason to leave me." Jake dragged his hand through his hair in frustration, his green eyes widening in disbelief. "Is that the way you're going to play it now? Make up lies about us? It won't work. I never hurt you. And I never hurt our baby."

"I wouldn't have taken our child and left you without a good reason."

"How do you know that?" he challenged. "You said you don't remember anything. Yet your memory is suddenly returning—just in time to paint me as the bad guy? I don't think so." He glanced at Officer Manning. "You can check me out. I'm an architect. I work in San Francisco, and I've never gotten so much as a parking ticket. I'm not a dangerous man. My slate is clean. I have nothing to hide."

"I hope that's true," Manning replied.

"It is. Right now my main concern is finding Caitlyn. How can I help?"

"I'd like to take the photograph of the child with me, so that we can broadcast a description of your daughter. If anyone saw Ms. Tucker with her child before the accident, that would give us a fixed time and location to work from."

"That picture is old. It was taken a couple of months before Sarah left," Jake said, his voice laced with bitterness. "Caitlyn would be much bigger now, sixteen months and a few days. She'd be talking and walking." His voice faltered as he drew in a sharp breath. "I missed a lot of her firsts, but I won't miss any more, Sarah. No more. I want my daughter back."

Sarah swallowed hard, his raw, painful words cutting her to the core.

Jake turned back to Manning. "The only reason I have that picture is because it was in my wallet. Sarah took the other photos with her when she left, or she destroyed them. If I hadn't had that one, I would have been left with nothing."

Officer Manning cleared his throat, breaking the thick tension in the room. "I'll give this back to you when I'm done." He took the photo from Sarah's hand. "We'll have to sort out the rest later. Why don't you come down to the station with me, Mr. Sanders? I can fill you in on our investigation, and you can tell me more about your relationship with Ms. Tucker."

Sarah wanted to protest. Who knew what lies Jake Sanders would tell the deputy? Then again, she didn't want to be left alone with Jake. Maybe it was better if he went down to the station. She would have some time to figure out what to do next.

"All right." Jake sent Sarah a meaningful look. "But I'll be back. We have a lot to discuss."

As the men left the room, Sarah knew she wasn't going to sleep again. She was going to do what came naturally to her—run. Her instincts told her to get out of the hospital. She needed to find her daughter.

Swinging her legs to the side of the bed, she gently put her feet on the floor and tried to stand up. Dizziness hit her again like a huge ocean wave dragging her under, and the pain behind her left eye was stabbing and intense.

She took several deep breaths, waiting for the pain to subside. It didn't, so she just ruthlessly pulled the IV needle out of her arm. Then she grabbed her clothes off the end of the bed and began to dress. It seemed to take forever, every movement painful. She had just finished tying her shoes when the door opened, and her heart sank.

"I knew you were going to run," Jake said, meeting her gaze head-on.

"Where's Deputy Manning?" she asked in a shaky voice.

"I realized as soon as I stepped out of the room that there was no way in hell I could leave you alone. I told the deputy I'd talk to him later. It's just you and me, Sarah." He shut the door behind him with a definite click. "Just you and me."

Chapter Four

Sarah instinctively backed up until her legs hit the bed and there was nowhere else to go. Jake moved forward until he was inches away from her. He towered over her by at least half a foot. He was too big, too strong, and too male. She felt an overwhelming sense of fear, but she couldn't let him see that she was afraid.

They were in a hospital, she reminded herself. There were doctors and nurses out in the hall. He couldn't hurt her here.

"Why don't you tell me where you're going?" he said.

"To find my daughter." She refused to be intimidated by this man. At the moment she didn't know if what he'd said about her was true or false. Until she did know, she was going to follow her instincts. Right now her instincts told her not to show any weakness.

"I thought you didn't know where Caitlyn was."

"I don't know where she is, but I can look. I can't just lie here and do nothing."

"Or maybe you're going to get her, so you can take off again," he suggested.

If she knew where her daughter was, maybe she would do that, because something was off between her and this man. She couldn't imagine behaving the way he'd described—unless she'd been desperate to escape. However, she couldn't help thinking that to remove all evidence of her existence before she left seemed more premeditated than desperate, more calculating than fearful. But she'd been afraid in her dream, and despite the bravado she was putting on now, she felt a sense of fear. There was danger somewhere—she just didn't know where.

"Nothing to say?" Jake prodded. He took another step closer to her. His breath whispered against her cheek, drawing goose bumps across her arms. She could feel the power in his body standing so near hers, and the air sparked with tension between them.

She cleared her throat and forced herself to look at him. "I told you I just want to find my daughter."

Jake didn't reply for a long, tense moment, his gaze deep and hard, his eyes searching hers for the truth. She wanted to look away, but she couldn't give in to the temptation. He would only think she was trying to hide something.

Finally he gave a frustrated shake of his head. "I don't know if you're lying or not. I used to believe I was good at reading people, but you . . . you proved me wrong. I never suspected that you had so many secrets. I was completely taken in, fooled in every possible way."

She was surprised he would admit to such a thing. He seemed like a proud, confident, arrogant man. Or was he playing his own game, trying to make himself look like a victim?

"I imagined seeing you a million times in the last seven months," he continued. "I thought about what I would say to you—what you would say to me. I expected that you'd have a big story to tell me, some logical explanation for your departure. I never anticipated a sudden case of amnesia. It's a good defense. You don't have to answer any questions, because you don't remember."

The cutting anger in his voice drew her chin up. She couldn't defend her actions before she'd woken up in the hospital, but she could stand up for her behavior in the past twelve hours. "I'm not faking the memory loss. I don't recall anything before I woke up in this bed. You're no more familiar to me than the deputy who was just here. I don't know you. I don't remember anything about our life together. You could be telling me a boatload of lies. I don't trust you any more than you trust me."

Jake picked up the photo of the two of them that still rested on the bed. "You need proof that we were together. Here it is."

"That woman's hair is lighter."

"You had blond hair when I knew you." His eyes

narrowed. "Come on, Sarah; you can't deny this woman is you."

She couldn't deny it. Despite the different hair color, and the cuts and bruises she now wore, the face was the same one she'd seen in the mirror. "Even if it is me, I don't remember having the picture taken. I don't remember being with you at all."

He shook his head in anger and frustration. "Fine, you don't remember. So I'll tell you the way it was. We had an intense, passionate relationship. We couldn't keep our hands off each other. We were together for two years, and I thought I knew you inside and out. Then I came home one day to an apartment I didn't recognize, a home stripped bare of everything and everyone. At first I thought something terrible must have happened, a stranger had come into our home and hurt you or kidnapped you and Caitlyn. But that didn't jive with the way you'd left the house so neat and tidy and utterly empty. I haunted the police station for weeks. I hung up posters all over the city. I pleaded on television for someone to come forward and tell me where you were."

"I don't know what to say." She felt damnation in each horrible word he uttered.

"Then just listen. Our friends, my coworkers, even one of the cops, suggested you might have had postpartum depression. No one came right out and said it, but I knew they were wondering if you'd harmed yourself and Caitlyn, too. But I kept telling them that you'd never hurt our child. You couldn't do such a thing."

"I don't believe that I did," she said quickly. "Officer Manning told me he found fresh milk in a bottle in the backseat of my car. Caitlyn has to be okay. She's just somewhere I can't remember."

"I hope to God that's true, Sarah."

"It has to be true," she said, hearing desperation in her own voice.

"Then maybe you left me for another reason. I don't care anymore what that reason was. What you did to me was unforgivable. And seeing you now alive and well only makes me remember how many hours I wasted worrying about you. The days kept passing, and I couldn't get any answers. The police gave up. No evidence of a crime, just a runaway girlfriend—that's what they called you. So I hired private investigators, one after another. They all came up empty. They told me to accept the fact that you'd left of your own volition, and you'd probably had help, because there was no trail whatsoever. Even my friends encouraged me to move on, forget the last two years of my life, as if I could do that. We'd made a family, you, me, Caitlyn. And you ripped it apart. You destroyed everything."

If Jake was faking the raw, bitter pain in his voice, the agony in his eyes, he was an incredible actor. But if he was telling the truth, it sounded like she was a terrible person, cold and so cruel. Sarah didn't know which scenario she preferred.

"I don't understand," she said helplessly.

"That makes two of us," he continued. "Because when I went looking for you, I discovered that everything you'd told me about your past was a lie. I ran down your supposed relatives on the East Coast. You said your parents died when you were young, and that you'd gone to live with a grandmother in Boston, but that person didn't exist. You told me you went to Boston College, but they never heard of you. You came into my life out of nowhere, and you vanished exactly the same way. I almost started to think I'd imagined you, made you up. I thought I was going crazy," he said with a wave of his hand.

"You're saying that I lied to you from the beginning?" she asked in surprise.

"That's exactly what I'm saying."

She put a hand to her temple as her headache deepened in intensity. Her senses began to spin, and her legs felt so weak she sat down heavily on the edge of the bed. Jake's face began to blur, and she twisted her fingers in the blanket and sheet so she wouldn't fall over.

"Are you all right?" Jake put his hand on her shoulder to steady her, and then yanked it away, as if he couldn't bear to touch her. His forehead drew into tight lines as he frowned. "Or is this another play in your game? Get me to feel sorry for you? Get me to go find the nurse or the doctor so you can leave?"

"I . . . I just need to catch my breath."

Jake's eyes narrowed. "You're white as a ghost. You look like you're going to pass out. This had better not be an act, Sarah. I can't take any more lies from you."

"It's not an act," she murmured, knowing that she couldn't faint. She had to stay awake so she could deal with Jake, not that it wouldn't be appealing to escape the fury in his eyes—if only for a few minutes. His anger and accusations were burning a hole right through her heart.

But some inner voice warned her not to assume that everything he said was the truth. She had to trust her own instincts. Words were just words, and Jake could have an agenda for wanting her to believe that she was a horrible person. He could be the one who was lying.

Jake pushed the call button for the nurse. "Let's get an objective opinion."

"I'm okay," she said. "It's a lot of information to take in all at once."

"Or you're giving yourself a minute to think up another story."

Before she could reply, the nurse entered the room, frowning when she saw Sarah dressed in her street clothes. "Now, where do you think you're going?" Rosie asked.

"To find my daughter," she said, even though she couldn't summon up the strength to get back on her feet.

"You need to rest," the nurse said. "Come on, now; lie down."

"I don't want to lie down," Sarah protested, but knew she was too weak to win this battle. Seeing the resolve in the nurse's face, she lay back on the pillows, stretching her legs out in front of her.

"That's better." The nurse untied Sarah's shoes and pulled them off. "Your body has been through a lot. You need to give yourself time to recuperate. Why don't I get you a sleeping pill?"

"No," she said immediately, hating the idea of losing any more control over her life. "I don't need a pill."

"Well, if you find the pain gets worse and you can't sleep, call me." The nurse glanced over at Jake. "Maybe you should let her get some rest."

Jake frowned but reluctantly nodded. "All right, but I want to talk to her doctor."

"I'll let Dr. Carmichael know you wish to speak to him," the nurse replied. She moved over to the window and drew the curtains, then flipped off the overhead light as she left, leaving the room in shadows, only a small stream of light coming from the part in the curtains.

Jake moved slowly toward the door. He paused, giving Sarah a long, speculative look. "I'll be right outside. Don't even think of leaving here without me."

Alone in the dark room, Sarah felt another wave of fear wash over her. Why couldn't she remember anything about her life? She could feel the love for her child deep in her soul, but the only image she had of Caitlyn was the child in the photograph. And Jake—she didn't remember him at all. Why wouldn't she recall a man with whom she'd been intimate, the father of her child? At the very least, why couldn't she feel the same love for Jake that she felt for Caitlyn? Had she loved him? Or was that just what he wanted her to believe?

Picking up the photograph of the two of them together at the carnival, she saw again the smile on her lips, the sparkle in her eyes. The emotion didn't appear forced or fake. Jake looked happy, too. There was certainly no love in his eyes now. He hated her.

Jake claimed that she'd lied about everything in her past. If she'd done that, she must have had something to hide. There must have been a logical explanation for why she'd left him and taken their child, and more reasons for why she'd been driving a car that didn't belong to her in an area of California in which she didn't appear to live. But what were those reasons?

It was no wonder everyone looked at her with suspicion. She was suspicious of herself. She might not have a memory, but she did have a brain, and adding up all the bits and pieces she'd learned about herself revealed a very disturbing picture. Unless she was a raving lunatic, there had to be someone else in that picture, someone who had given her a reason to do what she'd done. Was it Jake?

Although she'd been eager to get rid of him, now she couldn't help but wonder what he was doing. She didn't like the idea of him talking to the police without her, or even to her doctor. Shifting restlessly on the bed, she finally sat up and made another attempt to stand. She took it slowly, fighting through the dizziness as she got to her feet. Once she felt steady, she walked across the room to the door and opened it just wide enough to take a look around.

Her room was at the far end of the hall. Across from her was a stairwell. At the other end of the hall was the nurses' station, where several people in blue scrubs could be seen milling around. There were other random people in the hallway, but the most important figure was Jake, standing a few yards away with his back to her. He was talking on his cell phone.

She opened the door wider, trying to catch his conversation.

"I found her," Jake said. "Yeah, she colored her hair, but she couldn't get rid of those curls—those damn curls. There's no mistake." He paused for a moment. "The police have been searching for Caitlyn in the canyon where the accident occurred. What I need you to do is go there and check it out for me." He listened to the reply and then said, "She claims she doesn't remember anything. I'm going to check with Sarah's doctor. I'll get back to you when I know what I'm going to do about her."

Sarah shut the door, her pulse racing. Whom had Jake been talking to? And more important, what was he planning to do about her?

Jake sat down in a chair in the hospital corridor and leaned his head against the wall. The last time he'd been in a hospital was when Caitlyn was born—one of the happiest days of his life. That moment seemed like a lifetime ago.

Closing his eyes, he took a long, deep breath. He'd found Sarah, and the moment he'd anticipated for seven long months had not been at all what he'd expected. He'd prepared himself for a showdown, a battle for Caitlyn. He'd never once considered that he would find Sarah and she wouldn't be with Caitlyn. Where on earth had Sarah hidden their daughter?

He wanted to shake the answers out of her. He'd never felt such violence or anger toward a woman. Sarah had ruined him. And it appeared that she'd ruined herself too. She'd lost at least ten or fifteen pounds. She'd never been heavy, but now she was so thin she looked fragile, breakable. Her beautiful blond hair was a lifeless brown, her eyes filled with shadows, her demeanor nervous and wary.

Where was the woman he'd fallen in love with?

She was nowhere. She didn't exist, he reminded himself. The woman he'd lived with was a liar and a thief. He couldn't forget that. He couldn't let her get under his skin again. He had one goal now, and that was to find Caitlyn. Sarah was only going to be a means to that end, nothing more. He would stay with her until he had his daughter. He couldn't take the chance that she would run again.

Still, it took all the strength he had not to walk out of the hospital and join in the search for his child. But the police were doing their job, and Dylan was on his way to the accident scene. It was smarter for him to stay here and keep the pressure on Sarah.

So far Sarah had played the amnesia card exactly right. Her eyes had never once revealed any spark of recognition for him. Was she that good an actress? Could she really hide the truth so completely? Or was she truly without any memory whatsoever? It seemed impossible to believe that she could forget everything that had happened between them. She was probably faking it.

Opening his eyes, he glanced around the corridor and saw a young woman watching him. She had dark hair and eyes, and there was a pinched look about her white face, worry in her expression. When she realized she'd been caught staring, she gave him a nervous smile. "It's hard to wait," she said. "I hate hospitals. They're so depressing."

"Yeah, I know what you mean," he muttered shortly. He didn't feel like making conversation with a stranger. Fortunately they were interrupted. Jake got to his feet as a tall, gray-haired man paused in front of him.

"Mr. Sanders?" he queried.

"Yes, are you Sarah's doctor?"

"I believe so, if we're speaking about the woman in four-oh-seven with amnesia resulting from a car accident."

"That's right. Her name is Sarah Tucker. I'd like to find out more about her condition. What can you tell me?"

Dr. Carmichael stepped aside as someone pushed

a food cart down the hallway. He waved Jake into a nearby waiting room. "Why don't we speak in private?"

Jake cast a quick look down the hall. Sarah's door was closed. While he didn't trust her to stay put, he knew she was too weak to go far. Even if she ran, he would find her.

"I want the girl," the man said.

Sarah's heart stopped as she saw the man pull a gun out of his jacket pocket and take aim. His hand was calm; not a single tremor shook his fingers. She gazed at his wrist, mesmerized by the tattoo of a tiger. She'd seen that tattoo before. Where?

The gun suddenly exploded, and a rocketing blast reverberated through her body, ringing her ears, almost knocking her off her feet. She put a hand over her mouth, muffling her scream of shock and terror.

She couldn't believe what had happened. He'd done it. He'd actually pulled the trigger. Bright red blood streamed across the tile floor. God, how could anyone bleed so much and stay alive?

She had to get help. She had to say something, but she couldn't get any air into her lungs.

Suddenly the scene in front of her faded away, turning to blackness. She strained to see some light, but she was completely blind.

Someone was holding her down, covering her mouth and nose. She was going to be the next person to die. But he wasn't shooting her; he was suffocating her, she realized. In seconds it would be over.

Desperation broke through her paralysis. She pushed against the weight pressing on her, using her hands to swing at anything she could reach. Her fist connected with skin, bone. She heard a grunt, a curse, but the voice . . . it wasn't the same voice. Who was it?

Sarah's eyes flew open. A man stood over her, wearing blue scrubs and a mask over his mouth and nose. He had a pillow in his hand, the same pillow that had just been covering her face.

He was coming back after her. He was going to try again.

Chapter Five

Sarah screamed as loud as she could, raising her hands to fight off her attacker. The man struggled for a moment, then swore and dropped the pillow before running from the room. Gasping, Sarah put a hand to her mouth. Seconds later Jake burst through the door, a concerned expression in his eyes.

"What the hell is wrong with you?" he demanded.

"A . . . a man," she stammered, waving her hand toward the door. "Did you see him? He . . . he tried to smother me with that pillow." She pointed to the pillow now lying on the floor, her heart racing in triple time.

Jake looked down at the pillow, then back at her. Disbelief flooded his eyes. "What are you talking about?"

"I was asleep. When I woke up a man was holding that pillow against my face, so I screamed. Didn't you see him? He ran out of the room two seconds ago."

"I saw a male nurse come out of your room," Jake said slowly.

"That was the guy. He was dressed in scrubs."

"Are you sure you weren't dreaming?"

"I know the difference between a dream and reality," she snapped. But she had to admit there was a small niggling doubt in the back of her mind. She had been asleep. She'd been dreaming of gunshots and blood. Was she wrong? Had she just imagined that feeling of suffocation?

No, it wasn't her imagination. He'd put the pillow against her face. She could still taste the cotton fibers in her mouth. He'd tried to suffocate her.

"Oh, my God!" The reality of what had just happened settled in. "He tried to kill me." She looked at Jake in confusion, the horror of the past few minutes sinking into her brain. "Why would someone want to kill me?"

Jake stared back at Sarah for a long moment, doubt clouding his gaze. "You tell me."

"Obviously I don't know," she returned. "Could you at least go look for him?"

"Is this another trick to get me out of the room?"

"Are you out of your mind?" she asked in exasperation. "Forget it. I'll look myself."

"Hang on," Jake said with a frown. "If someone was trying to kill you, he's not going to be standing in the hall. He'd be long gone by now."

As Jake finished speaking, Rosie rushed into the room, looking worried. "What's going on?"

"There was a man in my room wearing scrubs," Sarah said. "He tried to smother me with that pillow." She pointed again to the pillow on the floor.

"What?" Rosie's jaw dropped in disbelief. "Are you sure?" she asked hesitantly. "You do have a head injury. Is it possible you might have imagined—"

"No, it's not possible. It happened. I know it did," Sarah said, desperation in her voice. Why wouldn't anyone believe her?

"Okay, okay. Calm down. I'll call security," Rosie said, holding up a reassuring hand. "I'm sure someone will be right up to talk to you about what happened."

"Are there any male nurses working on the floor right now?" Jake asked. "Maybe we could talk to them, see if someone had a reason for being in the room."

Rosie shook her head. "We don't have any male nurses on duty at the moment. But I'll ask at the nurses' station if anyone saw anything. I don't believe there were any further tests ordered, but it's possible one of the lab guys came in here—perhaps to draw some blood."

"He wasn't here to draw blood," Sarah said firmly.

"Before you go," Jake said as Rosie headed to the door, "has anyone called or asked about Sarah?"

Rosie hesitated. "I think there was a call earlier. One of the other nurses took it. Ms. Tucker was sleeping, and we had her phone turned off. The nurse forwarded the call to Dr. Carmichael's office. I can check with him."

"I already asked him if he'd spoken to anyone else, and he hadn't," Jake said. "However, it would be interesting to know if it was a man or a woman who called. Could you find out that much?"

"Of course," Rosie said with a nod.

Sarah looked at Jake as Rosie left the room, a half dozen thoughts running through her mind. "That call to the nurses' station could be from a friend, maybe whoever has Caitlyn, or . . ." She licked her lips as another idea occurred to her. "Or it could have been that man who just tried to kill me. He could have asked what room I was in. Maybe that's how he found me."

Jake frowned. "I don't understand what's going on here, Sarah."

"Neither do I. But until I remember my life, I need to protect myself." She made a quick decision. "Could you hand me my shoes?"

"You're not going anywhere."

"Look, last night someone tried to run me off the road. And just now when I was sleeping, I dreamt that I saw a man kill someone."

"Whoa, hang on a second," he said, raising a hand. "You dreamed that you saw a murder?"

"That's what I said."

"And then you woke up and someone was trying to smother you." He couldn't keep the skepticism from his voice. "I don't know, Sarah. Maybe you weren't all the way awake."

"That wouldn't explain why you saw a man leave my room," she countered.

"True," he said slowly. "But you could have misread his intent. The pillow fell on the floor during your restless sleep. He came in, picked it up, and was putting it under your head when you woke up."

"I know that sounds like a logical scenario, but that's not what happened." She paused, wondering why he was trying so hard to convince her that no one had tried to kill her. He hadn't been the man in her room, but she still didn't trust him. "Show me your arm," she said abruptly.

"What? Why?" he asked in surprise.

"Pull up your sleeve and show me your right wrist. In my dream the man who was holding the gun had a tattoo on his wrist. I want to know if it was you."

"You're crazy, Sarah. I've never shot a gun in my life."

"Then you won't mind showing me your wrist, will you?" she challenged.

Jake hesitated and then shoved up the sleeve of his leather jacket along with his shirt, revealing nothing but skin. "Satisfied?"

"About that," she replied. Until she knew exactly why she'd left him, she was going to keep her guard up.

Their conversation was interrupted by the arrival of an older man dressed in a business suit. "I'm Randall Jamison, head of hospital security," he said, his tone serious, his eyes concerned as he approached the bed. "What's the problem?"

Sarah related exactly what had happened, describing the man in her room as best she could. She also told him about her car accident the night before, and the possibility that the two events were connected. While Randall Jamison didn't appear to doubt her story, he didn't seem confident that they would find the person. Sarah had to admit that she wasn't giving him much to go on. It had happened so fast, the room in shadows, the man's face covered by a mask. She wasn't even sure she'd recognize the man if she saw him again.

"I've posted a guard outside your room," Randall said as they finished their conversation. "I'll also discuss the situation with Deputy Manning and see what else he wants to do in terms of an investigation."

"Thank you." After Randall left, Sarah picked up the pitcher next to her bed and attempted to pour herself a glass of water. She didn't realize her hands were shaking until she spilled half the water onto the table. She set the pitcher down and drank what little water she'd gotten into her glass. Then she took some tissues and mopped up the spill. All the while she could feel Jake's gaze on her. He seemed to be analyzing her every move, and she felt more than a little uncomfortable under his intense scrutiny. "What?" she finally demanded. "What are you thinking?"

"That you were always neat," he said, surprising her.

"Really? That's the first positive thing you've said about me." Her words brought the scowl back to his face.

"That's all I've got," he replied, obviously regretting his momentary lapse in anger.

"So what do we do now?"

"Hell if I know." He turned his back on her and walked over to the window. He pulled the curtains wide open, dispelling the lingering shadows in the room.

She was grateful for the light and relieved to deflect Jake's attention from her for at least a moment. She needed to regroup, get her wits about her. Unfortunately, her respite didn't last long.

Jake moved back toward the bed, taking a seat in the chair next to her. He leaned forward, resting his arms on his knees, clasping his hands together. "If you're in danger, then Caitlyn is, too."

She nodded. "I know. I'm really worried about her."

"Then, dammit, you'd better remember where the hell you left her," he said grimly. "Every second counts, Sarah."

"I'm trying. What else can I do? Everyone keeps telling me to sleep, but each time I do there's a new nightmare."

"Tell me more about this particular nightmare. What exactly did you see?"

She thought for a moment, wanting to get it right, not to miss any important details. "I saw a man holding a gun. On his right wrist was the tattoo of a tiger. He said something like, 'I want the girl.' I had the sense that I was watching from someplace nearby, and he wasn't aware I was there. I remember thinking I should try to stop him, to say something, but then the gun went off and there was all this blood. I was afraid to draw attention to myself. The next thing I knew I couldn't breathe, and I started struggling. When I opened my eyes a man was trying to smother me with a pillow. I screamed and he ran. Then you came in."

Jake's gaze met hers. "Was it the same man who was in your dream?"

She hadn't considered that possibility, but how would she know? "I didn't see the shooter's face in my dream, or if I did, it's hidden away in my mind. I suppose it's possible it was the same man, but they sounded different."

"Where were you in the dream? Was it a house, an apartment? Were you outside? What was surrounding you?"

"There was a tile floor—maybe a kitchen floor. I think I was in a house. I don't remember cupboards or tables or anything specific. I don't even know if it's something that really happened or just a bad dream caused by my head injury."

"Let's go with the theory that it's a memory. The man said he wanted the girl. . . ." Jake's voice faltered. "Do you think he was talking about Caitlyn?"

Sarah's pulse jumped. "I . . . I thought he was talking about me, but maybe you're right. Maybe he was talking about Caitlyn. Oh, God!" She put a hand to her mouth, her lips trembling. "I didn't think about that."

"You didn't see Caitlyn in your dream?"

"No. I wasn't aware of anyone but the man holding the gun. I don't even know who was shot. Obviously it wasn't me." She couldn't stand to think it was her baby. "There was a shadow," she said, focusing on a new detail appearing in her mind. "It was taller, bigger than a child. I'm sure it wasn't Caitlyn. There had to be someone else in the room, another adult. That's who was shot."

Jake jerked to his feet, pacing back and forth next to her bed. "I don't know what to believe. You lied over and over to me. Hell, you could still be faking this whole amnesia thing."

Anger swept through her. She was getting tired of defending herself, but she was going to do it one last time. "If I were faking, I wouldn't still be here in this hospital. I'd know where Caitlyn was. I'd know who my friends were. I'd be able to call someone to come and get me. I'd be able to look you in the eye and tell you exactly why I left you. More important, I wouldn't be sitting in this hospital bed waiting for someone to try to kill me again, now, would I?"

Jake looked like he wanted to argue, but was interrupted by Rosie. The nurse pushed the door halfway open and said, "The person who called about you was a woman, but she didn't leave her name. I'm sorry. That's all the information I have."

"Thanks," Sarah said.

"A woman," Jake echoed as Rosie left. "I hope it was the person who has Caitlyn, but if it was, where is she? Why hasn't she shown up here?"

"Maybe she's far away." Sarah frowned as Jake suddenly headed toward the door. "Where are you going? Jake?"

Jake ignored Sarah's call as he ran into the hall, remembering the woman he'd spoken to earlier. She'd said she was waiting for news about someone, but she'd been staring at him, watching him. Had she also listened to his conversation with Dr. Carmichael? They'd moved into the waiting room, but they certainly hadn't shut any doors. It was quite possible she'd heard every word they'd exchanged.

He strode quickly down the corridor, but there was no sign of her anywhere. He checked the waiting room. It was empty. He stopped at the nurses' station, where Rosie was working at a computer.

"Is there something else?" Rosie asked.

"There was a woman here earlier. She had brown hair. She was wearing jeans and a red sweater," he said, searching his mind for the details. "Do you remember her? She said she was waiting for news about someone. She was standing about three doors down."

"There were a lot of people here during visiting

hours," Rosie replied with an apologetic smile. "She doesn't stand out in my mind."

He sighed. Of course no one had seen the woman. That would have been too easy. He walked back down the hall and paused to speak to the security guard outside Sarah's room. "I'm Jake Sanders. I'm with the woman inside, Sarah Tucker. Will you let me know if anyone approaches you to ask about her condition? And make sure you check the ID on any hospital personnel. The man who attacked Ms. Tucker was dressed as a male nurse."

The guard nodded. "Yes, I'm aware of the situation."

When Jake reentered the room he found Sarah sitting on the edge of her bed, looking as if she were poised to flee. She hadn't put on her shoes, but they were close by, and she was still dressed in her street clothes.

"Where did you go?" she asked.

"I spoke to a woman earlier. She said she was waiting for news about someone, but I suddenly had the thought that maybe she was looking for information about you. She seemed to be watching me."

"Why wouldn't she have come to my room?" Sarah asked.

"Either she wasn't looking for you, or she got the information she needed about where you were, what your condition was."

"My condition?"

"Dr. Carmichael spoke to me about your amnesia.

I really have no idea if she heard anything or not, but she's gone now."

Sarah frowned. "Let's see. There are at least two other people besides you who are interested in me—the man who tried to kill me, and the woman who called to ask about me. I wonder if they're connected or acting independently."

He rolled his neck around on his shoulders, the tension of the past twenty-four hours tying knots in his muscles. When he'd jumped in the car to head south, he'd had no other expectation than to wrap his arms around his daughter and confront Sarah. Now the situation was far more complicated, and he was running as blind as Sarah was.

Sarah played with the bedsheet, twisting her fingers in the white cotton material. She wore no jewelry, no watch, no rings, no necklace. He wondered what she'd done with the jewelry he'd given her—what she'd done with everything. But there was no point in asking, not now, anyway.

He glanced at his watch—it was almost four thirty. He'd spoken to his brother over an hour and a half ago. Dylan should have checked in by now.

"You want to be out there, don't you?" Sarah asked. "In the search, looking for Caitlyn."

"Hell, yes, I'd like to be out there, but I can't, because I don't trust you not to run." She didn't bother to deny his statement, which only made him more certain that he had to stick close to her.

"I'd like to be out there, too. It's difficult to wait, to worry, to wonder."

Her words sent his blood pressure through the roof, and all the anger he'd been holding back blew sky high.

"You think it's hard?" he demanded. "You don't know anything about what's hard. I spent the last seven months in torture, wondering where the hell you were."

"I'm—"

"I don't want to hear it," he said with a wave of his hand. "You are responsible for everything bad that is happening. My daughter wouldn't be in danger right now if you hadn't left me without a word. I would know where she is. I would be protecting her, because I'm her father, a fact you conveniently seemed to forget. What you did was unforgivable. Indefensible. So don't even try, because I will never, ever believe a word you say."

Turning his back on her, he strode toward the window and stared out at the parking lot. He didn't even see the view before him. He was too busy fighting the desire to put his hands on Sarah and shake the truth out of her. So intense was his concentration, it took him a moment to realize that his cell phone was ringing. He pulled it out of his pocket and saw the number for the sheriff's department.

It was about time. "Hello?"

"This is Deputy Manning, Mr. Sanders. We've concluded our search of the canyon, and your daughter is not there."

Jake let out a breath. Finally an answer to something. He was relieved on one hand, but on the other hand he still didn't have his daughter.

"I met with your brother earlier," Manning continued. "He told me about the private investigation you ran on Ms. Tucker. I also did some checking myself, and Ms. Tucker has no fingerprints on record, no social security number, no credit cards, no paper trail. While it's concerning, it's not criminal—not yet, anyway. I'll stop by the hospital as soon as I'm done here. Security already filled me in on the alleged attack. Obviously Ms. Tucker is mixed up in something. Hopefully she'll get her memory back soon and will be able to answer our questions."

"What about my daughter? What else are you going to do to find her?"

"We'll discuss that when I get there. The good news is that your daughter wasn't in the car. She's probably tucked away somewhere safe."

"I hope so."

"What did the deputy say?" Sarah asked as he hung up the phone.

He turned back to face her. "They've finished the search. Caitlyn wasn't there. Manning will be down here shortly. He said he hasn't been able to verify your existence, that you've probably been living under another name."

She sat up straight, her brows drawing into a confused frown. "You mean I'm not Sarah Tucker?"

"That's the name you gave me. But like Manning, I never could find any evidence of your existence."

"How is that possible? I thought with the Internet these days, it was easy to find anyone."

"Not someone intent on hiding, someone very good at covering her tracks. When you disappeared, I discovered that the woman I knew didn't exist. You had given phony references to the café where you worked. You had no credit cards in your name, no bank accounts, not even a driver's license. I never thought to ask if you had a license when you told me you didn't have a car. I never thought to question where you kept your money. After you moved in with me, I paid all the bills."

He walked toward the bed, holding her gaze. "Every investigator I worked with suggested that you had help in disappearing, and that it wasn't the first time you'd pulled a vanishing act. You had to have had connections to construct an identity for yourself that allowed you to live freely and yet disappear completely when you were ready to go." He paused. "But someone somewhere knows who you really are."

"Maybe that's the person who's trying to kill me," she said.

"Maybe it is."

"And I won't see him coming, because I don't know who he is."

"Then you'd better get your memory back fast. I'm going to get some air."

Sarah stretched out on the bed and sank back against the pillows as Jake left the room. She was both relieved and terrified to be alone. She didn't know where the danger would come from next, but she was certain that whoever was after her was not through trying. She had to remember. She simply had to.

Squeezing her eyes shut, she searched desperately for a memory. But there was nothing. She knew there was only one way to get into her brain; she had to try to sleep. Her nightmares might be the only way to find her daughter.

Chapter Six

*The questions were so simple. He wanted to know her
name, where she came from, what she did, who she was.
He was so handsome, so sophisticated, so clearly out of her
league that she couldn't help but hesitate. Deep in her
heart she wanted to speak the truth, the whole ugly truth,
but she was afraid of the results. Things would change. He
wouldn't smile at her the way he was smiling now—not if
he knew who she really was. If she didn't give him the
right answers, he'd walk away. It had happened before.*

*What did it matter in the end? She would be who he
wanted her to be. She'd learned that important lesson
years earlier. Give them what they want, and then they'll
want you.*

Sarah woke up with a start, not sure how long
she'd been asleep, but the room was filled with dark,
late afternoon shadows. Blinking rapidly, she took in
the now-familiar surroundings of her hospital room.
The clock read five thirty. She'd been asleep for

about an hour. She'd been dreaming again—about a man. He'd been wearing a tuxedo. But his face remained vague, in the shadows of her mind. Was it Jake she'd dreamed about? Was it one of their early dates, when she'd first told him the lies about herself?

For some reason she didn't think so. Was it possible there was another man in her past? Someone else she had lied to? She frowned at that disturbing thought. What kind of a woman lied again and again? The only answer was that she had something to hide. And now she wasn't just hiding the past from others; she was also hiding it from herself.

Sitting up, she put a tentative hand to her head. The swelling had gone down, and her temple was much less painful. The dizziness also seemed to have eased. As she stretched her stiff limbs, she wondered where Jake was and, more important, what he was doing.

The door to her room opened, and she turned her head, expecting to see Jake, but it was another man. He was taller than Jake and thinner, dressed in a navy blue suit with a light blue tie that hung loose about his neck. His hair was brown but spiked and streaked with blond highlights, giving him a bit of a surfer look that didn't quite match his conservative attire. His eyes were a light brown, flecked with the same gold as his hair.

As he approached the bed, she tensed. Her first thought was that he was one of the doctors who had been called in to consult on her case, but there was something about the look in his eyes that bothered her. Her heart sped up.

"Who are you?" she demanded. "How did you get in here?"

Sarah reached for the call button as the man moved closer to her bed.

"Ready to call in the cavalry so soon?" he drawled. "I'm hurt. We haven't even talked yet, Sarah."

"I asked who you are," she repeated, unsure of what to make of his cynical, sarcastic tone.

"That's right. Jake says you don't remember anything or anyone. Very convenient."

"Not for me. How do you know Jake?"

"I'm his brother, Dylan," he replied, his gaze never wavering from her face. "Sound familiar, Princess?"

"Only in that Jake told me he had a brother," she replied. Now that she knew who he was, she threw back her shoulders and lifted her chin. She might have to answer to Jake, but she didn't have to answer to his brother. "And don't call me princess."

"What should I call you? I doubt Sarah is your real name, since I've spent the past seven months looking for you. My gut tells me you've been a number of people over the years, depending on whatever scam you were running. Otherwise we would have been able to track you down. But you were playing a game, a very good game—I'll give you that. You seemed so sweet and innocent, Jake's perfect blond angel, but that was just an illusion, wasn't it? Underneath that eager-to-please exterior was a woman who knew exactly what she was doing. You figured out everything Jake wanted, and then you gave it to him. You were smarter than I thought. But finally you made a mistake. You drove your car off the road and ended up where we could find you. So, game over." His gaze hardened. "Why don't you come clean, Sarah? Give Caitlyn back to Jake. Let him raise her. I'm sure a baby must be cramping your style."

"I don't know what you're talking about. What you say means nothing to me, and frankly, the person you're describing doesn't feel like me."

He shook his head, his eyes glittering in disbelief. "Doesn't feel like you—well, isn't that informative? Fine, you don't know anything about the past, so I'll fill you in. I walked away before. I kept my mouth shut, because Jake was stupidly in love with you, but I will not stand by and let you hurt my brother again. I will do whatever it takes to get Caitlyn back for Jake. And you won't stand in my way. Got it?"

There was no doubt about the threat in Dylan's voice. Sarah had one more enemy to add to the rapidly growing list of people who didn't like her.

The door opened, and Jake walked in holding two cups of coffee. His eyes were weary, his face showing a dark shadow of beard across his jaw. As he handed Dylan a cup, he frowned. "I told you to wait for me before you talked to Sarah."

"I wanted to see her for myself," Dylan said. "You're right: She looks like hell. But I don't feel one ounce of sympathy for her, and neither should you."

"I don't," Jake replied.

While they reconfirmed their dislike of her, Sarah eyed their coffees with envy. She could have used a shot of caffeine to raise her energy to face the night ahead, but she wouldn't ask Jake to get her a cup. He'd no doubt suspect some ulterior motive. Instead she asked, "Did you speak to Officer Manning again? He said he was going to come by, right?"

"He's downstairs," Jake said. "Look, Sarah, I don't know if Dylan told you, but he arranged for the local news channel to send a reporter over here. They want to do a short interview with you, ask for the public's help in identifying you and locating Caitlyn. It will air on the six-o'clock and eleven-o'clock newscasts tonight."

"But we already know who I am," she said, suddenly terrified at the prospect of going on camera and talking to a reporter.

"Someone may have seen you with Caitlyn at a rest stop or a restaurant, a gas station, somewhere that would help us pinpoint your location before the accident." Jake's eyes narrowed suspiciously at her hesitation. "Is there a problem?"

"Someone is trying to kill me. That's a problem," she said, panic rising. "I don't know if it's a good idea for me to go on television."

"It's no secret you're here in the hospital," Jake

said. "In fact, the more public you are, the more difficult you'll make it for someone to get to you."

Everything he said was true, but her mind still urged her to say no. "I think it's a mistake."

"Why?" Dylan shot out. "What are you afraid of?"

"I'm not sure. My instincts tell me to lie low."

"Well, my instincts tell me that we're going to need all the help we can get to find Caitlyn," Jake said. "You're going to do this if I have to carry you down there and force you to speak. This is a great opportunity for us to get the word out that Caitlyn is missing. I'm not going to waste it. And you have to be there, because you were with her. It's your face someone may recognize, not mine. It's also possible that whoever has Caitlyn will see the broadcast, realize you're not coming back, and step forward."

She knew he was right, and her reluctance was only making Jake and Dylan more suspicious of her—if that was even possible. She had no choice but to agree.

"All right. I'll do it," she conceded. "When is it?"

"Ten minutes, downstairs."

She swung her legs off the bed. "I need to use the restroom." She stood up slowly, her head spinning. Jake started to reach for her, and then thought better of it. Dylan watched her as if he were waiting for her to reveal something. Despite the fact that they weren't leaving her alone, she knew she was very much on her own. The two men were united—against her.

It was odd, but the feeling of being alone felt very true to her. She sensed she'd been on her own for most of her life. She'd told Jake her parents had died. That felt right. The rest, she had no idea.

When she thought she could move forward without falling, she put one tentative foot in front of the other until she had crossed the room. She reached for the restroom door with relief.

Once inside, she put her hands on the sink for balance and stared at her face in the mirror. The bruises around her eyes were darker, and the small cuts on her cheek were healing. Her brown hair was a mess, thick, tangled, curly, frizzed at the ends, completely wild. She felt a distinct feminine yearning for a hairbrush but settled for running her fingers through her hair, trying to get rid of some of the bigger tangles.

The familiar motion made her pause. She'd done this before. An image flashed through her mind. *Her hair was blond, and there'd been a man in the mirror, coming up behind her, his strong hands slipping around her waist as he nuzzled her neck with his lips. She could feel his warm mouth on her skin, his hard body behind hers.* She looked for his face in the glass, but it remained maddeningly out of reach.

It had to have been Jake. They'd been lovers, obviously. They'd had a child together. But had he been the only man in her life? She was twenty-eight years old, according to Jake. They'd been together two years. That left her early twenties up for grabs. She had to have been somewhere before she arrived in

San Francisco. She had to have had friends, relatives. Why was her past so elusive? Had she told so many lies that she didn't know what the truth was anymore?

Lies implied secrets, danger—had she done something horrific? Or had she seen someone else do it? Was she a victim or a villain?

She stared at her face in the mirror, determined to find something there that jarred her memory. But eventually her features turned into one unrecognizable blur. She didn't know who she was. But someone knew the truth about her. And they wanted to kill her. There had to be a reason why.

"You're sure Sarah isn't faking this amnesia?" Dylan asked as he dug his hands into the pockets of his slacks and paced around one side of the small hospital room.

Jake sighed. He didn't need his younger brother's overwhelming cynicism to make this any more difficult. "She's pretty good if she's acting," he prevaricated.

"Well, you already know she's good," Dylan reminded him.

"It's not just me. The doctor is convinced as well."

"Yeah, well, Sarah has a way of distracting men from the truth."

"Just say you told me so; then we can get it over with." Jake knew his brother had been biting back the words for the past seven months.

"I told you so," Dylan replied, meeting his gaze. "I knew Sarah was lying, but you wouldn't believe me, and you should have. I'm your brother. I have your back. And you know women are natural-born liars. But still you ignored all the warning signs."

Jake knew his brother wasn't just talking about Sarah. "She's not Mom."

"She's the same," Dylan said with a shrug. "She left, didn't she?"

Jake didn't want to go down that path. His brother's bitter feelings about their mother ran extremely deep. "Let's stay focused on the present, shall we?"

"Fine. Maybe something will come of the newscast. Although Sarah certainly doesn't want to do it—not exactly the actions of a woman desperate to find her child."

"She's scared," Jake admitted. "She's had a rough twenty-four hours. Someone has tried to kill her twice." He'd filled his brother in on the events of the past two days, and while Dylan still believed Sarah was no innocent bystander, he was at least beginning to believe that whatever she was involved in was bigger than her.

"Which is why going public is a good idea. We need to find out who has Caitlyn. And if Sarah is in danger, so is your daughter."

"I know," Jake murmured, his gut clenching at the thought. "I can't stand not knowing where she is."

"How are you handling being with Sarah again?"

Jake couldn't even begin to answer that question. His conflict must have shown on his face, because Dylan's mouth was already turning down at the corners.

"She's getting to you, isn't she? I knew it," Dylan said.

"Don't be an ass. She's not getting to me."

"I saw the way you looked at her when she got out of bed and stumbled. You almost reached for her. You wanted to help her."

"Reflex action," Jake said, avoiding his brother's piercing gaze. Dylan had a way of seeing through people's walls. That was why he'd been able to see through Sarah. But right now Jake didn't want his brother analyzing him or his reactions to Sarah.

"You have a bad habit of wanting to rescue people," Dylan said. "You spent half our childhood rescuing me, remember?"

"Yeah, well, someone had to. Look, she's not playing me, all right? I haven't forgotten what she did. But the situation is more complicated now. It's not just about Sarah walking out on me. There's a lot more at stake. Right before Sarah was attacked earlier, she told me that she dreamed she saw someone get shot. If she witnessed a murder, then that could be why someone is after her."

Curiosity sparked in Dylan's eyes. "A murder, huh? What else did she see in her dream?"

"She saw the arm of the man who was holding the gun. He had a tattoo of a tiger on his wrist. She couldn't identify where she was, but she felt like she was in hiding. The man said, 'I want the girl.' Jake drew in a sharp breath as the words reminded him that that *girl* could be his daughter. "Then he took a shot at someone."

Dylan's lips tightened. "Is that it?"

"Sarah saw blood, but that's all she remembers. When she woke up, there was a man in her room trying to smother her with a pillow."

"Right," Dylan said. "Well, at least some information is coming back into her head. Although she never seems to remember enough, does she—just little teasing bits. When did this alleged murder happen? While she was with you? After she left you?"

"I think it was before she left me—maybe the reason she ran."

"If it happened while she was with you, why wouldn't she tell you, go to the police, ask for help?" Dylan gave a warning shake of his head. "Don't start giving Sarah reasons for running off with your kid."

"I'm putting the facts together."

"Just don't manipulate the facts to paint the picture you're looking for. If you let that woman convince you that she's some innocent—"

"She's not going to convince me of anything that isn't true," Jake interrupted. "But I can't ignore what Sarah tells me. My daughter's life is at stake."

Dylan nodded, conceding the point. "All right. It's not much to go on, but I can look through the crime files. We might get lucky on the tattoo. It could represent some kind of gang affiliation. If it means something, I'll figure it out." He stopped talking as Sarah came through the door. "Was it the right wrist or the left?" he asked.

"What are you talking about?"

"The tattoo on the arm of the killer in your dream."

"You told him about that?" she asked Jake.

"Why not? It might help us figure out who you are."

"I guess," she said. "It was the right wrist, I think . . . I don't know. It's hazy now."

Jake could see that Sarah's vague reply only deepened the skepticism in Dylan's eyes.

"Of course it's hazy," Dylan said. "What else would it be?"

Sarah's back stiffened. She shot Dylan an angry look. "I don't care whether you believe me or not, but I've told the truth to every question that I've been asked since I woke up in this hospital room."

Jake was surprised by Sarah's strong response. It occurred to him that he'd never seen her react with anger toward anyone in the two years they'd been together. She'd always kept her feelings in check, her expression pleasant. She'd been a people pleaser, not someone who liked to stir things up, or even a person willing to continue an argument. She'd done everything she could to avoid conflict, usually by giving in.

But this new Sarah, who couldn't remember who

she was, had also forgotten how to stay neutral, how to keep herself from showing emotion. In some odd way he thought he might be closer to getting to know the real her than he had ever been.

Sarah slipped her feet into her tennis shoes and then sat down on the bed to lace them. Her hands shook, reminding Jake that she'd come very close to losing her life. She certainly wasn't faking the bruises and the injuries she'd suffered, nor the pain in her eyes. He told himself not to feel sorry for her. Sarah deserved the same kind of pain he'd been living through for the past seven months and more.

Sarah finished tying her shoes and stood up, facing him with determination in her blue eyes. "Where are we doing this?" she asked.

"There's a conference room downstairs. It's just going to be you, a reporter, and a cameraman."

"You're not going to be part of the interview?"

"I don't want to confuse anyone by suggesting that we were together. We want the public to think about whether or not they saw you alone, or you and Caitlyn together."

"They're going to put Caitlyn's picture on the screen during the live shot," Dylan added. "It's not up-to-date, of course, but maybe those blond curls will ring a bell."

Sarah nodded and threw back her shoulders as she headed for the door. "Let's go, then. I want to get this over with."

* * *

Every step Sarah took toward the downstairs conference room filled her heart with dread. She was going to do an interview that would be broadcast around the county. Who knew who would be watching her, listening to her? But this was a good opportunity to get the word out that Caitlyn was missing.

But was she missing? Or had she hidden her daughter somewhere?

The thought had been growing slowly in her mind. If someone were trying to hurt her and her daughter, wouldn't it have made sense for her to find a way to protect her child, put her in a safe place? However, if that place were somewhere close by, why hadn't anyone come forward to see her, to tell her that Caitlyn was okay? And if she had been in trouble, why hadn't she turned to Jake for help at some point in the last seven months?

She blew out a breath of frustration. She didn't have any answers, but she did know one thing for sure: She'd gotten herself involved in something big, something that made her a target for murder. And she prayed to God that her daughter wasn't in the middle of her mess. She had to find a way to make things right. Maybe this interview was the first step. But as they reached the conference room, every instinct she had screamed at her to run, to hide in the shadows, to stay out of sight, not to trust anyone or anything. Somewhere in her past she'd been betrayed by someone she'd trusted.

Jake caught her eye, a question in his gaze. "What's wrong?"

"I don't want to do this."

"You have to."

"Sarah is just stalling, trying to figure out how to protect herself," Dylan interjected. "She only cares about herself and what she has to hide."

"Maybe what I have to hide is the only thing protecting Caitlyn," Sarah returned, glaring at Dylan. "You told me you don't know who I am or where I've been. You don't know any more about me than I do."

"I know a liar when I see one," Dylan retorted.

"That's enough, both of you," Jake said, cutting Sarah off before she could reply. "This isn't getting us anywhere. None of us knows where Caitlyn is or why she's not with you, Sarah. But this is one thing we can do to try to move forward. And that's the only place I'm interested in going. So let's get this over with."

Sarah drew in a deep breath as they entered the conference room. An attractive blonde named Jillian Davis greeted them, giving Dylan a particularly flirtatious smile. They seemed to know each other from somewhere, talking about their time together on a previous story while the cameraman set up the shot. Finally Jillian turned to Sarah.

"I'll just ask a couple of questions," Jillian said. "Try to be as open as you can. Let the public see your desperation, so they will want to respond to your plea for help. This is going to be a live shot."

Live? That meant she couldn't screw up. She had

to get it right the first time. Sarah sat down in a chair in front of a big bright light. She could hear Jillian speaking to her cameraman about how much time before they started. Their voices faded in her head, replaced by a rush of panic. She closed her eyes, trying to find some calm, but then another disturbing image popped into her head. . . .

There were news trucks outside the building, reporters with microphones, light stands set up on the sidewalk. Every network in the city was waiting for the news.

"It's almost time to go," a woman said. "No one will see her leave, I promise."

She ignored the woman, looking over at the tall man in the center of the room, the one who was calling the shots. "I can't do this."

"It's too late to change your mind. From now on you're dead; do you understand? It's the only way out."

"Ms. Tucker. Sarah." The voice seemed to come from a long way away. "What's wrong with her? Is she going to be able to do this?" Jillian asked.

"Sarah, snap out of it."

Jake's voice broke through her reverie, and she jerked under the hand he had placed on her shoulder. Her eyes flew open. "What? What did you say?"

"I said we're ready." His gaze narrowed. "You disappeared right in front of me, went into your head. What did you see? What did you remember?"

Before she could answer, the cameraman was counting down the seconds, "Five, four, three, two, one, go."

Dylan dragged Jake out of the shot as the reporter

said, "This is Jillian Davis reporting live from St. Mary's Hospital, where an amnesia victim needs the public's help to find her missing child." Jillian turned to Sarah with an encouraging smile. "Tell us what we can do."

Chapter Seven

With a suspicious eye Jake watched Sarah stumble through her answers. Something had happened to her. She'd gone into herself, remembered something that scared her. Did it have to do with Caitlyn?

Sarah appeared to have gathered herself together now, but he could see that it was a struggle for her to speak. Her answers were short, clipped, and no matter what Jillian did to encourage a longer response, Sarah remained maddeningly brief in her replies. Finally it was over. The lights went off, and Sarah slumped in her chair.

Dylan shot him a pointed look, reminding Jake that his brother thought Sarah's behavior was odd, too. Nothing new there. Fortunately Dylan walked Jillian and the cameraman out of the room, leaving Jake alone with Sarah. He needed to talk to her before she got her guard back up.

"I didn't do well," she said, looking down at her hands. "I froze when it started."

"You froze *before* it started." He moved over to her, squatting down in front of her so they were eye-to-eye. "What did you remember? Don't try to lie. I know it was something."

"I was in a building, and there were reporters' news trucks outside. There were a couple of other people in the room, and they were talking about getting me out without anyone seeing me. I didn't want to go, but this man said I had to go, that I was dead, and it was the only way out." She raised her gaze to his, and he could see the fear in her eyes. "I had the feeling that whoever I was that night I was never going to be again."

Jake considered her words, his gut churning. Her statement only confirmed what he already knew—that Sarah had once been somebody else. But who?

"The fact that you were involved in something that the press was covering is very interesting," he said slowly.

Sarah nodded. "Yes, but I don't know where I was."

"Was anyone wearing a uniform? Could you have been at a police station? What about a courthouse? Did you see a judge, a court officer, a bailiff?"

"No one was wearing a uniform, just suits, nondescript suits," she said with a shrug. "I was in some sort of an office. It could have been in the courthouse or in a police station, but I can't say for sure."

"You saw faces this time?"

"They were vague, but sort of," she said.

"You're going to have to do better than that, Sarah."

"It was a flash, Jake. It lasted, like, ten seconds in my head. I didn't know it was coming. I couldn't get ready for it."

"Just think for a minute. Can you describe the people in the room?"

"Only that it was a man and a woman. The man was tall. He had a commanding air about him. It felt like he was in charge. They talked about getting me out through a side door."

It sounded to Jake as if someone had been trying to help Sarah hide. It could have been the cops, her family, friends—how could he know? But the fact that there had been news trucks implied that whatever she'd been involved in was big enough to warrant press coverage. That meant there must be a paper trail regarding that particular story, if he could figure out what the story was.

He stood up as Deputy Manning and his brother paused just outside the room, conversing with the hospital's head of security.

Sarah grabbed his arm. "Don't tell them what I just said," she pleaded.

Jake wondered why. "I'm not going to keep your secrets." But when Manning and Dylan walked over to join them, he decided to hear what they had to say first. He needed to think about Sarah's latest flash of memory, figure out what it might mean. He also wanted to ask her why she'd panicked at the idea of him discussing her memory with the police.

"I've spoken with Mr. Jamison in security," Manning said. "They don't have any new information on the man who entered your room earlier. They've talked to the employees on the floor, and no one saw anyone who didn't belong there."

Jake hadn't really expected a different answer. Sarah's description had been vague at best.

"We removed your car from the canyon," Manning continued. "It's in the impound lot. We found no other evidence or clues to your past in the vehicle. Except for the items belonging to the child, the car was clean. Our best hope is that tonight's broadcast will generate some new leads." He glanced from Jake to Sarah. "Is there anything else you can tell me?"

Sarah gave a brief shake of her head, barely glancing at the deputy. She certainly didn't appear eager to work with law enforcement, and it was clear she knew that Manning had his doubts about her. Who could blame him? Sarah was a mess of contradictions. Jake had lived with her for two years, but he barely recognized the woman before him.

"I'm not feeling well. I'd like to go to my room," Sarah said, sending him a pleading look.

He felt himself weaken at her desperate gaze. She was hurt. She was scared. And she wanted him to help her. He told himself he was concerned only because of Caitlyn. He didn't want Sarah to lose her grip on reality. Getting her memory back could be crucial to finding his daughter.

"I'll walk you up," he said as Sarah got to her feet.

He avoided looking at Dylan, afraid he would reveal too much.

"I'll check with you both in the morning," Manning said. "Hopefully we'll have some good leads to follow."

Jake put his hand on Sarah's arm as he escorted her out of the room. Dylan fell into step on her other side, the security guard following behind them. They didn't say a word as they made their way back up to the third floor.

Once inside her room Sarah kicked off her shoes and sat down on the bed with a weary sigh. She looked almost defeated, Jake thought. It wasn't just the pain of her injuries that was taking a toll—it was the fear running through her. And he suspected it was that fear that was keeping her memory at bay. How could he give her the courage to face the demons in her head, especially when he didn't know what those demons were?

She hadn't trusted him enough to tell the truth about herself when they were together, and she certainly didn't trust him now. Nor did he trust her. Where did that leave them?

There was a dinner tray on the bedside table, and Sarah picked up the aluminum cover to reveal a plate of chicken and mashed potatoes. Jake felt his stomach grumble at the sight. The food didn't look all that appetizing, but he couldn't remember when either of them had last eaten. "You should eat," he told her. "You need to get your strength back."

"I'm not hungry."

"Eat anyway. Do it for your daughter."

She reluctantly picked up her fork. "What about you?"

"He's coming with me," Dylan said. "Down to the cafeteria. No arguments. The guard is outside, and Sarah isn't going anywhere, right, Sarah?"

"Right," she muttered. "I wouldn't know where to go, and with someone trying to kill me, it's smarter to stay where I have someone watching out for me. I'm not an idiot, no matter what else you may think of me."

Jake hesitated, but his appetite won out. "Fine. I'll be back in thirty minutes. You'd better be here, Sarah."

"I will be," she replied, meeting his gaze.

There had been a time in his life when he'd never doubted her. Now he had nothing but doubts.

"Stop checking your watch. Sarah isn't going to run," Dylan said about twenty minutes later as he worked his way through a plate of spaghetti and meatballs.

"I'm not just worried about her leaving. I'm worried about who else might show up now that Sarah has gone public."

"What was with her during the broadcast? She looked terrified."

"Right before the interview Sarah told me she had a flash of being somewhere with the media nearby waiting for a story. She was being hustled out of the building in secret. She said she had the feeling she was going to have to disappear, to live under another name."

Dylan raised an eyebrow. "Sounds like a scene from a movie."

"Or Witness Protection," Jake suggested. The idea had been running around in his brain since Sarah had told him about the memory. "Think about it—if Sarah witnessed a crime, then she could have been asked to testify. Her life might have been in danger. And if her testimony was important, someone might have tried to hide her. Maybe that's why she lied to me about her past," he added, feeling as if the pieces of the puzzle were beginning to make sense.

"That's a lot of ifs," Dylan told him.

"True. But we know that Sarah saw someone get shot."

"Or that's what she wants us to think. She drops a few key details here and there and paints a picture that could be true or not."

Jake nodded. "You might be right, but let's go with the theory that her complete memory is lost and the bits and pieces that she's remembering are clues to her past. Do you have any contacts in Witness Protection?"

"I can look into it."

"Good, thanks. I'll stay with Sarah tonight. Tomorrow I want to go out to the accident scene. After that, if Sarah is well enough to leave the hospital, I'd like to take her down to LA. Manning gave me the address on the car registration. Apparently there is no one at that address who knows anything about the owner of the car, Margaret Bradley, or Sarah, but it's an apartment building, and Manning didn't check with everyone living there."

"Sounds like a plan."

"Not much of one, but all I've got," Jake said. "I just hope we get more leads from the broadcast tonight. I appreciate you setting that up. In fact, I appreciate everything you've been doing."

"It's no problem. I owe you, Jake. We both know that."

"No, you don't," Jake said quickly.

"Yes, I do," Dylan replied, meeting his gaze.

Jake saw a flash of pain flit through his brother's eyes and knew that despite his best efforts Dylan would be forever haunted and damaged by their past. What his mother had started with her sudden unexplained departure when Jake was ten and Dylan was seven, his father had finished with his brutal bullying of Dylan, who could never do anything right. Jake had tried to protect Dylan, but he hadn't always succeeded.

"Stop giving me that look; I'm fine now," Dylan said, reading his mind.

"Yeah, that's what you always say."

"Forget about me. We've got more important things to worry about. We need to get your kid back."

Jake threw a couple of dollars on the table and stood up. "Did you find a motel for the night?"

"I will when I leave here. Be careful, Jake," Dylan said as he got to his feet. "If someone wants Sarah dead, it's not a stretch to think they'd take you out to get to her."

Sarah couldn't believe she was actually missing Jake's presence. She'd spent most of the day wishing she could find a way to get rid of him. His never-ending suspicions kept her nerves on edge. But there was also something about his intensity, his determination to find his daughter, his strength and confidence that made her believe that if anyone could bring Caitlyn back to her, it was Jake. Not that he intended to hand his daughter over to her; she'd have to fight him for that. Surely, once her memory returned, she'd be able to do just that. But right now all she really wanted was to know that Caitlyn was safe. The rest would work itself out.

She flipped through the television channels with restless fingers. While her body was tired, her mind was still keyed up from the interview. She had done a terrible job. She'd felt as if every word she spoke was taking her down a path she didn't want to go. She'd gone against her instinct to stay in the shadows because of her desire to find her daughter; but somewhere inside she was terrified she'd done more harm than good.

Jake opened the door, and her pulse jumped at the sight of him.

When he came into a room she never knew what to expect. Most of the time he was extremely pissed off at her, but here and there she saw moments of softening, of kindness, or maybe she just wanted to see something good in him. She needed a friend, an ally, someone to trust, but was Jake that person?

He took off his jacket and tossed it over the back of the chair next to the bed. Then he sat down and stretched out his long legs in front of him, folding his arms across his chest. He looked like he was settling in for the night.

"Are you going to sleep in your clothes?" he asked.

"I think so," she replied. The hospital gown made her feel far too vulnerable. She wanted to be ready to flee at a moment's notice. "Where's your brother?"

"Looking for a motel. He has his computer with him, so he's going to get on the Net tonight and see what he can find out about some of the clues you've given us—the tiger tattoo and the idea that you may have been involved in some sort of press-worthy case."

"You told him about that?"

He met her gaze. "He's my brother. I'd trust him with my life—and yours," he added.

"He doesn't like me."

"No, he doesn't. He suspected you were lying to me long before you left, but I didn't listen. In fact, I kicked him out of our home and said he didn't know what he was talking about. Fortunately Dylan doesn't hold a grudge. As soon as you disappeared with Caitlyn he came back, and he's worked tirelessly to help me find you."

Sarah looked away from Jake's bitter gaze. She didn't want to talk about her disappearance. She didn't want to hear again how she'd destroyed their lives. Instead she wanted to go a little farther back, find a way to understand the life Jake had told her about. She hit the mute button on the television and asked, "How did we meet?"

He frowned. "That's not important, and I don't want to get into the past with you."

"You're going to have to, Jake. I need to remember my life, and you're the only one who has any information. Maybe something you tell me will bring my memory back. That's what we both want, isn't it?"

Jake sighed and stared down at the floor for a long moment. He cracked the knuckles on his left hand, then his right. As she watched him, something fluttered deep within her. She'd seen him do this before when he was stressed, and she had the feeling that she'd worried about him, which surprised her. Jake was a big, strong guy, smart, more than able to speak his mind and to stand up for himself. So where would the anxiety have come from? Love?

He'd told her that they'd had a passionate romance, but it was difficult to believe, not just because she didn't remember him, but also because he didn't act like he loved her. He was so cold to her. She got a chill whenever he came near. Had his love disappeared with her hasty departure from his life? Or had something happened before that?

"We met in a café down the street from my office," Jake said abruptly, lifting his gaze to hers. "You'd just started working as a waitress. I used to get lunch there on a regular basis. My architectural firm was down the street."

"What do you design?"

"Commercial buildings. But the day we met I was working on a personal project, a house I was planning to build. You were fascinated by the process and told me how much you loved houses, and you were dying to see some of the famous Victorians in the city. I offered to give you a tour, since you said you'd just moved to town and didn't know anyone. You didn't accept at first, but after a couple of invitations you said yes."

So she'd been cautious at first—that felt right to her. "Go on."

"The next weekend we spent all day Saturday looking at houses; then we moved on to the Transamerica Pyramid, Coit Tower, and the old bank buildings on Market Street," Jake continued. "When we were done, we went to dinner and talked for hours." He paused, an odd light coming into his eyes. "Actually, I didn't realize until after you left me how much I talked and you listened. At any rate, we went out again the next night for dinner, and by the weekend we were in bed together."

His words were so pragmatic, but the actions he described were romantic, passionate, whirlwind, and not at all cautious. "That fast?" she murmured.

"You said I swept you off your feet," he replied, his voice now laced with disbelief. "In retrospect you must have had an ulterior motive."

"Like what? Are you rich? Was it about money? Did I steal from you when I left?"

"You took a couple hundred dollars out of the dresser drawer in our bedroom, but you didn't have access to my bank account." He leaned forward, his gaze darkening. "The thing is, Sarah, I wouldn't have cared if you had taken every cent I had, if you'd left Caitlyn with me."

She wanted to defend her actions, but she couldn't.

"I kept thinking you'd have second thoughts," he continued, "that you'd come back or call or write me a letter. A couple of weeks after you left I received some hang-up calls, breathing on the other end, but no one would talk. It drove me crazy, but I didn't want to change my number in case it was you or it was someone who knew about you." He paused. "And then there was the break-in."

Her heart skipped a beat. "What are you talking about? What break-in?"

"About two weeks after you left, I came home and the back window of the apartment had been broken. Someone had come in, tossed the furniture, stolen some petty cash and my laptop computer. The police couldn't lift any fingerprints. They never figured out who did it." He took a breath as he met her gaze. "I know what you're thinking, that it was connected to your disappearance. I thought so, too, but another apartment in the building was also broken into. In the end, the police believed it was just your ordinary, run-of-the-mill burglar."

"It seems odd to me," she murmured, especially since she now knew that someone was trying to kill her. Had they been trying to kill her when she was with Jake, too? Was that why she'd run? Had they broken into Jake's apartment to find out where she'd gone, or to see if she'd left something important behind? If she'd cleaned out the apartment before she left, had she been trying to hide something?

"The timing felt coincidental," Jake admitted. "But the fact that two apartments were broken into made it seem more random."

"Which might have been what they wanted you to think."

"It's easier to see that now. At the time I didn't have any idea you had a secretive past or were in danger. All I had was a note saying our relationship wasn't working and you were leaving."

She sighed at his unforgiving tone. "Is there anything you can tell me about myself that's good? Just one little thing, like maybe I squeezed the toothpaste from the bottom up, or I made really great popcorn, or anything?"

Jake didn't look eager to comply with her request. "I can't remember."

"I'm sure that felt good to say. A taste of my own medicine, huh?"

He tipped his head in acknowledgment. "It's hard to swallow, isn't it?"

Silence fell between them. She couldn't bring herself to beg for more information, and it was clear that Jake couldn't get past the anger he felt toward her. It radiated off of him in thick, pulsing waves, making the air between them tense and uncomfortable. It was going to be a long night.

"You liked to take pictures," Jake said finally.

"Of what?" she asked.

"Buildings, landscapes, flowers, animals, pretty much whatever grabbed your interest. Not people, though. You never shot people. Even when Caitlyn was born, you seemed reluctant to take photos of her. I have no idea what you did with the ones you did take. They disappeared with you."

"What else?" she asked, eager for as much as he could give her. "What about your family? Do you have other siblings besides Dylan? Parents? Grandparents? Did we spend time with them?"

He gazed back at her, his expression still grim. "My parents divorced when I was ten. That's the last time I saw my mother. My father and I don't spend time together anymore. You never met him. We did, however, visit my grandmother a few times in the convalescent home. She liked you, but she had Alzheimer's, so God only knows who she thought you were half the time. Are we done? Because this is a waste of time. It doesn't matter who you were or what you did with me. What we need to figure out is where you've been the last seven months."

"I know, but how do we do that? All I have is a deeply ingrained sense of fear and the belief that I've been running for a long time."

"Maybe you have," he said. "I should have dug

deeper when you were with me. I should have asked more questions."

"Why would you? It sounds like we had a normal relationship."

"I knew better than to take you at face value. My parents' divorce was brutal, and the months leading up to it were a nightmare of accusations and lies. Afterward was no better. I grew up thinking it would be smarter to stay single and save myself a shitload of pain. But, no, I let you get under my skin. I broke every rule I'd ever made for myself, and you screwed me every way you could."

"I'm sorry I hurt you," she said, the words springing forth before she could stop them.

His eyes darkened. "How can you be sorry when you claim not to know what you did?"

"Because it's clear that I caused you pain. And it's obvious that I wasn't the only one in your life to do that. It sounds like you had a rough childhood."

"I'm not going to talk to you about my parents."

"Then tell me about mine," she said, changing the topic again in search of something that would give her a clue to her past.

"I don't know anything about your family. You said they were dead, that they died in a car crash and you went to live with your grandmother in Boston, but I couldn't find her or any record of her—or you, for that matter. So that was a lie."

She sighed. It seemed every question she asked eventually led to a dead end. "Are you sure there's nothing else I told you about my parents, like where we lived, or what they looked like, or what they did for a living?"

"You said you missed watching old musicals and movies with your mom. I think she was a stay-at-home mom. You didn't mention a job. Apparently when you were a little girl, your mother used to take you to a movie theater in the afternoons where—"

"—where movies were a dollar," she finished, excitement racing through her veins. "I remember that movie house. It was one of those big, old-fashioned theaters. We used to sit in the balcony in the front row. I'd put my feet up on the railing. Weird that I would remember that and nothing else."

"Maybe you remembered the movie house because there's nothing about it that scares you. But something terrifies you. There has to be a reason why your brain is protecting you from your memories."

"Is that the way you think of it?"

"How do you think of it?" he countered.

"I feel lost in my own head. It's strange. It's like you're telling me a story about someone I don't know. Some things you say feel right, but others don't. I'm trying to rely on my instincts, but I feel like I'm walking through a minefield."

"Because you mixed lies with truth, Sarah. That's why things don't add up. You should try to get some sleep. Maybe when you wake up you'll know who you are. And we can go get Caitlyn."

"How was I with Caitlyn?"

He cleared his throat. "Good. You were good," he

said roughly. "The two of you were inseparable from the moment I cut the cord and handed her to you."

"You cut the cord?" she echoed, the tender image at odds with the hard man sitting in front of her.

"Yeah, I did. I was there for every second of the fourteen hours you were in labor. And when Caitlyn was born, my life changed." His gaze settled on her face. "It was the best moment of my life. The worst was when I realized you'd taken Caitlyn and left me." He jerked to his feet. "I'm going for a walk."

"Jake . . ."

"What?"

"Did we really love each other?"

He paused by the door. "When you get your memory back, you'll know the answer."

"She went on the news," Shane Hollis said, adrenaline rushing through his blood as he turned off the television set in his motel room. He hadn't anticipated that she would go public. It changed everything, and it would make it more difficult to get to her. "She went on the fucking news," he repeated.

The silence on the other end of the phone disturbed him. He'd already failed several times. He knew he would have only one more chance at the most. If he didn't kill her, his own life would be over.

There had been a time when they were equals, brothers—or so he had thought. But what had started out as a game in their youth had taken turns he had never imagined. He stared down at the tattoo on his wrist, still remembering the day they'd gone in to get them. The tiger stood for fierceness, power, loyalty, brotherhood. He hadn't realized at the time that it also stood for murder.

He was in too deep now; there was no way out. The price of belonging to their elite group was blood on his hands that would never come off. He could only continue what had begun years earlier.

"I'm disappointed in you," the man said. "After all I've done for you."

Shane wanted to point out that he'd done far more in return, but he remained silent. The order of power in their group had been established long ago. The man on the other end of the line had known how to use each one of them to his own advantage. But he had made one critical mistake—a woman with long blond hair and blue eyes, a woman who still had to be silenced.

"I'll get her," Shane promised. "I just need some time. Besides, she doesn't remember anything. She's not a threat right now. We can wait until things cool down."

The pause at the other end of the line sent a chill down his spine. It wasn't his place to offer opinions.

"As long as she breathes, she's a threat," the man said. "She betrayed me. She must pay for that. I've waited a long time for her to die. I won't wait any longer."

"I'll get her, but there's someone with her—a man named Jake Sanders. He claims to be the father of her baby, but I never saw a kid."

"Maybe you weren't looking closely enough."

"What do you want me to do about the guy?" he asked, ignoring the criticism.

"Kill him, too."

His blood thundered in his veins. "What about the child?"

The line clicked, replaced by a dial tone. Shane closed his phone, knowing it didn't matter what he wanted to do. He would do what had to be done. If he didn't, someone else would.

Chapter Eight

Sarah was relieved to see the sun shining when she woke up the next morning. Unfortunately her optimism faded as she tried to remember something about herself that Jake hadn't told her, and she came up with nothing. At least she felt better. Her head didn't hurt, and moving it from side to side did not make her dizzy. *Thank goodness.*

She glanced at the chair where Jake had spent the night. It was empty now, but she suspected he hadn't gone far. During the night she'd been vaguely aware of Jake trying to get comfortable on the two chairs he'd propped together, but she doubted he'd been successful. She'd suggested he go to a motel, but it was clear he had no intention of leaving her until they found Caitlyn.

Getting out of bed, she made her way to the restroom to wash up. She was determined to get out of the hospital and go look for her daughter. She couldn't spend another day in bed doing nothing.

When she returned to the room, Jake and Dylan were waiting for her. Dylan had changed out of his suit and into a pair of worn blue jeans with a dark blue sweater. Jake also wore jeans and a long-sleeved black T-shirt. Despite their similar attire, the two men didn't look all that much alike.

Dylan was a golden boy, tan, handsome. Jake was rugged, less refined, more serious, less flippant. But there was a connection between them, an unspoken conversation that seemed to go on whenever they were together. They were united in their search for Caitlyn and in their feelings about her. Perhaps not completely united, she amended, seeing a softening in Jake's eyes as he looked at her. There had been a connection between them, too, one strong enough for Jake to go against his brother. If he had to choose again, would he make the same choice?

"I'm glad you're both here," she said, taking the first step. "I want to go to the accident scene this morning. I want to start looking for Caitlyn."

"So do I," Jake said. "I think we should retrace your steps from the site of the car crash back to LA, to the last-known address of the woman who gave you the car."

Sarah liked the idea of taking action, but she had one big concern. "Are you sure it's a good idea for us to leave the area? What if Caitlyn is around here?"

"She's not in that canyon," Jake said decisively. "She has to be somewhere else. And since no one has come forward from the immediate area, I'm guessing she's nowhere close by."

"What about the news broadcast last night?" she asked. "Did it generate any leads?"

"There were several calls." Jake glanced over at Dylan. "You have the details. Why don't you tell her?"

"The first call was from a gas station attendant about thirty miles from here," Dylan said. "He stated that he saw you fill up the tank, and you gave him two twenty-dollar bills for payment. You didn't bring the child inside, nor did he see a kid in the car. He admitted that he wasn't paying much attention. There were also a few calls from obvious cranks."

"What do you mean?"

"Well, one man said you're his daughter, and you owe him five hundred dollars. He's a homeless man well-known by the police, and he has no children. Another woman said you ran out on a bill at her coffee shop; she's also hoping to gain some cash by taking advantage of your memory loss."

"That's it?" she asked, feeling depressed. Wasn't there anyone who knew her? Who cared about her?

"Well, there was another woman who said you look like a friend of hers who disappeared eight years ago. She lives out by the coast, north of here, in San Luis Obispo. Manning talked to her, but said she had no facts to connect her friend with you, just a feeling. She wasn't completely sure she recognized you, and apparently she fancies herself something of a psychic. He thinks it's extremely doubtful there's any connection."

Sarah's heart had taken a jump at the thought of a

friend, but neither Dylan nor Jake seemed excited by the news. "You don't think she could be telling the truth, then?"

"I thought I'd drive out there and talk to her today," Dylan replied. "Just to be sure. We don't want to overlook any leads. It's a long shot."

Sarah blew out a breath, wishing there were more information, but in an odd way strangely relieved that there wasn't. Her reaction was wrong, she thought. She should have wanted someone to come forward and identify her, but her instincts told her it wouldn't be that easy. She'd taken great pains to hide herself away. "Shall we go?"

Jake hesitated. "Do you want to eat something first, see the doctor before we go?"

"I'm not hungry, and I don't need to see the doctor. He's obviously not going to give me back my memory. The sooner we start, the sooner we'll find Caitlyn." She glanced at Dylan. "Could you hand me my coat, please?"

He grabbed her coat off the chair and tossed it to her. She realized her mistake a split second too late. As the jacket flew through the air, the money slipped out of the unzipped pocket and landed on the floor in a wash of green bills.

"What the hell is this?" Jake asked as he knelt down to collect the money. He glanced up at her, shocked. "Good God, Sarah, there must be fifteen hundred dollars here."

"Fourteen hundred and forty dollars," she corrected. "I counted it yesterday when I found the money in my coat, and before you ask, I don't know where it came from. It was in a zippered pocket in the back of the jacket, almost like a hiding place. There was nothing else there."

Dylan grabbed the jacket and ran his hands through it, obviously intent on making sure she was telling the truth. "Nothing."

"That's what I said," Sarah repeated. "And I'd like my money back."

Jake gave her a hard look as he stood up, the wad of cash in his hand. "How do you know it's your money?"

"Well, it was in my jacket, wasn't it?" She took the money from Jake and stuffed it into the back pocket making sure the zipper was closed this time. "Are you ready?"

"More than ready," he replied.

"As soon as you leave this hospital, you're both going to be a target," Dylan said. "Are you sure you don't want me to follow you two down to LA, Jake?"

"I'd rather you follow up the lead with that woman who thinks Sarah looks familiar. There's a reason Sarah was in this area, and I can't discount the fact that maybe she was looking for some family or a friend or a place to hide," Jake said.

"I agree, but I'm still worried about you," Dylan said.

Sarah hated the way they were talking over her, but since she had nothing to add to the conversation she kept her mouth shut. She was relieved that they would be splitting up from Dylan. Dealing with Jake was hard enough; she didn't need his antagonistic brother around. Once Dylan had left the room, she let out a breath of relief.

Jake frowned. "I'm not going to go any easier on you than Dylan would," he warned.

"I didn't ask you to. But I'm not going to keep defending myself. Now you can drive me to the scene of the accident, or I'll call a cab. Your choice."

"Well, you do have all that cash," he said with a touch of sarcasm.

"I'm sure I have a good reason for having that money," she said, but despite her brave words, she wasn't sure at all.

After checking out with the nurse, who didn't look at all happy that Sarah was leaving without an official discharge from the doctor, Sarah and Jake walked into the hospital lot, where Jake had parked his sporty, dark gray Jeep Cherokee. As he opened the car door for her, Sarah glanced over her shoulder, her gaze darting nervously around the parking lot. She felt as if someone were watching them, but she couldn't see anyone. Still, the hairs on the back of her neck were standing up, telling her to be careful. She had only her instincts to rely on, and her gut told her that whoever had tried to kill her wasn't far away.

"What's wrong?" Jake asked, following her gaze.

"I don't know—something," she murmured.

Jake took off his leather jacket and tossed it on the backseat, then got behind the wheel. Once he was inside, Sarah flipped the lock button on the car. As soon as she'd done it a flash of uncertainty assailed her. Was she locking the danger out or locking it in?

For the first time since she'd woken up in the hospital, she was alone with a man, away from any other help whatsoever. There was no nurse nearby to come to her rescue, no security guard keeping an eye on her. Jake had told her not to trust anyone—but what about him? Could she trust him?

She cast Jake a quick glance as he started the car. She was suddenly acutely aware of everything about him, his broad shoulders, his strong arms, his long fingers gripping the steering wheel. Jake had a definite rough-around-the-edges appeal. Something stirred within her, a flutter through her abdomen, a tingle down her spine, a jolt of desire that shocked her. As her gaze drifted to his hands she could almost feel his fingers stroking her skin, running through her hair, touching her in intimate, arousing ways.

"What?" Jake suddenly demanded, his voice breaking through her reverie. "What are you remembering?"

Startled, she lifted her gaze to his, feeling a rush of warmth spread across her face. As Jake stared back at her his eyes darkened, and a flash of desire sparked and took hold. She shivered at the look in his eyes. He hated her, but he wanted her, and that made him hate her even more.

"Dammit, Sarah," he repeated. "What are you trying to do?"

She put her fingers to her lips. "I . . . you . . . you touched me," she said softly. "Kissed me."

"About a million times," he said huskily, his eyes narrowing on her face. "You're starting to remember us together?"

She knew he wanted her to say yes, but it wasn't that easy. "It was more of a feeling than a memory. I was looking at your hands, and I could feel them on me." She glanced away, uncomfortable and awkward. She'd once been intimate with this man. They'd made love. They'd had a baby together. And now they were strangers . . . except that her body was starting to recognize him even though her brain still refused to cooperate.

"That's it? That's all you've got?" Jake asked, frustration in his voice.

"It's something, isn't it?"

"I don't know. Maybe you've just decided to play me in a different way."

She sat back in the seat and crossed her arms as she stared out the front window. "What does that mean?"

"It means don't try to flirt with me," he warned. "Don't try to remind me that we once had something. That's over. Got it? You have no power over me whatsoever. Look at me, Sarah."

She really didn't want to, but there was no refusing the command in his voice.

"I don't want you anymore," he said bluntly, anger burning in his eyes. "I don't care about you at all. I just care about finding my daughter."

"I get it."

"You'd better." He turned his head, staring straight ahead now. "The attraction is gone. You're not going to seduce me into forgetting what you did to me, so don't even try. I'm in charge now. I'm calling the shots."

"Then why can't you look at me?" she asked. He'd wanted this moment between them. In fact, he'd demanded it. Yet, now that it was here, he couldn't look her in the eye. Was he afraid of what he might reveal?

"Because I can't stand the sight of you," he replied.

Was that the truth? Or was he trying to cover up the fact that his feelings about her were nowhere near as clear as he'd just stated? She sensed that he was far more conflicted than he was willing to let on.

Turning the key, Jake gunned the engine and pulled out of the parking spot with a squeal of tires.

She grabbed onto the armrest to steady herself. "I can see that you're in complete control," she said sharply. "Would you slow down?"

"I'm in a hurry to find my daughter. Then the two of us will be done."

They wouldn't be done; they'd just be beginning. Because there was no way she would let him walk away with Caitlyn without a fight. She knew she had a good reason for taking their child. She just had to remember what it was.

Jake slowed down as they passed through the small downtown area of Los Olivos, where a large banner on Main Street announced an upcoming wine festival. As they left town, heading toward the mountains that would eventually take them to the coast, the landscape grew more rural. They passed vineyards, olive groves, horse farms, and even a few celebrity ranches. The scenery was lush and calm, sunshine bathing the rolling hills in a peaceful light. It was hard to believe that just two nights ago she'd been running for her life on these very roads. Actually, according to Deputy Manning, she'd been driving in from the coast, so maybe there was no reason why she'd recognize the scenery. She'd gotten into her accident long before she'd reached this stretch of road.

As they turned off the main highway onto a much less traveled route, Sarah's tension began to grow. The road began to climb, winding through the mountains, the area becoming more desolate. The canyons off to the side were dark and deep.

"The accident scene is just up there," Jake said, consulting the notes he'd jotted down earlier. "Dylan said that coming from this direction there's a turnout about a quarter mile after the point where your car went over the side. We can park there."

Sarah didn't bother to reply. Her gaze was focused on the fluttering strip of yellow danger tape that clung to the edges of the smashed guardrail on her side of the road. From what everyone had told her, she'd been coming from the other direction. She'd taken the turn too fast, crossed the highway, and gone over the side, narrowly missing a car coming from the direction she was currently traveling.

Jake slowed down as they drove by the spot where her car had plunged off the side of the cliff. It was a steep descent down to the bottom of the canyon, the hillside filled with rocks, boulders, trees and other brush. He continued down the road until he could pull over at the turnout.

As soon as he'd parked the car, Sarah got out and walked over to the edge of the road where a waist-high rail prohibited her from slipping down the hillside. As she gazed into the canyon, she couldn't help wondering how on earth she'd survived the accident. She closed her eyes, trying to find some memory of the road, the canyon, the crash, of being trapped in the car.

"Sarah." Jake's voice interrupted her thoughts.

"I'm trying to focus," she complained, keeping her eyes closed.

He didn't reply, but she could hear his breath coming in impatient bursts, disturbing her concentration. She opened her eyes. "You're not helping. You're too close to me."

"Don't you remember anything?" he asked, his gaze boring into hers.

"Just give me a minute." She closed her eyes again, trying to at least relive the dream she'd had just before she'd woken up in the hospital. There had been a car in the rearview mirror, the lights drawing nearer. She'd pressed her foot down on the gas. She was running somewhere, looking for safety. But the rain was coming down harder; the windshield wipers could barely keep up. The turn in the road came quickly. The car began to slide. She hit the brakes, to no avail. Lights from the opposite direction blinded her. And then she was flying, terrified that when she landed it would all be over.

But where was Caitlyn in her dream? She never looked over her shoulder. Never heard the baby cry. Never once whispered a reassurance to her daughter that everything would be all right.

Caitlyn wasn't in the car. Sarah suddenly knew that with shocking clarity. When she'd looked in the rearview mirror, she'd seen the trace of a car seat— an empty car seat.

Her eyes flew open, her gaze connecting immediately with Jake's.

"She wasn't in the car," she said. "I saw the seat in the mirror. There was no one there. Caitlyn wasn't there."

He stared at her with grim eyes. "So where was she?"

"I don't know, but doesn't it make you feel better to be sure she's not down there?" she asked, waving her hand toward the wild canyon below. "And that no one took her from the car?"

"I still don't know if she's safe. I won't feel better until she's in my arms."

As Jake finished speaking, Sarah heard a car coming down the road. Her spine stiffened as she glanced over her shoulder and saw a dark sedan heading toward them. She suddenly realized how vulnerable they were standing alone on this desolate strip of highway. Not a car had passed since they'd arrived. She'd almost died here before. Was someone going to try again?

The sedan began to slow. She could see a man behind the wheel.

Jake grabbed her hand, yanking her toward his rental car. "Get in. Hurry."

She slid into the seat and was barely inside before Jake slammed the door and jogged around to his side of the car. He had just flipped the locks when the sedan stopped next to them.

Her heart pounded against her chest. "Start the car. Go," she urged.

"He's blocking me in," Jake muttered.

She stared past him at the man in the other car. He was dressed in a dark blue suit with a red tie. He had light brown hair, and he was rolling down the window on the passenger side. He motioned for Jake to do the same.

After a moment's hesitation, Jake lowered the window a few inches. "What?" he asked.

"Everything okay?" the man inquired. "Do you need me to call for help? Is your car all right?"

"We're fine. Thanks anyway," Jake replied, raising the window back up and starting the car.

The guy in the sedan stared at them for a moment, then shrugged and continued on down the highway.

Sarah put a hand to her heart. It was beating in triple time, her breath coming short and fast.

"Just a Good Samaritan," Jake said.

"I hope so."

He shot her a quick look. "Did you recognize him, Sarah?"

"No, but that doesn't mean I don't know him, does it?"

Sarah's question ran around and around in his head as Jake drove down the coast toward Los Angeles. Had there been something odd about the man who had stopped to offer help? Or was he just letting Sarah's nerves and his own imagination get the better of him? If the guy had wanted to hurt them, he'd certainly had the opportunity to do so. They'd been trapped on the side of that road, a mistake he would not make again. He checked the rearview mirror, knowing that he had to start thinking ahead. He couldn't let anyone sneak up on them.

Sarah hadn't said much in the past hour, but that wasn't unusual. She'd never been the type of woman to chatter. He'd liked that peaceful quality about her. He'd liked a lot of things about her, things that were starting to come back now that the haze of anger he'd been living under was beginning to dissipate. He was still furious that Sarah had walked out on him with Caitlyn, but he now knew there was more to her story. How much more he still had to discover. Aside from that, it was tough to spend every second breathing fire over her head. She was clearly terrified and worried and hurt. And they'd get farther if they found a way to work together instead of in opposition.

At least, that was what he was telling himself, and he didn't intend to look any closer at his motivations. He was just going to stay focused on finding Caitlyn. It felt good to be taking some positive, decisive action. He'd been stuck, running in place for seven months, and even for the past two days. Now he was moving again, and with some good luck for a change he'd have his daughter back by the end of the day.

Sarah's tension seemed to ease when they left the mountains and drove along the ocean south of Santa Barbara. The sun shone brightly over the breaking waves, with only a few stray clouds marring the blue sky.

"It's beautiful," Sarah murmured, her gaze on the sea. "I wish we could stop for a minute."

Her words were like an echo from the past. He tried to shake off the memories, but they came flooding back.

They'd been driving down the Pacific Coast Highway out of San Francisco, making their way to his boss's house in Half Moon Bay for a birthday party. He'd had on one of his best suits, and Sarah was wearing a cocktail dress and high heels. The sun was about to set when Sarah had said . . .

"I wish we could stop for a minute, Jake, walk on the beach, feel the sand between our toes. What do you say? Let's do it."

He smiled at the eager light in her beautiful blue eyes. "We're supposed to be at John's house in fifteen minutes."

"I know you hate to be late, but I think it will be worth it."

He wanted to tell her that his boss disliked people who were late. He wanted to say that they absolutely had to keep moving, that they could come to the beach another time, that this wasn't the moment. But suddenly it seemed as if this were the moment. That was the way it was with Sarah. She made him want to stop and smell the roses or the salty sea. She had an affinity for nature, and she was starting to rub off on him.

Before he could question his behavior, he found himself pulling off the road at the next turnout.

Sarah was out the door before he could tell her that they were just going to take a quick look at the ocean and be on their way. By the time he joined her at the edge of the sand she already had her shoes off.

When he'd first met her he hadn't thought of her as impetuous or impulsive; she'd been guarded, quiet, almost as if she were in hibernation. But now she was blossoming, coming out of her shell, and letting him see another side of herself. There were no haunting shadows in her eyes today, nothing to make him wonder what or whom she was thinking about.

"Take off your shoes, Jake," she said with a laugh. "Live a little."

"Sarah, we don't have time."

Her expression turned serious. "I know we don't, and we'll leave if you want to, but look—the sun is setting and the sand is still warm beneath my toes. It won't last much longer. It will be dusk soon—nighttime. The sea will turn dark and dangerous, but right now it's gorgeous."

Sarah didn't like the nighttime. She didn't like walking home from the movies to their apartment once the sun went down. She hated entering a dark house, and she had a terrible habit of flooding every room with light whether she was in that room or not. Whenever he'd asked her about it, she'd just laughed and said she'd always been a little scared of the dark. He could hear that tiny whisper of fear in her voice now, as if she were dreading the rise of the moon.

As he gazed at her, the breeze blew strands of her hair across her face. Sarah didn't seem to care. She was absorbed in the moment, her eyes closed as she lifted her face to the breeze and the sun. She was right. The sun wouldn't last long. It was already slipping over the horizon.

On impulse he took off his shoes, pulled off his socks, and joined her on the sand. She slipped her hand into his, her eyes still closed, and said, "I never want to forget this feeling. You and me together on a perfect sunny day."

"There are going to be a lot more perfect days," he said, turning her around to face him.

Her eyes opened and she smiled at him, but her smile wasn't nearly as bright. "I hope so, but you never know what's around the corner."

"Good things—that's what's around the corner." He didn't know when he'd turned into an optimist, but there was something about Sarah that made him want to believe in the future in a way that he'd never felt before. He'd spent most of his life concentrating on building a career, making sure he could support himself and whoever else in the family might need his help. He hadn't thought much about making a life with a woman—until he'd met Sarah.

"I hope so, Jake, but if not, we'll always have this moment. Sometimes that's all you have. I learned that a long time ago." Sarah put her hands on his shoulders and leaned in for his kiss. Her mouth was warm, soft, inviting, and he couldn't stop kissing her until the sun went down, and she shivered as the cold ocean breezes kicked up off the ocean.

"We'd better go," she whispered. She put her finger to his mouth and wiped off her lipstick. "Was it worth it?"

"Absolutely," he said.

"Jake?"

He blinked, realizing Sarah's voice no longer had the dreamy quality of the past. He glanced over at her. "What?"

"Where were you?" she asked, her eyes curious.

"In a dream," he said. "But it's over now. All over."

Chapter Nine

Dylan pulled up in front of a small clapboard cottage perched on the edge of the sea at Pismo Beach in San Luis Obispo. The house was white with blue shutters and a mix of colorful flowers in two long window boxes. As Dylan got out of his car, a blast of wind blew a chill through him. The sun was out, but the air was cold, and tall waves broke along the beach, the ocean still turbulent from the storm two days earlier.

He had mixed feelings about the sea. Some of his best memories were of his family's house on Orcas Island in the San Juan Island chain just off the coast of Washington state. But that house was also the last place he'd been with his mother. When they'd returned home his father had told him they were getting a divorce. The next day his mother was gone.

It was strange that Jake had once again suffered from a woman's quick and unexplained departure. Hadn't once been enough?

And Sarah hadn't just left; she'd taken Caitlyn. That baby was his brother's heart and soul. Dylan was going to get Caitlyn back for Jake if it was the last thing he did.

Walking up to the front of the cottage, he rapped sharply on the heavy wood door. He heard some dogs bark in the yard; then a moment later the door opened just a few inches, a gold chain in place. A woman peered out at him, but she remained in the shadows, and he couldn't get a good look at her.

"What do you want?" she asked warily.

"A little information. My friend was on the news last night. You called the police to say she looked familiar to you."

"The woman with amnesia?"

"That's right. We're trying desperately to figure out who she is."

"The deputy I spoke to didn't think there was a connection," the woman replied. "And my friend's name is Jessica. He said this woman's name is Sarah."

"She does go by the name Sarah, but it's possible she used to go by another name. She doesn't remember who she is. She was in a serious car accident. And her baby is missing. I'd really like to talk to you more about your friend, just in case there's a chance they're the same person. Can I come in?"

"Who are you exactly? You're not a cop."

"No, I'm a friend of Sarah's. Actually, she's involved with my brother, and the missing child is my niece. My name is Dylan Sanders."

The woman hesitated, then released the chain and opened the door. Silhouetted by the sunlight, she appeared younger than he had assumed, late twenties, maybe early thirties. She wore light blue capri pants and a long-sleeved button-down man's shirt that was white but streaked with yellow paint. Her hair was reddish blond and pulled back in a ponytail. Her face was thin, freckles dotting the bridge of her nose. Her eyes were a dark, deep sapphire blue that reminded him of the sea. He swallowed hard, suddenly realizing he was still staring at her. When he'd heard "crazy psychic lady," he'd pictured some odd-looking woman with a half dozen cats and maybe a bird on her shoulder, not this surprisingly pretty young woman.

"I'm Catherine Hilliard," she said in a soft, lyrical voice.

He cleared his throat. "It's nice to meet you. Do you have a picture of your friend?" Maybe he could clear up the situation with one photograph.

"Of course I do," she said.

"Could I see it?"

She stepped back and waved him farther into the room.

Dylan paused as he reached the center of the living room. He'd never seen so much junk in his life, a dozen or more glass figures dotting the tables, assorted wood boxes of every size imaginable, seashells, statues, books, magazines. Almost every available space was covered with something. Two cats slumbered on each end of the couch, and a bird chirped from a cage in the corner. Maybe his initial impression wasn't that far off.

He saw that Catherine had turned her dining room into an art studio. An easel was set up in front of a picture window that looked out at the sea.

"You're an artist," he said, crossing the room. On the easel was a portrait of a young girl sitting in a meadow filled with yellow wildflowers. The painting was only half-done, but the girl's light blue eyes were wide and startled, and a little familiar. An uneasy feeling ran down his spine. Were those Sarah's eyes looking back at him? "Is this your friend?"

"Yes," Catherine replied. "That's Jessica. I paint her all the time from memory. She's been gone eight years now—well, ten since I last saw her, eight since she officially vanished."

"What do you mean, officially vanished?"

"Jessica disappeared when she was twenty years old." Catherine traced one finger lovingly around the edge of the face in the portrait. "I miss her so much."

"Can you tell me what happened?" Dylan prodded, sensing that she was drifting away. For a moment he didn't think Catherine would answer. She seemed lost in a reverie. Finally she looked at him, her eyes filled with sadness and regret.

"Jessie called me about a week before she vanished. She said she was in trouble and that she'd made a horrible mistake. She was terribly afraid. That was the message she left on my answering machine. I was in New York at the time and away that weekend. By the time I got the message and called her back, Jessie was gone. I called her apartment nonstop for a couple of days, and then someone finally called me—her neighbor. The woman told me that Jessica hadn't shown up for work for the past four nights, nor had she been home, and they were worried about her. They'd found my number written on a piece of paper in her bedroom."

"I assume there was a search?" he queried.

"A short one. The police couldn't find any evidence of foul play, so they said it was possible she'd simply gone elsewhere. Eventually her file was set aside."

Dylan felt his stomach turn over. The way Jessica had disappeared was almost exactly the same way Sarah had left his brother.

"I flew to Chicago to look for her," Catherine continued.

"Why Chicago?" he interrupted.

"That's where Jessica was living at the time."

He shook his head, thinking this trip was going to be a waste of time, but then he reminded himself that no one knew where Sarah had been living before she arrived in San Francisco. Chicago was as good a town as any. "Never mind, go on," he said.

"I went to Jessica's apartment and the law office where she worked as a receptionist. No one had seen her in days. And no one seemed to know anything about her personal life, if she had a boyfriend, what she did after work. Jessica hadn't confided in anyone, which wasn't all that unusual, but her innate sense of privacy didn't help when she went missing." Catherine paused. "Jessica had told me a few weeks earlier that she'd met someone—the kind of man she'd always dreamed about. In fact, that's why she stayed in Chicago. She was originally only going to be there a few days. Jessica and this other friend of ours, Teresa, were driving across country—they were going to meet up with me in New York, but the car broke down. They didn't have any money, so they got jobs until they could fix the car. Then Jessica met someone and decided to stay."

"What happened to the other girl?" Dylan asked.

"Teresa didn't like Chicago all that much. She decided to go home to California. At least, that's the last I heard from Jessica. At any rate, I spent two weeks in Chicago, hoping Jessica would show up, but she never did. Eventually the police told me to go home. They said they'd contact me if anything came up. When I got back to New York, the dreams began to come every night. Jessie was calling to me, reaching for me, and she was so scared. I couldn't sleep for months. I kept thinking about how she hated the dark. I used to be the one she'd climb into bed with when she got scared, and that was a lot of the time. She didn't have it easy when she was a little girl."

"Why not?" he asked.

"Jessie's parents died when she was nine years old. She had no relatives willing to take care of her, so she went to foster care. I met her when she was eleven. We ended up in a home together in LA. We were there for almost four years, from the time Jessica was eleven and I was thirteen until we were fifteen and seventeen. Then the foster parents ran into hard times, and they split up all the kids in their care and sent us to different homes. I aged out of the system about six months later. We tried to keep in contact during the next year or two, but I had to work and Jessie was still in school. The next year I won a scholarship to an art school in New York, so I wound up moving across the country."

"And Jessica attempted to meet up with you a couple of years later, but got sidetracked in Chicago and disappeared," Dylan said. "And you think she looks like my friend Sarah. Is that pretty much it?"

"Yes." Catherine shrugged. "I might be wrong. Her hair color is different. Jessica's hair was blond. The woman on TV last night had dark hair."

"Sarah's hair used to be blond. Do you have any other pictures besides this painting?"

Catherine shook her head. "Sorry. No one takes pictures of foster kids, and even if they do, you usually don't get to keep them."

Her tone was matter-of-fact, but he could hear the edge of bitterness in her voice. "What happened to Jessica's parents?"

"They were killed in a car crash. It was a shock to her to suddenly wind up an orphan. She'd actually had a happy childhood until they died. She had a lot farther to fall than the rest of us when it came to expectations. I had to teach her a lot about survival. But I guess I didn't teach her enough."

Dylan frowned. Sarah had told Jake that her parents had died in a car crash. It was a small connection, but a connection nonetheless, and he had to admit the painting of Jessica bore a striking resemblance to Sarah.

"You're starting to think that your friend and mine are the same person," Catherine said.

"I don't know that I'd go that far."

"Because you're very guarded. You like to unravel other people's secrets, not your own."

He didn't like the way Catherine was looking at him, as if she had some sort of second sight. "We're not talking about me or my secrets," he said shortly.

"But you have some, don't you? Everyone does."

"Let's concentrate on whether or not the woman you saw on television last night is Jessica. You said the hair was different, but was there anything else that Sarah said or did that made you think she was Jessica?"

"It was the name she called her little girl. Jessie had a doll when she came to the foster home. It was the only thing she had with her from her past. The doll's name was Caitlyn."

Dylan drew in a quick breath, not sure what to think. "Is that why you thought your friend had suddenly come back from the dead? Or were you grabbing at straws because you felt guilty that you weren't around for Jessica before she disappeared?"

"I never said she was dead," Catherine stated. "In fact, a few months after she disappeared I got a note in the mail. There was no return address, no signature, just the initial J."

"What did it say? Do you remember?"

"Every word. It said, 'Don't try to find me. It's too dangerous. I'll love you forever. Stay safe and happy.' "

"Did you keep the note?"

"For a long time."

"But you don't have it anymore?" he asked, unable to keep the skeptical note out of his voice.

"Now you sound just like the doctors, suggesting that I see her face everywhere I go, that I hear her voice, that I make up stories because I can't accept the fact that I let her down."

"You've seen doctors?" he asked, his doubts returning.

"Two," she admitted. "I couldn't sleep for months after Jessie disappeared, because of the dreams, and my boyfriend told me I needed to get help so I could go on with my life. He didn't stick around to help me get there. He said I was obsessed and crazy. But that wasn't just because of Jessica. He didn't like that I could see things about him."

"What kind of things?"

"Just things that made him uncomfortable. I have a sense about people sometimes. And I get feelings about events that might happen."

"You're psychic?"

"And you're a skeptic. I'm not surprised," she returned. "Most people are, especially reporters like you."

"I don't think I said I was a reporter," he replied, feeling more than a little uncomfortable with her accurate assessment.

She gave him a little smile. "You are, aren't you?"

"It could be a lucky guess."

"Sure," she said. "Whatever you say. I'm used to people doubting me, getting nervous when they're around me."

And everything she was saying was making him nervous. Was she nuts or giving him a real lead to follow?

"It's funny that your friend's name is Sarah," Catherine continued. "Jessica had a grandmother named Sarah who lived in Boston. Jessie kept waiting for her grandmother to come and rescue her, but she never did."

Boston! His gut turned over. Sarah had told him she'd lived in Boston with her grandparents after her parents had died in an accident. Was that just a fabrication, an embellishment of the fantasy she carried in her head after she was abandoned? It was enough of a connection to send a jolt of adrenaline through his bloodstream.

"I think we'd better sit down and talk this out," he said decisively. "I want to know everything there is to know about Jessica, including her last name."

As Jake drove down the Pacific Coast Highway past Malibu and Santa Monica, heading for Venice Beach, Sarah soaked up the images of Southern California sunshine, swaying palm trees, in-line skaters, skateboarders, bicyclists, and joggers crowding the cement path that ran alongside the beach. Umbrellas, beach towels, and sunbathers filled the wide, sandy beaches, and surfers rode the large waves out by the Santa Monica Pier. It was a beautiful spring day, the kind of day that made her feel that something good was about to happen, that anything was possible. Her sense of optimism surprised her. But there was no denying the fact that she still had hope she'd find the answers to all her questions and that she'd hold her daughter in her arms very soon.

Her body had been battered. Her memory was in hibernation, but her fighting spirit was gaining strength. She was going to survive this. The voice in her head refused to let her think otherwise.

As they drove through the city she studied each street sign, each building, searching for something familiar to jog her memory. Her nerves tightened with each passing block. She began to feel on edge, wary. But she didn't know why.

She glanced into the side-view mirror, repeating an action she had done many times in the past few hours. Looking over her shoulder felt natural to her, too, as if it were part of her normal existence. Unfortunately there was a ton of traffic, and it was impossible to tell whether the cars behind them were on their tail or just going about their business.

"We're almost there," Jake said, checking the map they'd picked up at a gas station. "With any luck, maybe we'll find your past and my daughter before this day is over."

Sarah didn't like that he referred to Caitlyn as *his* daughter, but she'd save that battle for another time. She didn't know what to make of Jake or the way she'd left him. She wanted to believe she'd had a good reason, but so far that reason eluded her. She'd seen no hint of violence in Jake. Anger, yes, definitely. And his words could cut like a knife. But she'd never felt physically afraid of him. He could be putting his best foot forward, hiding his dark side, but she didn't really think so. His emotions were too raw, his pain too real. He hurt too much over the loss of his daughter. And even perhaps her own betrayal. Despite the fact that he professed not to care about her at all anymore, sometimes she wondered if he wasn't trying to make that true, rather than it already being true.

And then there were her own feelings, an odd stirring whenever she looked at him. On some elemental level she recognized him, maybe trusted him, perhaps even loved him. That thought shook her to the core. She couldn't love a man she couldn't remember, could she?

The silence and intimacy of the car suddenly became too much for her. Reaching for the radio, she turned it on, blasting the car with music. She flipped through a couple of stations until a familiar beat tugged at her memory. She knew this pop song. She'd heard it playing before. Where? Closing her eyes, she let the melody run through her head.

The music was coming from a bedroom down the hall. How odd, she thought. No one should be in there. As she reached the door, she saw that it was half-open. She gave a knock, a push.

She heard a shriek and didn't realize it was coming from her until the two naked people on the bed rolled over to look at her, shock and horror on their faces—or at least on the woman's face.

Betrayal ripped through her, and she ran from the room.

"This is the place," Jake said.

"What?" Her eyes flew open as Jake stopped the car and turned off the engine. "What did you say?"

"I said we're here." His brows drew together in a frown. "Where were you?"

"In the past. That song on the radio just now was playing in my head. I remember walking into a house, down a long hallway. I opened the bedroom door and there were two people having sex. I don't think they were supposed to be having sex."

"Who were they?" he asked quickly.

She licked her lips, wondering why their faces were now so vague. "I . . . I don't know. It's like the memory is just out of reach, hiding in the shadows. I felt a sense of deep betrayal." She thought for a moment. "Maybe it was my parents."

"So you were a child in this memory?"

"No, that doesn't feel right. I must have been an adult. And the fact that these two people were having sex mattered to me." A sudden thought occurred to her, and she turned to him with a question in her eyes. "Is it possible that you—"

Jake gave an immediate and definite shake of his head. "No, it wasn't me. I didn't cheat on you, Sarah.

I don't know why you left me, but you didn't leave because you saw me with another woman."

His green eyes were honest and true and, of course, angry, as if he couldn't believe she was questioning him about his fidelity after everything she'd supposedly done to him. "Okay," she said.

"You can't turn this around on me."

"I'm not doing that, Jake. I'm just trying to figure out where the memory might have come from. And at the moment you're the only man in my life, that I'm aware of. Did I ever mention any ex-boyfriends when we were together?"

"No. You said we didn't need to be one of those couples who shared every little secret." He uttered a bitter laugh. "Little did I know just how many secrets you were keeping." He tipped his head toward the street. "Why don't we table this for the moment and deal with what's right in front of us."

Looking around, Sarah noted that they were in a modest, working-class neighborhood on a street filled with apartment buildings a few blocks from the beach. "Which building did Margaret Bradley live in?"

"The three-story salmon-colored building about a half block down. I think there's a good chance that you may have lived in the same building. It's difficult to believe you'd be driving her car unless you knew her. I think she must have given you her vehicle because she wasn't driving anymore. She was in a convalescent hospital before her death, so that makes sense. It would also make sense that you were a neighbor or that someone who knew Margaret might also know you."

"I hope that's true."

"Only one way to find out. We start knocking on doors."

"Are you sure no one followed us here?" She checked the mirror once again. There was no one on the street, but quite a few cars were parked along the curb.

"I've been watching closely. I don't think we were followed, but if you did live in this area, whoever is after you might already know that."

"Maybe this is a bad idea. We could be walking into an ambush," she said.

Jake stared at her. "We could be," he agreed. "But I don't see that we have another choice."

"No, you're right. We have to find Caitlyn. And I'll do whatever it takes to accomplish that." Opening her door, she got out and waited on the sidewalk for Jake to join her. A man came out of an apartment building across the street with his dog on a leash. He headed away from them, and Sarah let out a sigh of relief. She felt tense and on edge, acutely aware that there could be danger anywhere, from anyone, and she had to be ready.

They walked down the street and up to the main door of the apartment building. It was locked. There was a row of buzzers next to a speaker.

"Deputy Manning said that the people in Margaret Bradley's apartment didn't know her or you; at least, they didn't know anyone by the name Sarah

Tucker," Jake said. "But we might as well start with them." He pushed the buzzer for apartment 310. When no one answered he tried the landlord. No response.

Sarah felt more uncomfortable with each passing minute. They were too vulnerable out in the open. "Maybe we should come back later. It's the middle of a workday. No one is home."

"Someone has to be home," Jake said, moving down the list of buzzers.

"They're not going to let in a stranger."

"They might."

A moment later a young couple came through the front door. They were each so busy talking on their cell phones that they didn't give Jake or Sarah a second look. Jake caught the door before it shut. "After you," he said. "We finally got a break."

"Those two didn't recognize me," she said, following him into the building.

"Nor did they care who we were. So much for living in a secure building."

"Where are we going now?"

"Third floor. Might as well start at the top."

As they approached the steel doors of the elevator, Sarah hung back, her stomach clenching with fear. "I can't go in there," she said shortly, her chest tight.

"In where?"

"The elevator. I can't go in that elevator." She backed away as an image flashed before her eyes.

She was holding two bags of groceries. The metal doors were closing, but at the last second a man's hand came around the edge of the door. He slipped inside. She'd seen him before.

A silent scream of terror ran through her. She began to shake.

Jake grabbed her arm, forcing her to look at him. "Sarah, what's wrong? Sarah, talk to me."

The elevator doors opened, and she bit down on her lip so hard she tasted blood. The open elevator revealed graffiti on the back wall, but otherwise it was empty.

"I've been in there before—in that elevator," she said. "A man got in just as the doors were closing. I don't know what happened next." She put a hand to her mouth as waves of terror washed through her. Something bad had happened in that elevator. "I can't get in there. I can't."

"Okay, all right. Take it easy," Jake said in soothing tones. "There's no one there now. But we'll go up the stairs."

She nodded, drawing in several deep breaths to slow her pounding heart. Jake pushed open the door to the stairwell.

"The good news is that you remembered being in this building," he said. "That's the most specific memory you've had so far. It's a good sign."

She tried to feel happy about it, but the flashback had only brought back the fear she'd felt when the man in the hospital had tried to smother her. She'd fought for her life before. What had she done to make someone want to kill her?

When they reached the top floor, Jake began

knocking on doors. They didn't have any success until they got to the last door. Sarah's heart skipped a beat as they heard footsteps.

"Oh, my God!" someone said in surprise.

Then the dead bolt turned with a decisive click and a woman opened the door. She appeared to be in her twenties and was dressed in black Lycra shorts and a tank top, her brown hair pulled back in a ponytail. She gave Sarah a broad, relieved smile. "Where have you been, Samantha?" the woman asked. "I was so worried about you."

Chapter Ten

"Samantha?" Sarah echoed in surprise. "Why did you call me Samantha?"

"That's your name," the woman replied, the smile on her face slowly fading. Her eyes narrowed. "What's going on? Your face is all bruised and cut up."

"I was in a car accident. But you know me, right? You know who I am. What's my name—my whole name?"

"Samantha Blake. Why are you acting so weird?"

"I have amnesia. I have no memory of who I am or where I live, and most important, I don't know where my daughter is. If you know me, you must know Caitlyn."

"Katie?" the woman asked, her glance flickering back and forth between Jake and Sarah. "Wow, this is so crazy. You're saying you don't remember me or anything?"

Sarah shook her head. "No, I don't. I'm sorry. Can you tell me your name and how I know you?"

"I'm Amanda Cooper. I've lived next door to you for the past four months. That's your apartment, three-oh-four." Amanda paused. "How did you get here if you didn't know where you lived?"

"The car I was driving was registered to a woman named Margaret Bradley, and this was her last address," Sarah answered.

"Right." Amanda shot Jake a suspicious look. "Who are you? I've never seen you before."

"Jake Sanders. I lived with Sarah for two years before she ran out on me with my daughter seven months ago."

Shock flashed in Amanda's eyes. She reached behind her for the door handle, as if she wanted to be ready to slam the door in their faces. "I'm going to call the police."

"Wait, why?" Sarah asked.

Amanda hesitated. "You should come inside, Samantha. And you should wait out here, Mr. Sanders."

"She's not going anywhere without me." Jake took hold of Sarah's arm, as if he couldn't trust her not to leave him behind.

Sarah didn't attempt to pull away. "Did I tell you about Jake?" she asked Amanda.

"You told me that there was a guy you were afraid of, someone who might hurt you or Katie."

"That wasn't me," Jake said firmly. "Sarah was never afraid of me. I did nothing but take care of her, protect her and my daughter. She was running from someone else."

Amanda frowned. "Why do you keep calling her Sarah when her name is Samantha?"

"When I knew her, she went by the name Sarah Tucker," Jake replied.

Amanda hesitated and then turned to Sarah. "I wish I knew what you would want me to do if you could remember your life."

"Jake is okay," Sarah said. "I feel I can trust him." She'd intended to say the words only in order to stop Amanda from calling the police, because instinctively she believed that calling the police was a bad idea and would only complicate matters. But as she spoke she found herself actually believing she could trust Jake. He wasn't going to hurt her. He wasn't the bad guy. Somewhere in her head, and probably more in her heart, she knew that. "I trust him," she repeated more firmly.

Jake's gaze met hers, and she saw something in his eyes that she couldn't define. She didn't know if he was pleased by her declaration or wondering whether or not she was trying to play him again. Not that it mattered. She was in the building where she'd lived. There had to be clues to her past here.

"I want to go to my apartment," she said. "But I don't have a key."

"I have one," Amanda replied. "Are you sure you don't want me to call the police? You were really scared the other night when that guy tried to get in the elevator with you. You told me that someone wanted to kill you, that you were in terrible danger."

Sarah's nerves tightened. Her memory of the elevator had been true and very recent. Maybe she was on her way to remembering everything. "Did I say who was after me?"

"A man from your past. And here you are with a man from your past."

"It wasn't Jake," Sarah said quickly.

"Was Sarah actually physically attacked?" Jake asked.

Amanda looked from Sarah to Jake, then back at Sarah again, obviously not sure how much to reveal. Finally she said, "No. Mr. Harrington, a tenant on the first floor, ran the guy off."

"Did I call the police?" Sarah asked.

"You refused. I couldn't change your mind."

"Where was Caitlyn? Was she with me?"

"No, I was watching her while you ran to the store," Amanda said. "She was fine."

Sarah let out a breath of relief. "What happened after that? Did the guy come back?"

"Not that I know of. I called you later that night, and you told me everything was fine, but you might take Katie and go away for a few days to visit some relatives."

"When exactly was that?"

"Tuesday. Wednesday morning when I knocked on your door you didn't answer."

"Weren't you worried about her?" Jake challenged.

"Of course I was," Amanda said defensively. Looking back at Sarah she said, "I called your cell phone, but it went to voice mail. I called the place where you work, but they said you weren't scheduled to be there, so I assumed you'd left town."

"I didn't say where my relatives lived?"

"No. You were very cagey about your past."

"So I left Wednesday morning and went somewhere," Sarah murmured, her initial hope beginning to fade again. "Where did you say I worked?"

"For a janitorial service, cleaning commercial office buildings at night. The name of the company is Gold Star Cleaners. It's over on Fifth Street, a few miles from here."

"Who watched Caitlyn for Sarah when she was at work?" Jake asked.

Amanda hesitated. She seemed more willing to answer Sarah's questions than Jake's. "Sarah took Katie along with her. It was night, and no one cared if Katie slept in her car seat while Sarah cleaned. She said it was a perfect setup. No one was around when she did her job, and she didn't have to pay for a babysitter."

It was also a great job for someone who wanted to live in the shadows, Sarah thought. Since she'd left Jake, she'd lived like a ghost in the night.

"And she never told you anything about me—the father of her child?" Jake asked, his voice edged with impatience and frustration.

"She didn't say one word about you. I thought you were probably the one she was running from, some kind of abusive boyfriend or husband situation. Maybe that's still the case, and she just doesn't remember."

Amanda's challenging statement hung in the air between them.

"That's not what went down," Jake said. "I didn't hurt Sarah. She left of her own free will."

Amanda didn't look convinced, but Sarah didn't have time to wait for Amanda to trust Jake. "I have to find Caitlyn," she said, bringing the conversation back to the single most important truth. "I must have left her somewhere, and I need to figure out where."

"Maybe with those relatives you mentioned," Amanda said. "Where did you have your accident? That could be a clue."

"Up north, about two hours from here, by Santa Barbara." As she answered the question, Sarah wondered if she'd made a mistake coming to LA. Instead of getting closer to her daughter, she might be even farther away. "Caitlyn could still be up there somewhere," she said to Jake.

"Maybe, but we need to check your apartment. There could be a clue there that will lead us in another direction."

"I didn't realize you'd gone so far away," Amanda said thoughtfully.

"I guess that means I didn't tell you about anyplace I knew of up north?" Sarah asked.

"You once said you loved San Francisco. Perhaps you were going there."

"That's where she was with me," Jake said.

Had she been running back to Jake and just hadn't made it? But no, Caitlyn hadn't been in the car. Would she have gone to Jake without their daughter? That didn't seem right.

"I wish I could help." Amanda offered her a compassionate smile. "I feel so bad that you don't know where Katie is. You must be dying inside. You love that kid more than life."

"I am dying." Sarah swallowed hard, a knot of emotion choking her throat. Amanda was the first person who'd actually felt empathy for her situation that was not tainted by anger or a sense of betrayal. It was nice to know that not everyone hated her, and some people actually knew she was a good mother. It helped to rekindle her faith in herself. "I can't stand not knowing where Caitlyn is. I have to find her. I have to make sure she's all right."

"I'm sure she's safe. You're a really good mother. You must have left Katie with someone you trust."

"I hope so. Can I have the key to my apartment, please?"

"All right."

"Wait," Sarah said quickly. There was something about the look in Amanda's eye that bothered her. "Don't call the police, okay?"

"Samantha, you need professional help." Amanda dropped her voice a notch as she added, "And you don't know who this guy is. He could be anyone."

"The police up in Santa Barbara know I'm with him, and they checked him out," Sarah answered.

"If anything happens to me, they know I'm with him. I don't want to slow things down by having to explain the situation over again to someone new."

"All right. I won't call the cops—yet—but I reserve the right to change my mind. Wait here and I'll get you the key."

Amanda disappeared into her apartment, shutting the door in their faces, leaving Sarah and Jake alone in the hall.

Sarah wrapped her arms around her waist as a chill ran through her. It was a warm day outside, but in this dark hallway, the corridor to her past, it was cold and a little scary. Was she ready for the truth? Or had her brain shut down because she couldn't handle it?

"I can't believe you traded what we had for this place," Jake muttered, digging his hands into his pockets as he gazed down the narrow hallway. "Whatever trouble you were in, you should have come to me. I would have done anything for you. I would have protected you. You didn't have to run to the other end of the state, take a job cleaning toilets at night, and drag my daughter around deserted office buildings so you could make a buck. If you didn't want to stay with me, you should have left Caitlyn behind."

She didn't know what to say to him. His words made perfect sense. Her actions didn't. But she obviously hadn't believed that he could protect her, or she wouldn't have run. If she was afraid for him, and was trying to save him from the danger that followed her, why would she have kept Caitlyn with her, exposed to potential harm? She couldn't answer that question either. She couldn't explain her actions to Jake, because she didn't understand them. Until she did it was pointless to try to justify her behavior.

"I have to believe that I made the right choice for my daughter," she said. "You want me to trust you, Jake, but I also have to trust myself. I don't think I'm a bad person. I have to go with my instincts. That's all I have."

Before Jake could reply, Amanda opened the door and handed Sarah a key. "I'd love to go with you, but I have to go to work. I teach a lunchtime aerobics class. I'll come back right after class, but before I leave, tell me what else I can do to help you, Samantha."

Sarah couldn't get used to hearing herself being called Samantha. Sarah felt more real to her, more true. She wondered if either of them was her real name. "What can you tell me about Mrs. Bradley?"

"You used to get her groceries, and she loved Katie. You visited her a few times in the rest home, and then she died. She gave you her car because she hated to see you taking the bus."

"Who lives in Mrs. Bradley's apartment?" Sarah asked.

"A single guy. I don't know his name. He's never around. He's in his forties. I don't believe you knew him, although I can't say for sure."

"Has there been anyone else around here looking

for Sarah or Samantha?" Jake asked. "In fact, let's go back to the guy in the elevator. What did he look like?"

"Samantha saw him; I didn't," Amanda replied. "She told me he had one of those beanies on his head and a sweatshirt with a hood, like the teenagers wear. He was white, I think. . . ." Amanda paused. "I don't recall anyone else coming by in the past few days. At least, no one knocked on my door. And while we were friends, you were really private. You didn't confide in me much."

Amanda sounded a bit resentful about her lack of sharing. Sarah wondered just how close they'd been. "Did I have any hobbies? Anyplace I went on a regular basis besides my job? Like a gym? You said you teach aerobics. Did I take your class?"

"No, you didn't want to leave Katie in child care. And you said you didn't have the cash to join the gym." She shrugged. "You did the usual stuff, went to the supermarket, the park, that kind of thing. I guess that's not very helpful."

"Where's the park?" Jake asked.

"It's about three blocks from here, toward the beach, on Jenner Street. Maybe you talked to some of the moms at the park," Amanda said with a new light in her eyes. "You did go there almost every morning."

"Thanks. That helps."

Amanda turned to go back into her apartment, then stopped. "You also liked photography. I thought you were really good, that you could make money at it if you wanted, but you said no. Once, I took you to an art gallery on Windham Place a few blocks from here—my friend Peter runs it—and I showed him some of your work, but as soon as we got close, you bolted. You told me to mind my own business and you wouldn't go in. I thought it was kind of weird at the time." She gave Sarah an odd look. "None of this rings a bell?"

"I wish it did."

"Well, my phone numbers are on the bulletin board in your kitchen. Call me if you need me."

"Thanks." Sarah headed down the hall to her apartment and slid her key into the lock, feeling a momentary sense of trepidation, but she pushed past it. This was her home. She had to go inside. As she opened the door she wondered if the memories would suddenly come flooding back, if fireworks would go off in her head, but when she walked into the room she felt absolutely nothing.

The apartment was a small studio. There was a double bed in one corner, a crib next to it, a small gray couch in the main part of the room, a TV the size of a toaster, a couple of beat-up end tables, and a kitchen that was little more than a small counter with a stove, a refrigerator, and a microwave. The room would have been completely sad if it weren't for the photographic prints tacked and taped across the cracked, dull walls. They were all landscapes, the beach, the city, the sunset. At least she'd tried to liven up the place.

This was her home, she told herself. There had to

be a clue to her past somewhere. Turning her attention away from the walls, she moved toward the bed. It was unmade. For some reason that bothered her. She felt as if she were the kind of person who always made the bed. She walked over to the crib and stared down at the pink blanket, the floral sheet, and a tiny white bear with a red satin ribbon around its neck.

As she picked up the bear, an image shot through her head.

Caitlyn had golden curls, long, dark lashes that framed her blue eyes, a soft mouth, and a dimple in her chin. She lifted her hands toward Sarah. "Mama," she said. "Up. Up."

Sarah swept her daughter into her arms and held her tight.

"Kiss, Mama," Caitlyn said, puckering her lips.

Sarah kissed her daughter's sweet lips and inhaled the scent of baby powder and lavender. Everything would be all right. She had to make it so.

Sarah didn't realize she was crying until the tears streamed down her cheeks and fell in big drops onto the sheet. She wiped her eyes and turned to see Jake staring at her.

"I remembered Caitlyn," she whispered. "I saw her in my head for the first time. I didn't just feel her; I saw her face, her beautiful face. And she talked to me. She said, 'Kiss, Mama.' " She sniffed as the tears flowed even harder.

"She was talking to you?" Jake asked in amazement. Then he shook his head in frustration. "Of

course she was talking. She's sixteen months old."
He drew in a long breath, his face tight as he battled
for control of his emotions. "What else?" he asked,
his eyes and voice impatient. "Where is she? Where
did you take her? What did you remember?"

She knew her next words would disappoint him,
but she couldn't lie. "I just saw that moment in time.
I was picking her up from this crib. That's all. I'm
sorry, Jake. I'm really sorry." And she was, because
she'd seen the pain in his eyes when he realized his
daughter had spoken her first words, and he hadn't
been there to hear them.

"I don't care if you're sorry. Sorry isn't good
enough. I need to find my daughter."

"I know. I'm trying."

Jake slammed his fist against the nearby wall, the
force of his action knocking one of the photographs
onto the floor. Sarah flinched but didn't move. She
knew he had to release his anger. And strangely
enough she wasn't afraid that he would turn his rage
on her. He wasn't the kind of man to hit a woman.
She knew that.

But other men would. She knew that, too.

How did she know?

It came from a dark place in her heart, a place
where she didn't want to go.

Moving across the room, she picked up the photograph from the floor. "This is the Golden Gate Bridge
in San Francisco."

"How can you remember that and not remember . . ." Jake shook his head, not even bothering to finish the question.

"Did I take this when I was with you?"

"Yes," he said shortly. "You shot all these pictures when you were with me. We went out every weekend. I grew up in San Francisco, but with you I discovered places I never knew existed. You dragged me down every back alley in Chinatown, every park, every narrow downtown street." He waved his hand toward the wall. "I'm surprised you brought these pictures with you. I certainly don't recognize anything else in the room. In this place you were Samantha Blake. And Caitlyn was Katie. I wonder how many people you've been in your life, how many places you've lived, how many times you've run."

His gaze burned into hers. In the past day he'd begun to look at her like he knew her. Now his suspicions had returned. And she had no way to fight them.

Turning her attention back to the photographs, she prayed for some clue to jump out at her, something that would trigger a memory. She moved down the wall, pausing in front of a two-story house. "Is this the house you were building?"

"No, that one belongs to a friend of mine. I designed the remodel. You shot the photos just before he moved in."

Sarah studied the picture, feeling a sense of warmth in the lines of the house, the lovely garden in the front yard. It was a home just waiting for a family, she thought. "Was your friend married?"

"A newlywed, and his wife was pregnant when they moved in."

"Do they love the house?"

"Why are you asking me these questions?"

She tilted her head to one side as images floated through her head. *She was walking down the street. It was twilight. The lights in the houses were on. Families were sitting down to dinner. In one window she could see a mother helping her child with homework. In another a man and a woman were holding hands over a candlelit supper. Inside, she felt a deep sense of longing.*

"Sarah?"

Jake's questioning voice brought her back to the present.

"I saw houses," she said. "At dinnertime. I don't know who the people were."

"No, you don't," Jake said, surprising her with the response.

"What do you mean?"

"We used to take walks at night when I got home from work. You loved looking in the windows. I teased you about it. You said it was a habit from childhood. You liked to see the way other people lived."

She thought about his words, wondering why they sounded right and yet a little wrong, too. She gazed back at the house he'd designed. "This is beautiful."

"You captured it well. You were a good photographer, Sarah. You loved to pick out the one detail that made the landscape different, like the empty beer can in this shot." He pointed to another picture on the wall—a bird nibbling at a fast-food wrapper. "You liked the contrast of nature with civilization. You would get into crazy positions just to catch the right angle, the perfect beam of light. You were passionate about it. Like Amanda, I suggested a couple of times that you turn it into a business, but you always blew me off, saying it was the digital age of camera phones, and everyone was a photographer."

"That is true, isn't it?"

"I think you had another reason. You didn't want to draw attention to yourself. You didn't want photos with your name attached. That would have been too public for someone intent on staying out of the light."

She looked into his face and asked the question she needed to ask. "Do you think I used you to hide?"

A pulse throbbed in his throat. "I think you used me, but I don't know why."

"How did I get pregnant? Did we plan it? Was it an accident?"

"An accident. The condom broke." His gaze darkened. "When you got pregnant you were shocked, agitated. I thought for a while you'd run out and get an abortion. You kept saying you couldn't have a baby. I tried to calm you down. It wasn't in my plan either, but it had happened, and we had to deal with it. And the last thing I wanted you to do was get rid of our child."

"You offered to marry me, didn't you?"

"Many times. You kept putting me off, telling me you wanted to wait until after Caitlyn was born. I figured eventually we'd get to it."

An image of a white gown flashed through her brain.

She was standing in front of a mirror wearing an off-the-shoulder wedding dress. A woman was taking measurements. Two glasses of champagne sat on the table. She could hear a man's voice in the background. He always knew exactly what he wanted for her, and today was no different. She glanced down at the diamond ring on her finger. It was three carats, huge. It felt heavy on her hand. Her pulse began to race. Sweat broke out along her forehead. Was she making a terrible mistake? She loved him. He loved her. Didn't he?

Sarah's breath was still coming hard and fast when she looked at Jake. "I just saw myself wearing a dress. You were there at the bridal salon. We were drinking champagne. You lied to me. We got married, didn't we?"

Chapter Eleven

"What the hell are you talking about?" Jake couldn't believe she was accusing him of lying.

"I saw us."

"You didn't see me." Jake's stomach began to churn.

"I heard a man's voice," she said. "Maybe it wasn't yours."

"I know it wasn't. If you married someone, it wasn't me. In fact, you told me you'd never been married, never even come close. Was that another lie, Sarah, another secret? Was it?" He jammed his hands into his pockets. "God! When is it going to end? When are we going to hit rock bottom with the truth?"

She stared at him with big, wide, confused blue eyes. He'd once thought she'd had the eyes of an angel. Even now he could see a shimmer of tears. Was her pained innocence an act? He'd been a fool before. He couldn't be a fool again. He couldn't let her get to him. He couldn't believe in her.

"Maybe I didn't go through with it. Maybe I ran away."

"You probably did run. That's what you do. I wonder how many other men you've left in your wake."

Sarah turned away from him, staring back at the photographs on the wall. Her shoulders were hunched in defeat, and he had to fight back an urge to put an arm around her and tell her everything would be all right. How could he want to protect her after everything she'd done to him?

He backed away from her, needing more space between them. Had she been married to someone else? Was that person the one who was trying to kill her, or just another victim of Sarah's drive-by lifestyle?

As he gazed around the shabby apartment, he couldn't understand why Sarah would have willingly traded in her life with him to live alone, raising a child while working as a night janitor. He'd been building her a dream house. She could have had everything she wanted. He would have given her the moon. He'd thought he'd made that clear to her.

But it hadn't been enough. She'd left him and come here. It didn't make sense. He'd told himself a million times that no reason could explain away what she'd done to him. But still he found himself wanting to know what had driven her to turn her back on something so good for something like this.

"I guess we should look through everything in the

apartment, see if we can find a clue," Sarah murmured, turning to face him.

Her expression was guarded now, as if she were afraid she'd revealed too much and didn't intend to let that happen again.

"Don't, Sarah."

"Don't what?"

"Think about holding out on me."

"Whatever I say makes you angry."

"So I'll be angry, but we'll have the truth between us. And it's about damn time that happened."

As he gazed into her worried blue eyes, he felt something inside him weaken. He'd loved this woman, loved her beyond the point of reason. He'd never felt so much passion for anyone. But he'd thought he'd known her, and it was clear now that he hadn't. He had to remember that. There was no going back.

Sarah looked away, but not before he saw a spark of desire, and it shook him to know that despite her memory loss she felt something for him. She was attracted to him. On some basic, elemental level her body wanted his. The chemistry between them hadn't gone away. For some reason that fact both exhilarated and infuriated him. He dug his hands into his pockets before he did something stupid—before he walked across the room and kissed her.

"I'm going to check the drawers of the dresser," Sarah said abruptly, moving quickly.

He could have followed her. He wanted to follow her. He wanted to put his hands on her and make her remember him. But he didn't move. He didn't trust himself not to go too far, not to get lost—in her. *Damn*. His own body was betraying his heart and his mind. He didn't like it. He wouldn't lose control. He wouldn't be a fool again.

Turning his attention away from Sarah, he focused on the apartment. The furniture appeared to be cheap, used pieces she'd picked up at a flea market or a garage sale. She certainly didn't need much to live on. She'd never asked him for anything either. Even after they moved in together she'd refused to change one thing in his apartment.

Looking back at their life together, he now saw all the little signs he'd missed. Sarah was never planning to stay. She hadn't intended to put down roots. Maybe she'd stuck it out as long as she had only because of the baby, the unplanned pregnancy. That must have thrown her off her game. And the house he was building had probably tempted her to some extent, but obviously not enough.

Shaking his head, he walked across the small room, trying to ignore the anger once again building inside him. He paused by the scratched-up wooden kitchen table. On top of a newspaper dated last Monday was a pencil sketch of a man in a beanie, a sweatshirt and a pair of jeans. It must have been the guy from the elevator. His pulse sped up.

"Did you draw this?" He held up the paper.

Sarah moved over to join him. She let out a little gasp of surprise. "Oh, my God. That's the man who was in my hospital room."

"Really? Because I was just thinking he was the man in the elevator with you earlier this week. The beanie, the sweatshirt—remember Amanda's description?"

"It was the same guy, then, because this man was the one who tried to smother me yesterday."

"Are you sure?" he asked, his pulse quickening at the link they'd discovered. "I thought you didn't get much of a look at him."

"The eyes are the same. It has to be him."

"You must have drawn this. Amanda said you were unwilling to call the police, so I doubt this was done by anyone else."

"You think I drew that?" she asked in amazement.

He nodded. "I'm not surprised it's a good sketch. You used to doodle when we were watching football games together. In fact, you used to draw this character with a cape and a big gold belt with all kinds of gadgets on it. What was the name you called him?" He shook his head as the name escaped him. "He was some kind of a superhero, Alexander or something like that."

Sarah stared back at him, an odd flickering in her eyes. "Alexander?"

"Does it ring a bell?"

"Not exactly, but it sounds a little familiar."

"You liked to draw faces. Funny, now that I think about it. You wouldn't use your camera to record actual faces, but you'd sketch people. Whenever I looked to see what you were doing, you'd crumple up the paper and throw it away. I thought you were just modest, but maybe you didn't want me to see the faces. I wonder if you were drawing the people from your past. You certainly didn't have any photographs of your relatives."

Sarah glanced back down at the sketch. "I don't remember drawing this, but maybe I did."

"Let's see, why don't we?" he suggested.

"What do you mean?" she asked warily.

He pushed a blank piece of paper across the table toward her. "Draw something."

"Like what? I don't remember anything. I can't draw a past that isn't in my memory."

"Maybe it's buried deep," he replied. "Sit down, Sarah. Give it a shot."

"Jake, this is a waste of time."

"Do you have a better idea?"

"Yes, search the apartment."

He could see not just reluctance in her eyes, but also fear. He'd noticed the conflicting emotions before. Sarah wanted to remember her past, and yet she didn't. No wonder her memory was still hidden away. She was sending her own brain mixed messages. "We'll search," he said. "But let's try this first."

After a moment's hesitation Sarah took a seat at the table. He sat down across from her and watched her stare down at the paper.

"I don't know what you think is going to come out of my head," she said. "It's as blank as this page."

"You're trying too hard."

"Now I'm trying too hard? Usually you don't think I'm trying hard enough."

"Just close your eyes and then draw whatever image comes to your mind. Let yourself go. I know you can do it."

She gazed back at him for long seconds, and he felt his stomach turn over with feelings he didn't want to feel.

"You have faith in me," she whispered.

He cleared his throat, not wanting to go down that road. "Draw, Sarah. Draw something you feel. Listen to your heart, not your head."

Sarah put the pencil to the paper but didn't make a move. She appeared lost in thought for several long minutes. He was beginning to think the experiment was a waste of time when she began to sketch, slowly at first and then with more purpose and enthusiasm. In a few minutes she was finished. She pushed the paper across the table and looked at him. "I feel as if this place is important to me."

He felt the blood drain from his face as he stared down at the picture she'd drawn.

"Jake? What is it? Do you know this place?" she asked, giving him a concerned look. "What's wrong?"

He didn't know if he could get the words out. He was quite simply stunned. "That's the house I designed for us, the one we were building together. You drew it better than I did." He looked into her eyes and felt the ice around his heart crack and melt. Sarah had remembered their house, the place where they were going to share their lives together, create a family. He'd never realized she'd studied the design in so much detail that she could actually re-create it as she'd done.

"I thought it was my home," she said.

"It was going to be. We hadn't finished it before you left. Since then . . . I've done nothing. I couldn't go through with it without you and Caitlyn. It didn't seem worth it. It would have been too big for me, too empty. The apartment was bad enough. Even though you'd removed all traces of your existence, I could still hear your laugh, see Caitlyn crawling on the floor, smell the hazelnut in the coffee you made every morning. Did you really think I could forget you just because you took your clothes out of our closet?"

"I'm sorry," she whispered. "I'm sorry for hurting you and ruining everything."

He saw her blue eyes fill and steeled himself against those damn tears. He couldn't stand watching a woman cry. "Don't. I'm not going to try to make you feel better."

"I don't want you to. I just wish I could at least explain why I did what I did."

"Nothing can explain it."

"Maybe not, but I am sorry. For what it's worth."

"It's not worth much," he said harshly, because even though he wanted to believe her, he'd already made that mistake more than once and paid a terrible price. He couldn't do it again. He was thankful Sarah didn't give in to her emotions. Instead she wiped her eyes with the back of her hand and stood up.

"I'd better keep looking for some clues," she said.

He watched her return to the dresser, going through each drawer with resolute determination. There wasn't much clothing in the drawers, as far as he could tell, just the basics. He wondered what she'd done with the stuff she'd taken from their home.

Standing up, he walked over to the closet and opened the door. He rifled through a couple of dresses, some jeans, a few shirts, but none of them looked familiar. Had she worn these clothes when she'd been with him? Then he saw the large plaid shirt in the back corner of the closet, a man's shirt, *his* shirt.

He caught his breath, imagining her in that shirt, the hem barely covering her ass, highlighting her beautiful long legs. He didn't have to pull the shirt out to know that the top two buttons would be gone; he'd ripped them off one night when he'd thrown her down on the bed and made love to her.

His breath came short and fast at the memory. *Fuck!* He didn't want to remember her in that way. He didn't want to see his hands on her breasts. He didn't want to remember what her skin tasted like, the way she moved restlessly beneath him, her soft mouth begging for release.

He slammed the door shut.

Sarah glanced over at him in surprise.

"Don't ask," he warned. He walked into the

kitchen and filled a glass with water from the tap. He probably would have been better off pouring the cold liquid over his head, but at least the water was cooling him slowly from the inside out. Finally, composed, he refilled the glass and walked back into the main room.

"I thought being here in my home would help me remember," Sarah said in frustration a moment later. She ran a hand through her hair, her fingers tangling in the curls.

Once again he was distracted by unwanted memories of wrapping the long strands around his fingers as he held her head to his. He blew out a breath and took another sip of water.

"It's not working," Sarah continued. "Maybe I wasn't here long enough—only a few months. What I need to know is who I was before I met you, where I lived, my name, everything. The trouble had to have started long before, because otherwise I wouldn't have lied to you." She sat down heavily on the chair by the kitchen table, as if her legs were about to give out on her.

Sarah was exhausted, he realized, noting the dark shadows mixing with the bruises on her face. She was probably still hurting from the accident, and certainly her sleep the night before had been as restless as his. They'd had only a couple of glazed doughnuts for breakfast. As much as he wanted to keep charging forward, he knew she needed a break.

"Let's get some food," he said. "You look like you're going to pass out."

"Do we have time? I feel as if every second that goes by means another second that Caitlyn is in danger."

"Yeah, I know, but your brain might work better if you eat." He considered their options. "I don't really want to leave here to go to a restaurant."

Sarah immediately nodded in agreement. "I would feel too vulnerable eating out somewhere, not knowing if someone was watching us."

"Why don't we order in some Chinese or pizza? What's your pleasure?" He walked over to the phone and saw a couple of take-out menus on the counter. "Looks like you've done this before."

"Chinese is fine. I'd like—"

"Mongolian beef, cashew chicken, and fried rice," Jake said, cutting her off.

She looked at him in surprise. "I was going to say that."

"I know. They're your favorites."

She cocked her head to one side, giving him a thoughtful look. "It's strange to be with someone who knows me better than I know myself."

"I don't think that's true at all," Jake said with a sigh. "I know who you pretended to be when you were Sarah Tucker. But I'm beginning to wonder if anyone knows the real you—including you."

Dylan didn't know what herbs Catherine Hilliard had put in his hot tea, but the drink had a kick to it. He was feeling energized and ready to get down to business. Unfortunately Catherine had told him that any further questions would have to wait until after she took her dogs out for their afternoon run. The dogs in question were two golden retrievers who apparently loved the ocean. From his vantage point on her deck, he could see her throwing sticks into the water, the dogs bounding in enthusiastically, with no regard for the rough, cold waves.

Catherine didn't seem to care when the dogs shook water all over her. She was certainly an earthy sort of woman in her paint-spattered clothes and her bare feet. He didn't know what to make of her—or her story about her friend Jessica, but he definitely knew that he wanted to learn more about both of them.

As Catherine and the dogs moved farther down the beach, he let out a sigh. It was obvious they weren't coming back anytime soon, which meant more waiting, and he hated to wait. The open door to Catherine's cottage beckoned to him. After her initial wariness, she'd offered him nothing but hospitality. He couldn't believe she'd left him—a total stranger—alone in her house without any concern for the security of her belongings. He could have stolen everything of value in the cottage since she'd poured him a cup of tea, told him to relax, and taken off down the beach. Then again, there didn't appear to be much of value in her home. Aside from one very small TV on her kitchen table, there were no other electronic devices that he'd seen, no computers or stereos or MP3 players—nothing, unless they were tucked away in the bedroom.

Unable to resist the lure of his own curiosity, he walked back into the house, through the kitchen, and into the dining room where her easel was set up. He knelt down and looked through some of the paintings that were piled up against her wall. What he saw surprised him. He wasn't much of a judge of art, but there was certainly a sinister tone to Catherine's work. He frowned as he studied one dark painting after another. The colors were reds, blacks, browns, the images abstract, some with ghostly appearances, others that seemed purely evil.

There was a definite mood to her work, anger, restlessness, frustration, and a sense of injustice. At least those were the emotions he felt when he looked at her paintings. How could such a pretty young woman paint such black moments?

The painting on the easel, showing Sarah's look-alike sitting in a beautiful meadow, was a departure from Catherine's other work. It was almost as if Catherine wanted to protect her memories and images of Jessica by permanently putting her in a calm, restful place.

Which brought him back to his original question: Was Catherine's friend Jessica really Sarah?

"I see you've made yourself at home," Catherine said.

Dylan turned in surprise. She'd come in so quietly he hadn't heard her. His instincts were usually much sharper. She must have left the dogs outside.

"Yes, thanks for the tea," he replied. "It had a kick to it."

"You looked like you needed a boost."

"I rarely need a boost," he said.

She smiled at his cocky statement. "So you're one of those men who thinks being tired is a weakness."

"I'm not tired," he countered. "I'm concerned about my brother's child. It's important that we find her as soon as possible."

"I know. I've been thinking about the fact that your friend and my friend could possibly be the same person. It seems amazing to me that Jessica would have a baby, though. How old is the little girl?"

"Sixteen months," Dylan replied.

Catherine shook her head. "It's so difficult to believe. In my head Jessica is a young girl. But she's not. She's twenty-eight years old now. So much time has passed since I saw her."

"Let's not let any more time pass," he said quickly, sensing that Catherine was the type of person who could get lost in her own head. Hell, maybe that was what she and her friend Jessica had in common. "Let's get back to business. You told me that Jessica made her cross-country trip with another girl. Tell me more about her."

"That was Teresa Meyers. She was in foster care with us, too. She was the same age as Jessica, but totally different in personality. She prided herself on being a tough chick, you know what I mean?"

He nodded. He'd run into more than a few of those in the field of journalism. "Where is Teresa now?"

Catherine shook her head. "I don't know. I tried to find her after Jessica disappeared in Chicago, but I couldn't locate her. She didn't go back to any of her previous addresses, and quite frankly I didn't have the money to hire anyone to look for her."

"So Teresa knew how to disappear, too? What? Did they take you aside in foster care and give you a hands-on guide for how to vanish without a trace?"

Catherine shrugged away his sarcasm. "They didn't care enough to do that. Kids in foster care don't have roots. If you're not a cute baby someone wants to adopt, you float around the system, moving from house to house, with no regard for any kind of permanence or feeling of security. That's the way Jessica, Teresa, and I grew up. It's what we were used to. We didn't worry about telling people where we were, because there wasn't anyone to tell. No one gave a damn."

Despite her matter-of-fact tone, anger burned in her eyes, and Dylan felt like a shit for his comments. "I apologize."

"You should. At any rate, I don't know where Teresa is. Nor do I know where Jessica is. That's the bottom line."

"But they could be together. They could have kept in touch after Teresa left Chicago?"

"Yes, but if Jessica knew where Teresa was, she kept the information in her head, because it wasn't written down on any of the papers in her apartment. Although she did have her purse with her when she disappeared."

"Really?" Dylan said, surprised by that fact.

"As far as we can tell, yes. That's the clue that led the police to speculate that there was no foul play involved."

"Well, I think there's only one way to answer your questions and mine. You need to come with me to LA to meet Sarah, to see if she's Jessica. We can go right now. I'll drive."

Catherine's hesitation disturbed him.

"What? You don't want to go?" he asked in amazement.

"Of course I want to go, but I have a job. I teach an art class at the local community college on Friday afternoons, and today is the midterm exam. I can't miss it."

"What time is it over?"

"Five o'clock."

He didn't want to wait until the end of the day. They were three hours north of LA, and at this rate they wouldn't be able to meet up with Jake and Sarah until later in the evening. But he had no choice. Catherine was his best lead. "We'll go after your class."

Catherine stared back at him, uncertainty in her eyes.

"What now?" he asked.

"It has occurred to me over the years that maybe Jessica had a reason to disappear, and by trying to find her I might be putting her in danger. I wonder if I did exactly that when I called the police last night.

It might be better for me to wait here. If Jessica wants to find me, she'll find me."

"Maybe she doesn't know where you are. You were in New York when she disappeared."

"That's true. But if she wanted to track me down, she'd look here. I lived here for a couple of years when I was a little girl. I used to tell Jessica about the sand dunes on Pismo Beach and the beautiful waves. It was a happy place for me. I think she'd come here if she were looking for me. And my name is listed in the phone book."

"Perhaps she was coming here," Dylan suggested, his nerves tightening at the thought. It would give Sarah a reason for heading north from LA. She could have been on her way to find Catherine. "Sarah doesn't know who she is," he reminded Catherine. "She needs someone to tell her. If she's Jessica, you could be the one person to bring back her memory. And it's important, not just because her child is missing, but because someone is trying to kill Sarah."

"What?" she asked in shock. "You didn't say that before."

"Her accident wasn't random. Someone ran her off the road, and someone tried to smother her with a pillow in the hospital yesterday. That's the truth." He gazed into her eyes. "You can see I'm telling the truth, can't you?"

"Yes, I can see that. But what you haven't told me is why you're trying to help someone you don't like. What do you have against Sarah?"

"She wrecked my brother's life. She took his kid and ran away seven months ago. Watching him search for his daughter . . ." Dylan couldn't even finish the statement. Seeing Jake's pain had just about killed him. He hadn't been able to do anything to help his brother, the brother who had quite literally saved his own stupid life. But he had a chance now, and he wasn't going to blow it. He needed Catherine to trust him, and she wasn't a woman to trust easily. He couldn't fake it with her. She was far too perceptive. "I don't like Sarah, but I'm not interested in hurting her," he said truthfully. "I just want to help my brother get his daughter back."

"I never had a brother," Catherine said. "I used to wish I did. Someone who would have protected me the way you want to protect your brother. All right. I'll help you. I'll go to LA with you tonight. But I'm as loyal to Jessica as you are to your brother. If I have to make a choice between them, I'll choose her."

"And I'll choose him," Dylan said.

"Then we understand each other," she said.

"We do." And what he understood was that he didn't trust her any more than she trusted him. He would bet his life that Catherine knew how to run and hide as well as Sarah did.

Chapter Twelve

Sarah felt much better after their late lunch. Jake hadn't said anything while they ate, and for that she was grateful. She needed a break from the constant onslaught of questions. A lot had happened in the past few days. She needed to process the odd facts that had come back to her and see if they made any sense. She started to clear their plates, but Jake waved her back.

"I'll clean up," he said. "You sit. Save your energy for the big stuff."

"Thanks." She watched him take care of the food and dishes with quick, quiet competence. There was a confidence about his movements, as if he were used to taking care of himself—which she supposed he was.

She wondered what his life had been like before they met. Aside from his job, she knew next to nothing about him.

"How old are you?" she asked.

"Thirty-three," he said shortly as he rinsed off a plate and set it on the counter to dry.

Which made him five years older than her. "Where did you grow up? San Francisco?"

"Yes."

"What did you like to do in your free time?"

Jake walked back to the table, looking none too pleased by her questions. "Why do you want to know about me? It's not going to help you remember your life."

"Probably not, but I'm curious. And you never know—something you say, something you shared with me before, might spark a memory."

"You're reaching, Sarah."

"Okay, so I just want to fill in some blanks. Are you going to talk or not?"

Jake sat down with a sigh. "You never used to be so nosy."

"I didn't?"

"No. You weren't one of those women who wanted to know every last thing about me. I thought at the time how lucky I was."

"But you don't anymore."

He shook his head. "Because now I understand that you didn't ask me about my life so that you wouldn't have to answer questions about yours. You said, 'Let's keep the past in the past,' and I said, 'Sure, why not?' I had no idea that you had so much to hide."

"What about you? Were you hiding anything from me?"

The odd look that flashed through his eyes surprised her. And when he said, "Of course not," she didn't believe him.

"Jake?"

"I didn't have a great childhood. I don't like to talk about it. I'm not hiding anything." He frowned. "Fine, here's the abbreviated version of my life. As I told you before, my parents divorced when I was ten and Dylan was seven. My mother left, and my father raised us, so to speak. He wasn't really around that much. He was a businessman, an investment banker. Everything for him was about numbers and bottom lines. He didn't have patience for anything that didn't add up. He had high expectations that were impossible to meet, especially for Dylan. He was rough on my brother. He made life impossible for him. Every night the dinner table was a battlefield."

"So you tried to make things easier," she ventured.

"It didn't work. My father and brother couldn't get along, and to be honest my father was a bully. He'd go after any sign of weakness. Even when Dylan was just a little kid, my father would taunt him about his failures, if it was missing a ground ball at second base or marking the wrong answer on a math quiz. Sometimes I'd try to distract him by doing something even worse."

Sarah leaned forward, resting her arms on the table. "Like what?"

He shrugged. "Anything, spilling something on

the floor—he hated that—turning on the TV when we were supposed to be studying." Jake stared down at the floor. "Whatever."

"You are totally lying," she said. "You didn't do those things—Dylan did. You just tried to take the blame for him."

His head jerked up. "That's not true."

"I don't think it's in you to screw up. You have this innate sense of right and wrong."

His gaze burned into hers. "When it comes to you, yes."

"When it comes to everything," she countered. "Even if you tried to mess up to distract your father, I bet you didn't do a very good job."

"Okay, we're done."

"No, no, wait," she pleaded, realizing she'd shut him down. "Okay, I'll buy your story."

"It's not a story."

"Tell me the rest. Please."

He drew in a deep breath and then said, "Things got worse for Dylan when I went away to college. My father kicked him out of the house when he was sixteen. Dylan wound up coming to live with me. He slept on my living room couch for two years in an apartment I shared with a few other guys. I got him signed up at the local high school and that was that. He was my responsibility."

"Your father didn't try to get Dylan to come home?"

"Hell, no. I think he was happy we were both gone. He threw some extra cash at me until Dylan was eighteen, and then he said he was done supporting either one of us."

"Your father sounds like a harsh man."

"Cold as ice."

"It's no wonder you're such close brothers. I'm sure Dylan would do anything for you." Their tight relationship also explained why Dylan was so protective of Jake when it came to her.

"We'd do anything for each other," Jake amended.

She gave him a thoughtful look. "I came between you, didn't I? You said something about that before."

"Dylan didn't trust you, but I wouldn't listen to him. He'd always been a cynic about women. He never got over my mother walking out on us. He went crazy when you moved in with me, and especially when you got pregnant. He pressured me to ask you more questions, to make sure I knew who you were before I married you. But I didn't want to ask you questions. I didn't want to rock the perfect boat we were on. So I blew him off. I told him to get out of my life if he couldn't be happy for me. I didn't see him again until the day you disappeared. He came back as soon as he heard you and Caitlyn were gone."

"You chose me over your brother. I'm amazed."

"It just goes to show how insane I was. But Dylan was right. I was wrong. I should have done everything he said." Jake drummed his fingers on the tabletop. "In my job, I focus on every detail. I know how important it is to have a foundation that's strong, that won't cave in; otherwise nothing else matters. But in my personal life, with you, I screwed up. I didn't worry about building a foundation. I didn't care about the details. Our relationship was built on shifting sand, and look what happened. It collapsed. Why was I surprised?"

She didn't know what to say. She was still stunned to know that she'd been able to rip apart such a tight bond between brothers. Jake must have really loved her. And she must have loved him, too. But if she had loved him, why had she let him send away the brother he adored? Jake must have told her before how he had practically raised Dylan. She had to have known how close they were.

"Did I know at the time that Dylan disliked me?" she asked. "Did you tell me about your conversation with him?"

"Not completely," he admitted. "You knew a little, but I didn't want to hurt your feelings."

Because he had a big heart, she realized. He'd protected his brother and he'd protected her. Jake was a good man. Why on earth had she left him? There had to be something he wasn't telling her about their relationship.

"What did we fight about?" she asked.

Jake stared at her. "Nothing."

"Seriously?"

"You weren't a fighter. You didn't complain. You didn't argue about anything."

"Wow. I sound like an incredibly boring doormat of a person. Why did you like me?"

Jake sighed. "You weren't a doormat. We didn't fight because we were in sync. We liked the same movies. We read the same books. We were never bored with each other. We didn't talk about a lot of personal stuff, but we talked about everything else. And you have a great sense of adventure, Sarah. You once read an article about all the public stairways in San Francisco. There are three hundred and something of them, by the way. You decided that we would find all of them and climb them. And we did. I had grown up in the city, but I'd never seen it before, not until I met you." He paused. "You made me stop and feel the sun on my face. It sounds stupid, but I'd never done that."

No, because he was a goal-obsessed person, and right now he was chafing with impatience at having to tell her things about their past when all he really wanted to do was find Caitlyn.

"Thanks," she said simply. "It's nice to know something about myself."

He shrugged. "Whatever it takes."

The muscles in his face tightened, as if he regretted the small confidence they'd shared. She doubted she would get anything more personal out of him. But she didn't want their conversation to end. She felt as if every word he spoke was lightening up the darkness in her head. "This is helping," she said.

"Why? Are you starting to remember?"

"The memories feel closer."

"What does that mean?"

"I don't know, Jake. Just keep talking. Tell me about your mother."

"I don't talk about her."

"But why did she leave you behind? Don't mothers usually get custody?"

"She obviously didn't want custody," he replied. "I think she was so beaten down by my father over the years that she just couldn't keeping fighting. She used to drink, take sleeping pills. I'm sure she was trying to escape from my father."

"Did he abuse her?"

"I never saw him physically hurt her. I even remember some good times. But one day they were just gone. And then so was she. She wrote us a long letter and that was that. Over the years she did sign her name to a few birthday cards or Christmas presents, but that was basically all the contact we had with her."

"It seems strange that she would just leave you like that."

"Really? It seems stranger to me that *you* would think it was strange," he said pointedly, his gaze burning into hers. "Obviously you had no problem walking away without a word."

Sarah felt the sting of his accusation. She didn't like how closely his mother's story seemed to parallel her own. Frowning, she asked, "Did I know this before about your mother?"

"Oh, yeah, you knew. It apparently didn't matter to you. Or maybe you realized that leaving me without a word was the perfect way to kill me without actually taking out a gun. I didn't think you had it in you to be so cruel."

His tone was vicious, but there was as much pain as anger in his words. Her eyes began to water, and she felt as if she were on the verge of crying again, but she couldn't cry, because Jake would think she was pretending, trying to get his sympathy, when in fact she felt like crying because of what she'd done to him.

He was right. It was unbelievably cruel to replay his mother's departure. She had hurt him so badly, this man she had supposedly loved enough to live with and have a child with. How could she have done such a thing? She didn't feel inside like the tough, cold bitch he described. Yet how could she deny the facts?

"I think I hate myself as much as you hate me," she murmured.

"That's impossible." Jake's face was grim, his mouth taut, the pulse in his neck beating hard and fast. He jumped to his feet so fast the chair toppled over backward. "We're done with this conversation. Whatever we had is gone. I want it to stay that way."

It was his last, belated statement that made her realize how conflicted he was about her. She was almost afraid to ask, but somehow the words came out. "Do you mean it's not completely gone?"

"Well, it is for you, isn't it?" he countered.

"Maybe it's not. Maybe when I remember who I am, I'll remember that I'm still in love with you."

He stared at her for a long moment. "I did love

you, Sarah," he said, his voice husky with emotion. "I thought you were the perfect woman, only you turned out to be a figment of my imagination."

"What we had together was real," she argued.

"No, it wasn't. Everything you said was a lie."

"Not everything. I'm a real person, even if my name keeps changing. What I like to eat is the same."

"So Sarah Tucker and Samantha Blake and God knows who else like Mongolian beef and chicken fried rice. Who cares?" he snapped.

"I do, because maybe who I am down deep is the same, too." She paused, searching for the right words. "I feel a lot softer than the person you describe. I feel as if I've been hurt, too, like the pain is really big, and if I let it out, it will be too much."

"Do you want me to feel sorry for you?"

"No, I want you to understand."

"Understand what? At the moment neither of us knows the truth about you. You can't explain your actions, and I can't understand. That's where we are, Sarah. You have to find a way to get through the block in your head. If it's fear and pain, you have to battle through it."

"I don't know how to do that."

"Yes, you do. I watched you climb three hundred and seventy-two stairs with shaky, exhausted legs and a determined spirit. You know how to make it to the top. You're not a quitter."

"I'm afraid," she murmured. "I'm scared of finding out that I left you as cruelly as you said I did, that something terrible is happening to my daughter while I'm locked up in this lost world in my head. I'm terrified that whoever is trying to kill me will succeed if I don't remember him before he finds me again." She began to tremble and shake, and she couldn't seem to stop. She was so cold. She felt so lost. And maybe she hadn't felt like quitting before, but she did now. The mountain facing her, filled with doubts and lies, seemed insurmountable.

After a moment Jake came over to her, hauled her to her feet and into his embrace, pressing her head against his chest, wrapping his arms tightly around her. She inhaled the scent of him and her body began to warm. As the long, silent minutes passed, she leaned on him, absorbed his strength, and for the first time since she'd woken up in the hospital she felt safe.

At some point their embrace changed. She became acutely aware of Jake's heart beating against her chest, the points where their bodies touched, the way their hips fit together, their legs entwined. Jake stroked her back, creating a line of fire that ran down her spine.

His breathing changed, quickened. She wanted to move, but she couldn't possibly take a step away from him. Her body went from relaxed to tense—but it was a different kind of tension, a different kind of need.

Jake put his hand under her chin, forcing her head up so she would have to meet his gaze. "Damn you, Sarah."

She sucked in a quick breath at the look of raw desire in his eyes. "We shouldn't," she whispered.

"Hell, no," he agreed as his thumb ran roughly around the edge of her mouth.

Her lips parted. She hadn't meant it as an invitation, but he took it as one, crushing her mouth with his own in a harsh kiss that was a mix of anger and passion. She didn't know where one emotion began and the other ended. She just knew she didn't want the kiss to end. But it had to end. It needed to end.

Jake pulled away first, his breathing ragged, his eyes glittering. He gripped her arms, his fingers tightening so hard she could feel their imprint on her skin. Then he moved her away from him and released her, taking a couple steps back, putting some distance between them. For long moments all they did was stare at each other. Then Jake turned on his heel, stomped into the bathroom, and slammed the door.

She let out a breath, sinking down on her chair as she heard the shower go on.

Had he always kissed her like that? No wonder she'd gone to bed with him so fast. Her entire body was on fire. But she'd almost made a huge mistake. She couldn't make love with Jake. She didn't know him. He was a stranger to her now.

But the problem was . . . she felt as if she did know him. Her body recognized him, even if her mind didn't, and her heart wanted to reach out to his. She felt an emotional connection as well as a physical one. And Jake felt something, too.

Despite everything she'd done to him, he still wanted her—and he hated himself for it. She knew his shower would be long, cold, and punishing.

For several minutes she just sat, breathing in and out, trying to calm down, but she could still taste Jake on her lips, feel his hands on her arms. At last she had a memory of him, a very recent memory, and it was overwhelming.

Finally her heart settled into a reasonable beat, and she forced herself to concentrate on what she needed to do next. Without Jake's presence she tried to relax, visualize herself in the place she had called home for the past few months. There had to be a clue to her life somewhere in this apartment. She'd slept here every night. She'd eaten at the table, cooked in the kitchen, watched her baby sleep in the crib. Her gaze swept back and forth across the room.

Something bothered her. Something played at the back of her mind.

The details were off. Was it in the arrangement of the furniture? Was there a crooked photograph? Was there something about the way the curtain hung over the window? She walked slowly across the room, turned, and came back again. The floorboard creaked beneath her feet. She stopped and took another long look around the apartment.

What had Jake told her before?

That when she was taking pictures, her mind always went to the odd detail that made the photograph more interesting.

There were three small throw rugs on the floor

that gave some color and life to the worn brown carpet. One was in front of the apartment door, the other in front of the kitchen door, and the third by the window.

Why wasn't it in front of the bathroom door? It would have made more sense to put it there.

She walked over to the window and knelt down, then in one fluid motion picked up the rug. She'd done this before, she thought. There was a heater vent hidden under the rug. Why would she put a rug over a heater?

She reached into the slats of the vent and pulled the metal piece up, once again feeling that odd sense of déjà vu.

Putting the metal grate aside, she peered into a small, dark hole. Reaching in, she took out a pile of cards and rocked back on her heels to see what she had. She laid the cards out on the floor, shocked to see that they were driver's licenses, each one with a different name, a different address, but all with the same face—hers.

Chapter Thirteen

"What's all this?" Jake asked from behind her.

Startled, she had to resist the urge to scoop up the identification cards and hide them away, but it was too late anyway.

Jake knelt down next to her, wearing only his jeans. Water still glistened on his shoulders, and his hair was spiked and damp. He picked up one of the licenses.

She licked her lips. In the picture her hair was blond, her name was Kelly Grimes, and the address placed her in Las Vegas. The next one he studied appeared to be a younger version of her with red hair. Her name was Stephanie Hamilton, and her address was in Palm Springs. There were a half dozen more identities.

"How did you know these were here?" Jake demanded, lifting his gaze to meet hers. "Were you just waiting for me to leave the room?"

"No, of course not."

Skepticism filled his eyes. "Sure. You just happened to find these while I was in the shower."

"Jake, if I had known they were here, I would have found a way to get rid of you for longer than a shower, and I wouldn't have been kneeling here like an idiot waiting for you to discover yet another bad secret about me."

"So what did happen?"

"I thought about what you told me, that I was always aware of odd details. As I looked around the apartment, I kept thinking there was something out of place, and it was this rug. Who puts a rug in front of a window?"

Jake peered back into the hole, reached in, and pulled out a pile of papers and a bunch of Social Security cards. "Dammit."

"What are those?" she asked, not getting a clear view, as his broad shoulders were in the way.

"Birth certificates for a half dozen little girls. Someone went to a lot of trouble to get you and Caitlyn identities that you could switch around and around." He paused and shook his head in disbelief. "You had help disappearing, Sarah. A lot of help."

"Because I'm in a lot of trouble," she whispered.

"I think so. And you've been doing this for a while," Jake added, going back through the licenses. "You look at least five to six years younger in this picture."

"It started before you, then." She'd suspected that, but here was confirmation.

"Yes." Jake gazed into her eyes. "But for two years you stayed put; you had a baby, a life with me. Was it always a temporary thing or did something happen to make you run again?"

"I wish I could answer that."

"Maybe you would have run sooner if you hadn't gotten pregnant," Jake mused. "Perhaps that's why you stayed as long as you did. You had to make it through the pregnancy, deliver Caitlyn, and get back on your feet. The pregnancy changed your plans for a few months, that's all—which was probably why you were so agitated when you found out you were having a baby."

"But why would I need to keep moving?"

"That's the million-dollar question, isn't it?" He gazed back at the birth certificates. "You had these made in the past sixteen months, which means you had to see someone to get them—either in San Francisco or here in LA. Since the names match up on several of the licenses done before Caitlyn was born, I'm betting it was the same person you'd gone to before, a long-term connection."

Sarah picked up the cards and certificates and slipped them back into the hole, then replaced the vent and the rug and stood up.

"Why did you do that?" Jake asked.

"Uh . . ." she faltered. "What do you mean?"

"You hid everything away again."

Sarah glanced down at the rug. "I don't know. Habit, I guess. I wasn't thinking."

"Maybe your habits are the key to your past. When you're not thinking, you rely on your instincts."

"I guess." She rubbed her temple with her fingers. Her headache had been steadily growing the past hour and was now a throbbing ache behind her left eye. "What do you want to do now?"

"I think you should take a shower," he said. "Change your clothes. Brush your hair. Clear your head. Take a few minutes for yourself."

She was surprised by the suggestion. "Do we have time?"

"We'll make time. You have a headache, don't you?"

"A little one," she replied, dropping her fingers from her face. "It's not important."

"You used to get headaches, migraines, when you were with me. You hated to take medication, and you wouldn't go to the doctor. You always chose to tough it out. I guess you had to avoid anyplace where they might ask for insurance. When you had Caitlyn, I paid the hospital bill."

That was probably true. There would have been questions to answer, papers to fill out, and she obviously hadn't wanted to leave any kind of trail. It was hard to believe the facts she was learning about herself. She felt as if she'd stepped into someone else's life. Then again, maybe that was exactly what she had done. Had the names and addresses on the fake IDs hidden away in the vent belonged to real people? Her head pounded with pain.

"I will take a shower," she said, heading toward the bathroom. She needed a few minutes to regroup and she needed to do that away from Jake.

As Sarah closed the door, Jake pulled on his shirt and buttoned it up. He mentally ran down the list of people in their social circle, wondering whom Sarah could have contacted in San Francisco to make her fake IDs. But there was no one she knew that he didn't. She'd been new to town, or so she'd said, when they met. After that, his friends had become her friends. Still, she had ventured out on her own during the day to do things all women did, get her hair cut, go to the supermarket, the post office, the bank. She could certainly have incorporated visits to someone else during those times. It wasn't as if they'd been together every second.

Checking his watch, he pulled out his cell phone, hoping Dylan had come up with some new information.

"Hello," Dylan said a moment later. "I was just about to call you, Jake."

The optimistic note in his brother's voice gave him a lift. "I hope that means you have some news."

"Well, I have a strong suspicion that Catherine Hilliard's missing friend, Jessica, is Sarah."

Jake felt a surge of energy run through his body. Maybe they were finally going to catch a break. "What have you discovered?"

"Catherine doesn't have photographs of Jessica, but she does have a portrait that she painted from memory, and the girl looks a lot like Sarah."

"I don't know, Dylan, a painting?" he asked doubtfully.

"Just listen. Catherine's friend Jessica disappeared eight years ago. She was living in Chicago at the time, but she was originally from California. About a week before she vanished, Jessica left a message for Catherine saying she was in some trouble. Like Sarah, Jessica disappeared without leaving any clues behind. She was twenty years old at the time of her disappearance. Which would make her twenty-eight now."

"The same age as Sarah," Jake said.

"Yeah. I just got on the Internet, and I looked up the newspaper articles on Jessica's disappearance. One had a grainy head shot that doesn't definitively look like Sarah, but it's close. Her hair is much shorter, straightened and blond, but the features are similar. In the articles, the police say they have no idea what happened to Jessica. The woman had no known enemies. She worked as a receptionist in a law firm, a temp job, so no one knew her very well. Her neighbor said she thought Jessica was dating someone, but she never met him. She just heard them out in the hall a few times. However, no boyfriend came forward to look for Jessica. It's all very sketchy."

"So the only thing we really have is that this woman looks a little like Sarah."

"There are a couple of other facts that support my theory, like that Jessica's parents died in a car crash, same as Sarah's."

"Anything else?"

"Catherine says that Jessica grew up in foster care with her."

"Foster care? Sarah certainly didn't mention that. I don't know, Dylan. It sounds very circumstantial or coincidental."

"Maybe she didn't tell you because it was part of the past she wanted to hide from you. Jessica also had a doll named Caitlyn and a grandmother in Boston named Sarah. I don't know about you, but I think that's a few too many coincidences."

Jake's mind raced with the implications. "Okay, so what's next?"

"I want to bring Catherine down to meet Sarah. I think if they're face-to-face we'll know for sure."

"That sounds like a good idea. When can you get here?"

"Unfortunately, not until late tonight. Catherine is teaching an art class, and she can't miss it. I doubt we'll get on the road before six o'clock. And it's probably a three-hour drive from here. What's happening on your end?"

"We're at Sarah's apartment. We found a pile of fake IDs and birth certificates for Sarah and Caitlyn," he replied. "Sarah has been a dozen different people over the years, and it appears that she's been on the run for a while."

"That would jive with Catherine's story."

"Yes, it would. And if Sarah is Jessica, and she really grew up in foster care, then that could explain her lack of relatives. It would also give us a concrete place to start looking for her past. If she was in the foster care system, there have to be records."

"Agreed. I also want to dig further into the Chicago connection. Jessica had neighbors, coworkers, friends there. Someone has to know more than we do."

"You'd think so. By the way, Sarah's neighbor here in LA called her Samantha."

"Another alias."

"Yes. Her neighbor also told us that someone may have tried to attack Sarah earlier this week, which could have triggered her run up the coast. There's a sketch of the attacker here in the apartment, and Sarah seems to think it's the same guy who was in her hospital room."

"I wonder if Sarah was running here to see her old friend Catherine," Dylan suggested. "Although, aside from a cryptic unsigned note, Catherine said she's had no contact from Jessica in the past eight years. It's possible I'm completely off base here. I hate to get your hopes up, Jake."

"Well, until we know for sure, keep working the contact."

"I will. I'll let you know when we get on the road."

Jake felt a rush of optimism as he ended the call. If they could trace Sarah to this Jessica, they would be a lot closer to finding out the story of her life, why she'd disappeared eight years ago, and what kind of trouble she'd been in. Maybe Chicago was where it had all started.

Slipping his phone back into his pocket, he looked around the apartment once more. Was he missing something? Sarah had zoned in on the hidden vent beneath the carpet. Were there other hiding places? Would she have been paranoid enough to use more than one location to secret away the clues to her past? The answer to that question was a definite yes.

He walked through the apartment, running his hands along the walls to see if he could find anything out of the ordinary. Nothing jumped out at him. He walked back to the bed, to the crib. He'd been trying very hard not to look at that crib, because it was the one piece of furniture in the room that really bothered him. Now he knew he had to face it head-on.

He moved over to the crib, putting his hands on the rail. Gazing down at the mattress, he could picture his daughter lying there with her blanket and her bear and her thumb in her mouth, and the image brought a knot of emotion to his throat. He couldn't believe how much time had passed since he'd seen Caitlyn. She would be so much bigger now, talking, walking, a little person.

Would she remember him? When she saw him again, would she know he was her father? Or would he be a stranger to her?

It killed him that she probably wouldn't recognize him now. She'd been away from him almost as long as she'd been with him, half of her short life.

Sarah had stolen so much from him—time he

would never get back, moments he would never experience. He hated her for that. But the separation between him and his daughter was coming to an end. He would get Caitlyn back, and when he did he would never let her out of his sight again.

As for Sarah . . . he didn't know what he would do about her. It had been easier to hate her when she was gone, when he wasn't with her, when the good memories had been overwhelmed by the bad ones.

His gaze caught on a piece of fabric underneath the blanket. He moved the blanket aside and was shocked to see what appeared to be a rolled-up T-shirt—a man's shirt, he realized as he picked it up. He unrolled the material, stunned to see the Cal Berkeley logo on the front. This was his shirt—one of his favorites, in fact. Sarah had once teased him about how often he wore it. She'd even snapped a photo of him wearing it as Caitlyn slept on his chest after her feeding. And here was the shirt in his baby's crib.

Why? Why had Sarah tucked his shirt into Caitlyn's bed?

Had she wanted to give their daughter some memory of her father, some tactile sense of his presence in her life? Or was he grasping at straws, wanting to believe that Sarah had cared a little about the fact that she was separating father and daughter?

What did it matter? Even if she had taken his shirt for some sentimental reason, it didn't change anything. Still, he found himself raising the shirt to his face, inhaling deeply, and wondering if he could really smell Caitlyn's scent or if it was just his desperate need to feel some sort of connection with her.

He set the shirt back down in the crib and gripped the railing as a rush of emotion swept through him. He'd stuffed the pain down deep, refusing to let it come to the surface. It was the only way he'd gotten through the days, the weeks, the months. And he couldn't let the pain overwhelm him now. He couldn't get lost in the memories. He had to find Caitlyn. He was so close to getting his daughter back. So damn close.

"I'm coming, baby," he murmured. "I'm coming to get you."

Turning away, he walked back to the kitchen table and sat down. He picked up the sketch of the man Sarah had drawn and focused on the facial details. Aside from his dark eyes, his other features weren't particularly exceptional or memorable. Jake would put the man's age to be in his thirties, maybe forties. He dressed like a thug, but did that describe who he was, or simply provide a good disguise? The multiple attempts on Sarah's life led Jake to believe that whoever was after her was powerful and determined. Was it this guy? Or was this man just the hired gun?

Whoever was after Sarah certainly hadn't given up over the number of years that she'd been gone, especially if the trouble had begun in Chicago eight years ago. What would make someone want to hunt her down and kill her after all this time?

For some reason the dangerous reality hadn't sunk in for him until this moment. Now it hit him hard. Someone wanted to kill Sarah, and he had to keep her alive, not just for her own sake, but also for Caitlyn's.

The only fact that made him feel marginally better was the belief that if the person who was after Sarah already had Caitlyn, they would have said so by now. They would have used Caitlyn to get to Sarah, which meant Caitlyn was still safe—for the moment. Who knew how long that would last? The bad guys knew more about Sarah's life and past than Jake or Sarah did.

So, what next? Sarah's place of employment, he figured. She might have made a friend there, someone she'd confided in, although he found it doubtful. She'd lived with him for two years and never told him any of her secrets. Why would she tell some other night janitor any truths about herself? Still, it was the only lead they had in this part of town. And he had to hope that Caitlyn was somewhere close by. It was certainly possible that Sarah could have found herself a babysitter without giving away her secrets, and that babysitter could have come from her workplace.

He looked up as Sarah emerged from the bathroom in a pink floral robe that had been hanging on the back of the bathroom door. She grabbed some clothes out of her dresser and closet and disappeared again.

It was a good thing, too. Seeing her bare legs peeking out of that robe and the shadow of cleavage between her breasts had made him hard in an instant. He had to get over this insane physical attraction to her. She'd practically killed him with her actions. He should not want her in any way whatsoever.

Only he did. And that was the damnable truth. For the past seven months he'd done nothing but concoct beautiful plans of revenge and torture for her. But now he was confused. Nothing was adding up as he'd expected. In some ways Sarah was as lost as Caitlyn was. And when Sarah looked at him with a plea in her beautiful blue eyes to somehow find a way out of this mess, he wanted to swoop in and rescue her. But who would he be rescuing? Who was the real Sarah? He sure as hell shouldn't sleep with her until he knew the answer to that question.

The bathroom door opened again. Sarah had put on clean jeans and a cream-colored sweater over a camisole top. Her hair was still damp and curling wildly, despite her efforts to brush and straighten it. Her eyes were clearer now, and her bruises didn't seem so intense. She'd removed the bandage from her forehead, revealing a long deep cut just below her hairline.

"I feel better," she said. "That was a good idea. What have you been doing?"

"I spoke to Dylan. Does the name Catherine Hilliard ring a bell?"

Sarah thought for a moment, then shook her head. "Why? Who is she?"

"The woman who called in to the news broadcast

last night. She says you look like a girl she lived with in foster care—a girl named Jessica." He watched her closely to see if she flinched or responded in any way, but she simply gave him her usual blank expression.

"Are you saying I grew up in foster care?"

"If you're this girl Jessica, you did."

"Then I don't have a family?" Shadows of disappointment filled her eyes.

"You told me your parents died when you were young. Maybe that's why you were in foster care, although you also said you lived with your grandparents in Boston, which wasn't true."

"Why would I lie about that?"

He shrugged. "Catherine told Dylan that her friend Jessica disappeared from Chicago eight years ago, in much the same manner you disappeared from me."

"Chicago?" Sarah rubbed her temple again. "My headache is coming back."

"I'll bet. Maybe your head hurts because you can't keep track of all the lies. At any rate, Dylan is going to bring Catherine here to meet you. Hopefully if you're face-to-face, your memory will return."

"Hopefully," she echoed. Sarah glanced at the clock on the wall. "It's almost four. I wonder why Amanda never came back."

It was a good question. Amanda had acted concerned for Sarah, even wanted to call the police, but she hadn't rushed back after her lunchtime class to check on her friend. Why was that? "Where did Amanda say she worked?" he asked.

"Something about a gym."

Jake got up and walked over to the kitchen wall. There were several numbers listed, including Amanda's cell and work. He pulled out his cell phone and dialed the first number, then handed the phone to Sarah. "She'll be more likely to talk to you."

A moment later Sarah shook her head. "No answer."

"Try the other number," he suggested, reading it off the paper to her.

"Yes, hello," Sarah said. "I'm looking for Amanda. Is she there?" She paused. "Okay, thank you." She hung up the phone. "I'll call back later. The gym said she isn't working today, but I thought she told us she had a lunchtime aerobics class. That's odd."

"She's the only close friend of yours that we've identified," Jake mused. "And she used to watch Caitlyn."

Sarah's gaze met his. "She also didn't let us into her apartment. She shut the door when she went to get the key."

Jake jumped up, cursing himself for missing the obvious.

Sarah beat him down the hall to Amanda's door. She pounded hard on the wood, calling out Amanda's name, but there was no answer. "What if Caitlyn is in there?" Sarah asked, desperation in her voice, in her expression.

"She's not there now," he said, his own nerves on

edge. "Look, Sarah, even if Caitlyn was with Amanda earlier, Amanda would have taken her somewhere else as soon as she got rid of us. She would have wanted to put some space between us until she knew what to do."

"Why? Why wouldn't she just give my daughter to me?"

"Because you don't remember who you are. You didn't know your name, and Amanda didn't recognize me," he said. "Damn, I was a fool not to think of this earlier."

"Break the door down," Sarah ordered.

"What?"

"You heard me. I said break the door down." She gave him a determined look. "Caitlyn may not be there now, but she might have been there before, and I want to know for sure. If you won't do it, I'll find a way to do it myself. There must be something I can use to—"

"I'll do it; hang on." He took a step back, then launched forward, slamming the door with his shoulder. It shuddered but didn't break. He tried again, using every bit of strength that he had. The door cracked and then flew open. He stumbled into the apartment.

Sarah pushed past him, searching the small area for any sign of their daughter. The floor plan was basically the same as Sarah's place, although Amanda had added more color with fake flowers and cozy, bright blankets on the couch and bed. Sarah zeroed in on a set of plastic keys lying on a table. "Caitlyn's," she whispered, her heart in her eyes.

Jake saw the pain of her loss, and knew that at least that emotion was real. Sarah still had a deep connection with their daughter, even if she couldn't remember anything else.

"Take a breath," he advised, directing the words at himself as much as at Sarah. His heart was beginning to pound, and all kinds of crazy theories were running through his head. "You visited over here with Caitlyn. Amanda said she'd babysat for you. It doesn't mean anything that those keys are here."

"What about this?" she asked, picking up a child's picture book. "You think I casually left these things behind?"

"Maybe not. I don't know, but there's no real proof Caitlyn was here a few hours ago, which is what you'd like to believe."

"Amanda said she had a lunchtime class, and she didn't. She lied about that."

"Maybe she has a second job at another gym." He didn't know why he was trying to defend or explain Amanda to Sarah, but deep in his gut he just couldn't believe that Caitlyn had been with Sarah's next-door neighbor for the past few days. "Think about it, Sarah. If someone attacked you in this building, you would not have left Caitlyn here while you drove up the coast. You wouldn't have believed she would be safe, not after that man tried to get into the elevator with you."

Sarah stared back at him, unblinking, as she

processed his words. He could see the light dim in her eyes when the logic took hold and the hope faded. Finally she nodded. "I can't argue with your reasoning, but I still think it's strange that Amanda didn't come back. She seemed so suspicious of you and worried for me. That doesn't make sense."

"Well, one thing is clear to me—when we go to your workplace next, you're going in alone. You might get a better reception that way. It's possible Amanda would have said more to you if I hadn't been standing right next to you."

"Amanda could still know where Caitlyn is and just have been afraid to tell me," Sarah suggested.

"It's a possibility. We can try to find her. You have her cell phone. You can leave her a message. Maybe she'll call back."

"What should we do about the door?" Sarah asked. "We can't leave her apartment open."

"We'll try the landlord before we leave. Maybe he can nail the door shut until she gets home, and we'll leave a note, some money to fix it."

They walked down the hall and back into Sarah's apartment. Jake noticed that Sarah was still clutching the toy and the book. She couldn't seem to let the items go, and he couldn't blame her. They were a tangible link to Caitlyn.

"Why don't you pack up some clothes in case we don't come back here for a while," he said.

"Why? Where are we going?"

"To where you worked—maybe back up the coast. Who knows? Caitlyn isn't here, and I'm not sure it's a wise idea for us to stay long. Obviously the person who is after you knows where you live."

"It seems so hopeless. I thought my memory would be back by now."

"Don't quit on me, Sarah. I need you in this all the way or we'll never find Caitlyn. You can't give up."

She bristled at the idea, as he'd known she would. She immediately gathered herself together, throwing back her shoulders, lifting her chin, a new light back in her eyes. She might not be willing to fight for herself, but she would do battle for Caitlyn.

"I'm not quitting," she said. "I would never do that, not while my daughter is in danger."

"Our daughter," he corrected.

She ignored him and moved to the closet. She pulled out a duffel bag, grabbed some clothes from the dresser and closet, and then went into the bathroom for personal supplies. She had barely returned when an alarm went off in the building. A series of shrill bells rang through the apartment.

"That's the fire alarm," he said in surprise.

"Yes," Sarah agreed, putting on her coat. "We need to get out of here."

He grabbed her by the arm. "Wait. I want to see if there's any smoke." He walked over to the window and saw gray smoke billowing up around the side of the building. When he turned, Sarah was right behind him.

"It's real. It's a fire," she said.

"Yeah, a very convenient fire," he muttered.

Her eyes met his. "You think someone set it deliberately?"

"It's a good way to smoke us out of the building—literally."

"It's obviously a real fire. We can't stay here. We're on the third floor, Jake."

"Let's go. Get your bag." He jogged over to the front door and put his palm against the wood. It was still cool. He turned back to see Sarah stuffing Caitlyn's blanket and bear into her bag. She grabbed his shirt, and then stared at it in bemusement. "What's this?"

"It's mine," he said shortly, meeting her quick, questioning gaze. "And no, I didn't put it there. You must have taken it with you when you left me. I used to wear it all the time." Sarah hesitated, then put the shirt into her bag. "Pull your sweater over your mouth and nose," he advised. He opened the door slowly, coughing as smoke blew through the hallway from an open window at the end of the corridor. He tried not to breathe as he took Sarah's hand and headed toward the stairs, praying he was making the right choice.

The smoke was so thick he could barely see where they were going. Sarah's hand tightened in his, a sign of complete and utter trust. They were in this together, for better or worse. He put his hand on the door to the stairwell. It was warm but not hot. He pushed it open. The air was dense and dark, but he didn't see any flames.

He grabbed the railing with one hand as they

made their way down the stairs quickly but carefully. They were almost to the second-floor landing when a figure came out of the smoke.

The man wore bulky clothing, baggy pants, and a hooded sweatshirt, and there was something in his hands. A gun. They'd run straight into an ambush.

Chapter Fourteen

Jake stopped abruptly, shielding Sarah with his body as he quickly assessed the situation. They were trapped between the fire behind them and the gun in front of them. Sarah's hand tightened in his, and he could feel her body shaking, her breath on his neck. She was depending on him to get them out of this alive. He needed a plan, but there was no time to make one. The man was raising the gun, his finger on the trigger.

Jake let out a yell as he launched himself at their attacker, praying the gun wouldn't go off and hit Sarah.

The man stumbled backward in surprise, but he recovered quickly, coming at Jake with a fury that he didn't expect, slamming Jake's head against the wall. He saw stars and felt blackness begin to descend, but he forced it back.

"Run, Sarah," he urged.

His words turned his attacker's attention on

Sarah. The man fired a shot at her just as she ducked past him, running down the stairs.

Taking advantage of the man's momentary distraction, Jake hit him from behind, this time knocking the gun out of his hand. They wrestled on the landing, both trying to get control of the gun, which had slid against the opposite wall.

The man was strong and knew how to fight. Jake battled back. He had to give Sarah time to get away.

Their bodies rolled over and over as they each struggled for dominance. They were close to the stairs now. If he could just shove the guy down the stairs, he might still get out of this alive.

The smoke was getting thicker. Jake could feel the heat of the fire emanating from the walls. His lungs were burning.

Suddenly a blast of cool air hit him in the face. There were men coming up the stairs. Firemen. *Thank God!*

His attacker jerked away. He gave Jake one last push as he ran down the stairs, nearly knocking over one of the firemen on his way down.

"Are you all right?" a fireman asked him, grabbing him by the arm.

Jake stumbled to his feet. He couldn't speak. His lungs were filled with smoke. The fireman helped him out of the building. He prayed that Sarah had gotten away, that she wasn't still waiting outside, and that their attacker hadn't caught up to her.

Finally they reached the street. He gulped in deep breaths of the cool, fresh air. Dozens of people were milling around in front of a fire truck that blazed with red and blue strobe lights.

"I'm okay," he said as a paramedic came up to him. But his gasp only led the paramedic to slap an oxygen mask over his nose.

"Breathe," the paramedic instructed. "Sit down."

He sat down on the grass, taking in much-needed air. All the while his gaze raked the area. He couldn't see Sarah anywhere. He needed to find her. He pulled the mask off his nose. "I'm all right," he repeated.

"You're bleeding," the paramedic said. "And the oxygen will do you good."

Jake put his hand to his head, and his fingers came away wet with blood. He must have cut himself on something in the stairwell.

"Let me take a look at that cut."

Jake pushed the paramedic's hand away from his face. "I'm fine. I have to find someone. My . . . my wife," he said, the words coming out before he could stop them. He didn't bother to correct himself. "She came out of the building right before me. Did you see her? Long, curly brown hair, blue eyes?"

"Sorry, buddy, I just got here, but I think everyone is out. Come on, sit down. You need treatment."

"No, I have to find her." He jogged down the sidewalk, looking for Sarah or the guy who had attacked them. When he got to the spot where the car was parked, his heart sank.

The car was empty. He glanced around him. Where the hell was Sarah?

* * *

A storm was coming, Dylan realized as he got out of his car. Dark black clouds were blowing in off the ocean. The temperature had dropped twenty degrees, and he shivered as he made his way up to Catherine Hilliard's front door. It was half past five. He hoped she was home and ready to go. He was impatient to get down to LA.

After she'd left for her class, he'd settled in at a coffee shop down the road. In addition to swilling down three cups of strong coffee, he'd gotten on the Internet and begun researching Jessica's disappearance. He'd also done a little digging into tattoos, specifically of the tiger variety. It hadn't surprised him to learn that tattoos could be linked to various gang organizations as a symbol of their fidelity. In fact, the tiger tattoo, which many believed to stand for fierceness, power, and loyalty, could also be traced back to specific groups linked to the Russian Mafia. Dylan sincerely hoped that Sarah's would-be killer was not part of that organization, but at the moment he couldn't discount any possibility.

Knocking again, he wondered what was taking Catherine so long to answer. Her yellow VW Bug was parked in front of her garage. She had to be home. And her house was small. He could go from one end to the other in about thirty steps. Trying the knob, he turned it in his hand. He'd never been one to ignore an open door, so he walked into the cottage, calling out for Catherine. There was no answer.

Crossing the room to the desk, he rifled through

the drawers of her desk, feeling only a slight twinge of guilt at invading her privacy. Any woman who left her door unlocked was fair game, he rationalized.

The phone on the desk suddenly rang, and he jumped. He stared at it for a long moment and then picked up the receiver. "Hello," he said.

He heard someone take a breath; then the phone slammed down and there was nothing but silence. Obviously the caller had not expected a man to answer. That was odd.

He was just hanging up when the front door opened and Catherine walked in. Her golden-red hair was windblown, her cheeks stained with pink, her eyes a deep, mesmerizing shade of blue. He drew in a quick breath, shocked by his physical reaction to her. She wasn't his type at all, he reminded himself. Nor was he here to get involved with her. She was just the means to an end—the end being Caitlyn and his brother back together.

"Your door was open," he said.

"And a lock would have stopped you?" she countered, a challenge in her eyes.

"Maybe not, but it might have slowed me down. Do you always leave your door open when you go out?"

She hung up her coat on a hook by the door. "I just ran next door to see if my neighbor could watch my pets while we're gone. But we're going to have to wait until morning."

"Why?" he asked sharply. "You said you'd go

tonight. Why have you changed your mind? Don't you realize how important this is?"

"I do, but it's starting to rain, and the storm will be severe. If we leave tonight, we won't make it."

"Of course we'll make it. It's just a little rain. I can handle it."

"I saw an accident," Catherine said slowly, quietly.

"What do you mean, you saw an accident?"

She stared back at him, the answer in her eyes—an answer he didn't want to believe.

"You mean, like, in a vision?" he asked.

"Yes."

It sounded like an awfully convenient vision to him. "Look, we'll drive carefully, slowly."

"I'm surprised those two words are in your vocabulary, because you're neither slow nor careful. But I am. And I can't go tonight. Tomorrow—in the morning. That's when we'll go."

He didn't want to wait until morning. There had to be something he could say to change her mind, but he had barely finished the thought when a flash of lightning was followed by a rumble of thunder that ran through the house like a freight train. She was right. The storm was upon them. It was a good three-hour trip down the coast to LA, and despite what he'd said, it would be a brutal drive in the pouring rain. Sarah had almost lost her life making such a trip during the last storm. Perhaps they should wait. Still, he itched to get on with it, to make the final connection.

"You're impatient," Catherine said.

"Well, you don't have to be psychic to see that," he said dryly, realizing he was tapping his foot. "I don't like to wait. I've spent way too much time waiting for people to . . ." He didn't finish his sentence, not sure why he'd even started it. He never spoke about his past.

Catherine gave him a speculative look, as if she were reading his mind. He didn't like it. "Fine, we'll go tomorrow," he said quickly. "First thing in the morning. In the meantime you can tell me everything you know about Jessica."

"I'd be happy to." Catherine sat on the couch, pulling down the afghan and wrapping it around her shoulders. "But first I have some questions for you."

"Like what?" He took a seat on the chair across from her.

"Tell me about your friend Sarah's baby. What does she look like?"

"Like the most beautiful baby you've ever seen, blond curls, blue eyes, little pug nose. Caitlyn smiled all the time. I told Jake she was going to be a man-killer when she grew up. He'd have to watch her every minute once she hit high school. He was crazy about that kid. When Sarah took her away, he just about went over the edge. I'm sure he feels even worse now, knowing that Caitlyn is in danger from whoever is after Sarah."

"I can't imagine my friend putting her child in danger on purpose," Catherine said. "Jessica loved babies. She couldn't wait to grow up and be a mom. She wanted so badly to re-create the family that she'd lost. I used to encourage her to think more about a career, a job. She said she didn't have enough money to pay for college, which I know was true, but I think she could have found a way if she really wanted it. She just didn't see her future in academics, and she didn't want to waste her time there. I couldn't blame her. I went to art school. I made painting a priority over finding a job that would pay me a lot of money."

"Going to school would have been too much work. Sarah liked shortcuts."

Catherine shook her head. "Jessica learned early on that life can change in a heartbeat. There's no point in wasting time doing something you don't love. You have to live for the moment."

Dylan leaned forward, clasping his hands together. "I don't know if we're talking about the same person, but I'll tell you this: Sarah isn't living; she's hiding. I talked to my brother earlier today. Since Sarah left him, she's been living in a run-down apartment working as a night janitor. Does that sound like someone who's grabbing hold of life? She walked out on Jake, who makes a good living as an architect. They were building a house together, for God's sake. Jake was willing to give Sarah anything she wanted, and still she left. It's pointless to even try to please a woman, because it's impossible."

Catherine tilted her head. "That last bit sounds like a personal statement."

"Just calling it like I see it."

"You must not have met the right woman."

"Oh, believe me, I've met a lot of women."

"I'm not talking about one-night stands. I'm talking about personal relationships where you actually learn each other's last names."

"Hey, I've gotten plenty of last names."

"But I'm betting not much more than that."

"We're not talking about me," he returned.

"You don't like to talk about you. It's always about other people. Is that why you became a journalist—so you could ask the questions?"

He didn't care much for her assessment, even though it was close to the mark. "Let's get back to your friend Jessica."

"I don't know why Jessica or Sarah, if they're the same person, left your brother the way she did, but I am sure of this—Jessica knows how to survive. She had to learn early how to protect herself, because once her parents died, once she went into the system, she was on her own. If you want to survive in foster care, you have to figure out how to fit in. You have to be a chameleon. You have to be good at reading people, predicting who's going to be a danger to you. You have to learn how to hide, how to run, and how to find help. Just because someone puts you in a house with a roof over your head doesn't mean you're in a good home. The monsters aren't always in the closet or under the bed. Sometimes they're right in front of you, only everyone thinks they're the good guys."

Catherine spoke as if she had had firsthand experience with those monsters. Dark shadows filled her eyes, and he could hear the edge of bitterness in her voice. He wondered if her sinister paintings were an expression of the blackness in her soul. The question came out before he could stop it: "Is that why you paint monsters?"

She caught her breath, and for a moment he didn't think she would answer.

"Yes," she said finally. "I'm afraid if I don't let them out, they'll swallow me whole."

The fear in her voice forged a connection between them. He'd faced a few monsters in his own time, and he knew what it felt like to be afraid, to feel young and powerless. But he wasn't that scared kid anymore. He could take down any monster that came his way. Apparently Catherine didn't feel quite so confident. He felt an odd urge to reach out to her, to offer his protection, but that was crazy. He didn't know what she was involved in. Hell, she could be as messed-up as Sarah.

He sat back in his chair, realizing they'd gotten off-track. And since Catherine was now working on biting one nail down to the quick, he suspected she was just as interested in changing the subject as he was. He was surprised when she glanced up at him, catching him in midstare.

"You bite your nails," he said, feeling somewhat stupid at the observation.

She pulled her hand away from her mouth. "Bad habit. Do you have any?"

"None that I intend to share," he said lightly.

She offered him a small smile, breaking the tension between them. "I've been thinking about what you said before, that you can't understand how Sarah could have taken her child with her when she ran away from your brother, but it makes sense to me if Sarah is Jessica. There is no way on this earth that Jessica would leave a child of hers behind. She wouldn't abandon her daughter, no matter what the stakes. She grew up without a mother; she wouldn't want that for her child."

"What about growing up without a father? Isn't that just as bad?"

"That depends on the father."

"Jake is a good guy. The best. He loves his kid beyond belief." He paused. "There's nothing you can say that could justify what Sarah did."

"I didn't say that she was right. I just said I understand why she did it." She gave him a thoughtful look. "What was your family like? Did you have the perfect childhood?"

"Not even close. My father was a shithead. My mother was gone. And Jake was the only one who kept me sane. He knows what it's like to grow up in a bad family. He wouldn't want his baby to grow up without him either. Sarah doesn't have a monopoly on that kind of fear. And Sarah didn't give Jake a chance to help her. He would have walked through fire for her."

"Really? I've never met a man who would do that for a woman."

For some reason her cynical statement unsettled him. He had the insane desire to want to prove to her that he was just such a man. But Catherine was already talking again.

"Jessica wouldn't have expected your brother to help her," Catherine continued.

"She should have. She was with him for almost two years. If she couldn't figure out what kind of a man he was by then, I don't know what else he could have done. But let's move on. Jake told me that they found numerous fake IDs and birth certificates in Sarah's apartment in LA. She had to have gotten those from someone. Do you have any idea who could have done that kind of work for her?"

Catherine didn't answer right away, and he felt a stirring of excitement in his gut. She knew something.

"If you know, you have to tell me," he said.

"There was a boy when we were growing up," she said slowly. "His name was Andy Hart—he could come up with any ID you wanted. He was a computer-hacker genius and had a lot of other not-so-legal talents, even when he was just a teenager."

"Andy Hart," Dylan repeated. "Any idea where he'd be now?"

"Probably somewhere in Southern California, but I have no idea. That's where he was when I knew him, but it was a dozen years ago."

"We need to find him."

"How?"

"Well, barring a very convenient psychic vision on

your part, I'm guessing the Internet. My laptop is in the car. Mind if I work here?"

"Would it matter if I did? And if you continue to mock my visions, I won't tell you what I saw about you."

He didn't like the odd light in her eyes. "You didn't see anything about me."

"Didn't I?"

Catherine's gaze didn't waver as she stared back at him, and he felt an odd sense of uneasiness. Still, he ignored it. This wasn't about him; it was about Jake and Caitlyn. Their future was the only one he was interested in at the moment. At least, that was what he told himself as he dashed outside to retrieve his computer.

Jake walked back and forth on the sidewalk next to his car, scanning the area for Sarah or the guy who had jumped them. Another fire truck had just arrived, and the firemen were working hard to contain the fire. Had the fire been set deliberately to lure them out of the building? Or had it also served another purpose, a way to destroy anything and everything in Sarah's apartment?

There hadn't been anything there, he told himself—nothing except those fake IDs, and those couldn't be valuable. Had they missed something? Was it not just that someone wanted Sarah dead but rather that they wanted something from her?

No, that didn't make sense. If she had something they wanted, they wouldn't have tried to kill her;

they would have tried to kidnap her or ransack her apartment while she was out of town. Certainly the other attempts on her life had been solely about getting rid of her. It was more logical to think that the fire had just been a distraction to lure them into the open. And it had worked. Fortunately, they'd managed to evade getting shot, but what was he going to do now?

He'd lost Sarah and he still didn't have Caitlyn. He was right back where he'd started. It was his fault. He'd told Sarah to run, and she'd done just that. She could have hopped on a bus, taken a cab. She could be anywhere now.

A kid on a skateboard came down the street, stopping in front of him, his attention on the fire. "Whoa, dude. That's cool."

Trust a teenager to think a fire destroying the homes of a dozen people was cool.

"Your name Jake?" the kid asked.

"Yes," he said, surprised and wary.

"Some chick told me to give you this," the kid said, handing him a piece of paper. He then got on his skateboard and headed closer to the fire action.

Looking around to be sure no one was watching, Jake unfolded the paper and saw only a few words—*Barney's Ice-cream Parlor, Fourth and Beach Street*. The message had to be from Sarah.

Chapter Fifteen

Jake got into his car, started the engine, and made a quick U-turn. He headed down the block. They'd come in on Beach Street, just a few blocks away. He checked his rearview mirror every few seconds, hoping he wasn't leading anyone straight to Sarah. With any luck the guy who'd ambushed them had already taken off. Jake wished to God he'd had time to force the guy to say why he was after Sarah, or who he was working for. That would have to wait for another day. At this point he had no reason to doubt that there would be another time. The attacks on Sarah were relentless. No one was giving up. How long would they be able to fend them off?

Jake parked his car in the small lot next to the ice-cream parlor and made his way into the store. It was filled with kids and families, and in the very back corner at a small table sat Sarah. As soon as she saw him, Sarah jumped to her feet and ran over to him. "Are you all right? You're bleeding. I was so worried about you. I was so afraid you wouldn't make it. . . ." Her voice trailed away, as if she couldn't finish the terrifying thought in her head. She searched his face with anxious eyes. "You're hurt."

"I'm fine," he said. "The firemen arrived just in time."

"Are you sure you don't need to go to the hospital?"

"Positive. I'm just glad you found a way to tell me where you were."

"I sent that kid with the note to look for you, but I wasn't sure he would be able to find you in the crowd. I didn't even know if you had made it out of the building. I shouldn't have left you there. I should have stayed."

"No, you did the right thing," he told her, leading her back to the table. "I wanted you to go."

Sarah shook her head in self-loathing. "I took the easy way out. You could have been killed."

"If you hadn't gone, we might both be dead, and then where would Caitlyn be?"

She didn't look convinced. "When I left the building, I saw the fire truck coming. I hoped they would be able to save you, since I couldn't. Then I thought I should get away, but I didn't want to go too far."

"You did everything right. You picked a crowded place with lots of people, and a seat at the back where you could see whoever came in the door." He wasn't surprised she'd known what to do. Her self-protective instincts were finely tuned. "This is what you do, Sarah—you hide; you protect yourself."

"What happened to that man? Did you . . . did you kill him?"

"I wish," he muttered. "We were wrestling for the gun when the firemen came in. The guy bolted. The firemen forced me out of the building. I never saw him again after that."

"So he's still free, still out there somewhere?"

"Yes." He met her gaze. "And I don't think he's finished with you yet."

"I don't think so either. Did you get a better look at him?"

"It was difficult to see anything, but I suspect it's the same guy. My instincts tell me that he's just the front man. He didn't talk to you like he knew you. He didn't use your name. He didn't give you any idea why he wanted you dead."

"That's true."

"You pissed someone off, Sarah. Someone has been tracking you for years. And I suspect that guy was sent to take care of you." He cleared his throat and then winced at the pain.

"I'll get you some water." Sarah retrieved an empty cup from the guy behind the counter and then walked over to the drinking fountain.

When she returned, he took the drink out of her hand and drained it in one long, soothing swallow. Sarah watched him with concern in her eyes. He'd seen that look on her face a few times when they'd been together, but always when she'd been worried about Caitlyn—the first time Caitlyn got the croup, then when she got the flu and ran a high fever.

They'd stayed up all night together, taking turns rocking Caitlyn, putting cool towels on her forehead, giving her sponge baths. Sarah had been distraught with fear that something bad would happen to her daughter. And he had tried to reassure her, but the truth was that he'd been just as scared. Finally the fever had broken, and Caitlyn had bounced back in record time. He thought it had probably taken Sarah longer to get over that illness.

Now she was looking at him with the same fear, as if she were afraid for him. He'd thought she'd completely stopped caring what the hell happened to him when she'd walked out on him. Could he trust the expression on her face now?

Sarah pulled a napkin out of the dispenser and leaned forward. "Do you mind if I get some of that blood off you?"

Before he could reply, she gently touched his forehead and cheek with the napkin. Her moves were unbelievably gentle and tender. He closed his eyes for a moment. She was so close to him he could feel her breath on his face, the brush of her breasts against his arm, the scent of lavender lotion on her skin. He was taken back in time to another place, when he'd watched her rub that sweet-smelling cream onto her skin before she came to bed. It had taken months to get that scent out of his head. Her scent. Her taste. Her touch. It was painful as hell.

He grabbed her arm and opened his eyes. "It's okay," he said.

She looked at him for a long, long moment, a myriad of emotions flitting through her eyes, and then she finally sat back in her chair.

He let out a breath of relief.

"That cut doesn't look too deep, but you might need a stitch," she said quietly.

"It's fine."

"You don't always have to be the tough guy."

"Yeah, I do."

She gave him a half smile. "Then you'll be happy to know you're developing a black eye."

"I guess we'll be twins," he said.

Her smile broadened, the tension of the last few hours finding a release in his small joke. "I guess we will." She paused, her expression growing serious again. "How bad was the fire when you left?"

"Bad. I don't know what they'll be able to salvage."

"I feel terrible for everyone who lived there. It's my fault. That fire was set deliberately to get to me."

He couldn't deny the obvious. "He got tired of waiting for us to come out, and he wanted the advantage. I guess we don't have to worry about Amanda's door anymore."

"She could lose everything in that fire."

"But not her life," Jake said. "At least we know she wasn't inside her apartment."

"Thank God for that." She fell silent for a moment. "I want to say thank-you, Jake."

"There's no need."

"Yes, there is. You stood in front of me and faced that gun, and then you jumped that guy without any regard for your own life. You could have been killed." Her gaze sought his. "Why? Why did you do that? You hate me. Why would you try to protect me?"

"You're the mother of my child. I need you to find Caitlyn," he said, but he knew that wasn't the whole truth. The need to protect Sarah ran deep within him. He hadn't been thinking at all when he'd stepped in front of her. It had been pure instinct.

"Well, I'm still grateful."

"Why didn't you keep running? You've got money. You could have left me."

"I couldn't just leave you like that."

"You did before," he said pointedly.

"Well, I couldn't now. You see—"

He cut her off with a wave of his hand. "Don't—don't say anything else." He suddenly felt as if this conversation were more dangerous than the gun he'd faced earlier.

Sarah tilted her head to one side. "I never did—did I? Say anything else."

"What does that mean?"

"You said before that we didn't argue; we didn't fight; we didn't disagree on anything. That seems odd to me. Who's like that? Don't most people disagree on something? Don't most couples argue, even if it's only over who's going to take out the trash or do the dishes?"

He frowned, not liking the fact that she was picking up on something he'd failed to see for almost two years. "Obviously you didn't want to rock the boat."

"Nor did you," she pointed out "Did we each do everything the other wanted?"

"You more than me," he admitted. "At the time I thought you were perfect."

"I guess I'm not perfect anymore."

No, she wasn't close to perfect now, not at all the ideal woman he'd come to believe he was involved with. Now she was a mess of complicated emotions and behaviors. But for some bizarre reason, he was actually starting to like this version of Sarah. Despite the fact that someone had tried to kill her again, she was already back on her feet, ready to get down to business, not nearly as shaken by the events of the past hour as he would have expected her to be. Maybe he'd never given her enough credit for her quiet strength. She'd so often let him take the lead in their life together. He hadn't realized until she'd left how little he knew of her own opinions. He'd seen their relationship purely from his own point of view, never stopping to consider that he was doing more talking than listening.

"Why are you looking at me like that?" Sarah asked.

"I'm trying to figure you out."

"Are you having any luck?"

"Not much," he admitted. "Knowing how you've lived these past seven months makes me realize how strong and independent you are. You hid yourself away from danger, found a place a live, a job where you could take Caitlyn, a way to make enough money to survive. I don't think I saw your strength before."

Sarah clasped her hands together on the top of the table. She gazed into his eyes "I do feel like I'm a survivor, as if I've been doing just that for a very long time. Maybe I didn't seem strong when I was with you because I didn't need to be. You took care of me, didn't you? Just the way you did on the stairs earlier. You have protective instincts."

"I tried to take care of you, but obviously you didn't trust me enough to tell me what kind of trouble you were in. You should have trusted me, Sarah. You should have given me a chance to fix things."

"I don't know why I didn't. I know it makes no difference to you, but I trust you now. That's why I didn't keep running this time, Jake, because we're in this together now. While I can't change the past, I can at least do the right thing from here on out."

He saw nothing but sincerity in her eyes. He wanted to trust her again, but what she couldn't remember he could, and those painful, unending days still burned bright in his memory. "Are you ready to go? I think it's better if we keep moving."

She gave a nod. "While I was waiting for you I looked in the phone book for the address of the place where I worked—Gold Star Cleaners. They're on Fifth and Harrison. I asked the guy behind the counter, and he gave me directions. We can go there now if you want."

"Might as well. We certainly can't return to your apartment."

She swung the duffel bag strap over her shoulder and followed him out to the car. They stuck close together as they entered the parking lot. The weather was changing, the sun vanishing behind thick, dark clouds. There was an ominous feeling to the early evening air that only heightened his tension. Once inside the car, Jake flipped the locks. He had just started the engine when his phone rang. He saw his brother's number on the screen. "It's Dylan," he said to Sarah as he answered the phone. "What's up?"

"There's a huge storm hitting the coast up here, so Catherine and I aren't going to make it down there tonight. I'm sorry, dude. I can't get her on the road. She thinks it's too dangerous to make the drive until morning."

Jake wasn't happy to hear that. He'd been hoping that the woman Dylan was talking to might jog Sarah's memory. "Have you found out anything else?"

"A couple of things. Catherine gave me a lead on a kid they knew in foster care who worked the backside of the law manufacturing fake IDs when he was in high school. His name is Andy Hart, and I'm on the Internet now trying to find him. I also dug a little deeper and found an address for Sarah's former social worker, Eleanor Murphy. According to Catherine, Eleanor was a kind woman who tried to keep in touch with the kids she followed. There's a slim chance Sarah might have contacted her if she was in trouble."

Dylan felt a rush of excitement at the news. "Great. Where does she live?"

"Manhattan Beach, not too far from where you are now, I believe, which could be a coincidence or the reason why Sarah moved to Santa Monica."

Jake grabbed a pen from the console between the seats and wrote down the address Dylan rattled off.

"There was also another friend of Sarah's—or Jessica's—who was with her in Chicago about a month before she disappeared—Teresa Meyers. So far I haven't found her, but I'm still looking. What's up with you?"

"There was another attempt on Sarah's life. A fire was set at her apartment building. A guy was waiting for us in the stairwell. We got into a fight. I got the gun away, but he escaped when the firemen came into the building. So he's still out there."

"Shit!" Dylan swore. "Where are you now? Are you both all right?"

"We're in the car, and yes, we're fine."

"I should get down there."

The last thing Jake wanted to do was drag his brother any further into this mess. "No, you're more helpful staying with Catherine, researching on the Net. That's what I need from you right now."

"I can do that down there."

"The morning is fine. We'll meet then. Is there anything else?"

"The tiger tattoo. I found some gangs, including

the Russian Mafia, who use tiger tattoos as their symbol of affiliation. There could be more than one person after Sarah. And they could be very dangerous."

Dylan's words only confirmed Jake's suspicions that there were some powerful people who wanted Sarah dead. And he was the only one standing between her and them—whoever they were. "Thanks. I'll talk to you soon."

Sarah felt a growing sense of unease as Jake finished his conversation with his brother. She could hear bits and pieces about someone named Jessica.

Jessica. The name sounded familiar, and with the familiarity came a deep sense of loss.

"Sarah?"

Jake's voice intruded on her thoughts. She blinked and looked up at him. He was watching her again with those penetrating green eyes of his that made her feel like he could see right through her. Only he couldn't. No one could. Not even she knew what was in her own head.

"What did Dylan find out?" she asked.

"He gave me some names of possible people from your past: Andy Hart and Teresa Meyers, two kids you may have lived with in foster care. And Eleanor Murphy, who was apparently your social worker."

She took in what he was telling her like a dry sponge absorbing every bit of water. It seemed that Dylan was piecing together a past for her, foster care, friends. Jake seemed to think his brother was on the right track—so why didn't the names mean anything to her?

"Nothing, huh?" he asked.

"I'm not sure."

"Sarah, I know you're scared to remember, but you have to try."

"I think I must be a terrible coward," she murmured.

"That word doesn't describe you at all. Maybe you've just reached your limit on fear. The blow you took to the head sent your memories into hibernation, and that's where they want to stay. But we have to drag them out, Sarah. Because of Caitlyn."

"I know. I need to embrace the facts you just gave me and try to believe them. Try to make them work for me. I'm someone named Jessica who grew up in foster care after my parents died. And these people, Catherine, Teresa, and Andy, were my friends." Maybe if she kept saying their names, she'd remember them. "What else?"

"There are some gangs who use tiger tattoos as a sign of their affiliation. Some can be traced back to the Russian Mafia."

"The Mafia?" she echoed. How could she be involved with the Russian Mafia? It seemed unbelievable, and yet there was something about his statement that made her nerves tingle and her chest tighten. She felt a rush of panic as she struggled to breathe. She pressed the button to roll down the window, but her window was locked. "Please, Jake, I need some air."

Jake rolled down her window, watching as she drew in some much-needed gulps. Her pulse steadied, but it was still beating fast.

"Better?" he asked.

"Yes."

"Good. We must be coming close to the truth, because you're getting more scared."

"Yeah, I can't wait to see what happens next," she said, trying to make light of her terrifying fear. She felt as if she were standing on the edge of a cliff. One false step and she'd plummet to her death.

"What comes next is that we get Caitlyn back," he said.

She wished she could share his confidence, but she couldn't beat down the feeling that things were going to get worse before they got better. "What do we do now? Go to where I worked?"

"I think we should first talk to the social worker, Eleanor Murphy. Apparently she doesn't live too far from here. Maybe seeing someone from your past, if you are Jessica, will jog something loose."

Eleanor Murphy lived in a quiet, modest neighborhood of single story ranch-style homes that butted up against a busy LA freeway. An old blue sedan sat in the driveway. The lawn was badly in need of cutting, and three newspapers rested against the front door.

"Doesn't look like anyone's home," Sarah said, noting the closed blinds.

Jake rang the bell. He waited half a minute, then rang it again.

"Jake, look," Sarah said, her gaze catching on a broken window at the corner of the house. Shattered glass lay on the ground. A piece of plywood covered where the window had been. Her nerves tightened. Something was wrong. She backed down the stairs, her hand to her mouth, feeling as if she were going to be sick.

"Sarah, what are you doing?"

"Leaving. We need to leave."

"Why?"

Sarah was in such a panic to get away, she stumbled on the cement path. As she stared down at the jagged crack, her mind fled back to the past.

Her pink shoelaces were untied. She wanted to stop and tie them, but someone had hold of her hand and was pulling her toward the driveway.

"It will be all right, Jessica. The next house will be better. You'll see."

"Can't I just stay with you?" she pleaded. She didn't want to get into the car. She didn't want to meet another family. She wanted to go back inside the house, where it was warm and cozy and smelled like chocolate-chip cookies. She wanted to sleep in the big leather armchair with Mrs. Murphy's cat, Whiskers, on her lap. "I'll be good," she said. "I promise. I won't be any trouble. You won't even know I'm there. I can be really quiet."

Mrs. Murphy stopped and squatted down next to her. She had the warmest brown eyes Jessica had ever seen.

And crinkly lines around her eyes and her mouth, especially when she smiled. But she wasn't smiling now. She looked sad, too.

"I'm sorry, honey, but it's against the rules for me to keep you. It's my job to find you a good home. The Garrisons are a wonderful family, and they have a few other foster children. You'll have brothers and sisters and a mother and a father. That's more than I could give you, sweetie. It won't be like the last place." *She stroked Jessica's hair.* "I wish I could keep you. But I will always, always be here if you ever have a problem. You have my phone number, and you know my address, right?"

Jessica slowly nodded, her eyes filling with tears. She wasn't supposed to cry, but she couldn't help it. "I'm scared."

"Trust me."

"Sarah." Jake took hold of her arm and gave her a little shake.

She stared up at him, still lost in the past. "I'm her," she said.

"Who?"

"Jessica."

Chapter Sixteen

"I was here when I was a little girl. My name was Jessica then." Sarah swallowed hard at the realization. She waited for her memories to come flooding back now that she knew her name, her past, but where was the rest? "That's all I know," she said in amazement. "Why don't I remember everything?"

Jake's eyes filled with disappointment and frustration, and he bit down on his bottom lip, probably to stop himself from swearing at her. She didn't blame him for his anger. She wanted her memory back now.

"Okay. You said you were here. Why?" he asked.

"I stayed here in between foster homes. Mrs. Murphy was taking me to another house, and I didn't want to go, but she said I'd be safe and that if I ever had a problem I could come to her. I felt like I cared a lot about her."

"Maybe you did come to her. Maybe you came here when you ran away from me."

"Do you think so? My memory was from so long ago. I was a child."

Jake looked back the house. "We need to get inside."

"We can't break into her house."

"Someone did," he said, tipping his head toward the broken window.

"It was probably just a baseball or something."

"Maybe there's a back door. Or a hiding place for a key." He put his hands on his hips as he stepped back and surveyed the porch.

Her heart skipped a beat. "What did you say?"

"A hiding place for a key," he repeated.

She swallowed hard, something tugging at her memory. "Third flowerpot on the right," she said.

Jake moved down the steps and glanced at the flowerpots lined up along the front path.

"In the dirt," she said, "not underneath the pot."

He dug his hands into the dirt and pulled out a key. "Good job, Sarah."

"I don't know how I knew that."

"Doesn't matter. We're going in."

"It still feels wrong. This is someone else's home, and maybe someone I haven't seen since I was a child."

"She told you where you could always find a key. I don't think she'll get angry if you're here."

Jake slid the key into the lock and opened the door. Sarah felt another wave of fear wash over her. Was her uneasiness coming from the past or the sense that something was wrong with this little house and the broken window?

She stepped into the living room and paused, staring around at the comfortable furnishings. There was a big brown leather chair in the corner with a rumpled afghan on the seat, just like the chair in her memory. She wandered over to the fireplace mantel. There were dozens of photographs, all children. Her gaze caught on one in particular, three girls, one blonde, one redhead, one brunette. They were sitting on a merry-go-round at a park. Across the bottom of the photo were scrawled two words: *My girls.*

Her heart stopped and she picked up the photo and pressed it to her heart. She knew those girls—what were their names? "Catherine and Teresa," she said, looking at the picture again. "And that's me in the middle."

Jake moved across the room to join her. He took the photo from her hand. "You must be about eleven or twelve. What else do you know?"

His eyes were encouraging, supportive, but her memory was seeping in slowly, uncertainly. "We lived together at the Garrisons'. Catherine was the oldest. She took care of me. She's the redhead. Teresa was a tomboy. We were all really different, but we had one thing in common: We were alone in the world, except for one another." She let out a sigh. "Mrs. Murphy was kind, caring. She tried really hard to make things right."

Sarah stopped talking to gaze around the room. "I wonder where she is. Something is wrong." She shook her head as new details in the room jumped out at her: the coffee mug with the red lipstick stain on the table in front of the couch, the half-eaten bagel on the plate next to it. "Mrs. Murphy never left food out."

She picked up the plate and mug and headed toward the kitchen, following her instincts. But as she pushed open the kitchen door, she stopped dead in her tracks. On the floor was a large dark red stain that looked like . . . The mug fell from her hand. "Oh, my God!"

Jake pushed past her. He knelt down next to the stain, then stared up at her. "It's blood."

She put a hand to her chest in horror. "Something happened to Mrs. Murphy."

"Do you know that, Sarah, or are you guessing?"

"I . . . I'm not sure."

Jake got up and walked over to the counter. "Goddammit!" He held up a small bib with the word *Angel* written across the front. "This is Caitlyn's."

Images snapped through her mind like the photos from a camera. *She saw herself handing a bottle to Caitlyn. Mrs. Murphy was stirring something at the stove. She wanted to stay, but she knew she couldn't bring danger to the woman who had been like a mother to her. She was going to get herself an apartment, a place to stay.*

"You were here," Jake said. "Caitlyn was here in this house. When?" His eyes were wild as he came back to her. Is this where you brought Caitlyn on Wednesday? Is this where you ran? Is that Caitlyn's . . ." He choked on his words as he stared back down at the dark red stain on the tile floor.

"No, Jake, that's not Caitlyn's blood," Sarah said. "It can't be."

"But you don't know, do you?" He thrust the bib under her nose. "Take it. Smell it. Try to remember."

She took the bib from his hand, her fingers curling around the material.

She tied the bib around Caitlyn's neck. Caitlyn was throwing Cheerios on the floor—the floor, the otherwise clean floor.

"The blood wasn't there when I was here. I know it wasn't." She froze as a third voice suddenly came from behind her.

"You remembered," Amanda said.

"What are you doing here?" Sarah whirled around in surprise.

Amanda had on a navy blue Nike sweat suit and tennis shoes. A large ring of keys hung from one hand. "I went home and found the apartment building on fire. The firemen told me it looked like arson, and you were nowhere to be found. I thought you might come here once you got your memory back."

"It's not all the way back," Sarah said. "Jake's brother tracked my past to foster care and Mrs. Murphy. So I came here to find out if she knew who I was."

"So you still don't remember?"

"Just bits and pieces of being here when I was a child."

"Where is she?' Jake asked Amanda. "Where's Mrs. Murphy?"

"In the hospital. Someone broke into her house on Monday night. She's been in a coma ever since."

Sarah stared at Amanda, realizing her neighbor had not been honest with them earlier. "You lied to me before. You said we'd met when I moved into the building, and you didn't know anything about me, but if that's the case, how do you know Mrs. Murphy?"

Amanda hesitated, an odd light flickering in her eyes. "That wasn't a lie. We did meet when you moved into the building, but Mrs. Murphy knew about the apartment because of me. I was one of her foster kids, too. She told me that you needed a place to stay and someone to be a friend. She introduced you as Samantha Blake, although I guess that wasn't your real name."

"Why didn't you tell me this before?" Sarah demanded. "My daughter is missing, and you withheld information—why?"

"Because of your amnesia, and because of him," Amanda said, nodding in Jake's direction. "I don't trust him, and I don't think you should either."

"Where is my daughter?" Jake asked, steely determination in his voice. "You know, don't you?"

"You have to tell us," Sarah added quickly. "Caitlyn is in danger."

"You said you had to hide Katie away. That's all you told me."

"Where is Mrs. Murphy?" Jake interrupted.

"St. Francis Hospital—it's a few miles from here, on Russell Street off the Coast Highway. She was beaten up pretty bad, and the doctors don't know if she'll recover."

"Why would someone do that to such a sweet woman?" Sarah asked.

"The cops don't know. Maybe a robbery. This area has been going downhill. Lots of drugs. Someone might have thought they could get some quick cash out of Mrs. Murphy."

Sarah's heart went out to the gentle woman in her memory, but she didn't believe for a second that this was a random robbery. "This had to do with me," she muttered. "The timing is too coincidental. Mrs. Murphy knew where I was. Maybe that's how the guy in the elevator found me. Are you sure you've told me everything?" Sarah asked Amanda. "We called your work earlier and they said you didn't have any classes today."

"It was at a different gym from where I usually work," Amanda said. "Teaching aerobics isn't exactly a full-time job; I pick up classes all over the place. I was later getting back than I thought I would be." She paused. "I still can't believe someone set fire to the building. Everything I owned is gone. I have nothing but the clothes I had in my car and at the gym."

"I'm so sorry," Sarah said. "I'm sure the fire was set to get me out of the building."

"You must be in a hell of a lot of trouble," Amanda said. "But at least you escaped. Everything else can be replaced. I'm used to starting over. I can do it again. Where are you going now? Can I help?"

Sarah glanced at Jake. His gaze was fixed on Amanda, suspicion in his eyes. He didn't believe her. Why not?

"We're not sure," Jake said, answering for her. "What about you?"

"The Red Cross is offering temporary shelter. I'll probably check that out. Why don't you come with me?" Amanda suggested. "Let your ex hang on his own for a while, just in case he's not who you think he is."

"I can't do that," Sarah said, not sure why Amanda was trying to get her on her own. The fact that Amanda had lied to her once concerned her. "Let me make sure I have your cell phone number in case I need to reach you."

"I'll put it in my phone," Jake said as Amanda gave him her number. "And why don't you take mine as well in case you think of anything else that might help us find Caitlyn." He recited his number for her.

Amanda turned to leave. "Stay safe, Samantha."

"I'm going to try."

Sarah waited until she heard the front door of the house close before she spoke. "What do you think?"

"That Amanda was hiding something," he said. "None of her emotions ring true."

"I agree. Her apartment just went up in smoke, and she didn't seem all that concerned."

"She knew Mrs. Murphy but wasn't that upset about what had happened to her."

"Maybe she's just had time to come to terms with it," Sarah said, not sure what they were both trying to get at. Obviously Amanda had rubbed them the wrong way.

"She had an explanation for everything, but no real answers," Jake said. He put his hands on his hips and let out a sigh. "I certainly wasn't expecting her to show up here. Let's take a look around. If you came here with Caitlyn, maybe you left some other clue behind as to where you were going next."

They walked back into the living room. Sarah stood in the middle of the room. Her gaze moved to a music box on the end table by the window. The lid was up. She crossed the room, knowing what she was going to find. "It's empty," she murmured.

"What was in it?" Jake asked

"Money. Mrs. Murphy always kept cash under the fake bottom. It was for emergencies—for her kids." Sarah looked at Jake. "This wasn't open when we first got here."

"Maybe that's why Amanda came."

"You're right. She wasn't looking for me; she was looking for cash. Let's go to the hospital. I want to see Mrs. Murphy."

An hour later Sarah walked into a room on the third floor of St. Francis Hospital. Eleanor Murphy was lying on her back in a bed by the window. Her brown hair was streaked with gray. Her eyes were closed, but her lids were purple with the same bruises that filled the space across her cheekbones. Her skin was fair and dotted with freckles. Her arms and legs were immobile. If it weren't for the faint movement of her chest, Sarah would have thought Mrs. Murphy was already dead.

It was her fault the woman was in a coma. Someone had wanted to find her, and they'd used Mrs. Murphy to do it. Had they tortured the woman to get the information out of her? It certainly looked like someone had used her face as a punching bag.

It was suddenly too much for Sarah to take in. She turned into Jake's embrace, resting her head on his chest, closing her eyes against the pain and guilt sweeping through her.

Jake put his arms around her body and gave her a reassuring squeeze. He stroked her hair and said, "It's going to be all right."

The words echoed those she'd heard over and over again in a lilting Irish brogue.

"You're going to be all right, Jessica. You're going to grow up and have a happy life, and one day you'll have a family of your own. I can see it now as clearly as I can see you. You just have to have faith, child. The bad times will pass. There's only good coming your way."

Tears filled her eyes as Mrs. Murphy's words rang through her head. The voice was so loud, she turned her head to make sure Mrs. Murphy wasn't actually speaking to her, but she was as still as she'd been before.

"She used to take care of me in between houses.

248

She'd be the one to pick me up and buy me an ice cream or a hot chocolate, and then we'd go somewhere else. She'd always tell me it was going to be all right. I just had to wait and see." Sarah paused. "I believed her every time. I couldn't stop believing. Catherine and Teresa used to tell me that I had to give up making wishes, but I couldn't stop."

"Not even when you were an adult," Jake cut in. "You wished on everything—birthday candles, stars that were probably airplanes, but what the hell, you wished on them anyway. You were superstitious, too. You couldn't walk under a ladder, and when a black cat crossed in front of us, I thought you were going to have a heart attack."

"I remember throwing salt over my shoulder and knocking on wood," Sarah continued. "Catherine said I was a fool; no one was listening to my wishes or prayers, and it was a waste of time. Teresa said dreams were for suckers, and she wasn't going to let me be a sucker. The two of them were going to make me into a street kid."

"Sounds like you're remembering more and more."

"I hear their voices now in my head." She gave him a quick look, hoping he didn't still think she was holding out on him, but there was no more suspicion in his eyes, just weariness and perhaps a little bit of hope that they were getting close. "But those girls, Mrs. Murphy, they were from a long time ago. I was with you at least two years, and before that I was in

Chicago or God knows where. I'm not remembering anything important—anything that's going to get us closer to Caitlyn."

"You're getting your memory muscles warmed up," he said.

"Why are you being nice to me all of a sudden?"

"Am I? That wasn't my intention."

"You just can't help it. You're a good guy."

"You used to think so," he said roughly, his voice sending a ripple of awareness down her spine.

She turned away from his gaze, rattled by the sudden spark of attraction between them. She couldn't let herself get sidetracked. Drawing a deep breath, she focused on the woman in the bed. A moment later she said, "I remember Mrs. Murphy from my past, but not from last week or last month, even though it's clear I was in her house with Caitlyn at some point, and she obviously helped me get an apartment. I must have kept in touch with her over the years. I wonder why I didn't mention her to you. I wonder why I kept the foster-care stuff a secret from you."

"Whatever put you in danger happened before you met me," Jake said. "You didn't want anyone to be able to trace your past. Apparently that included me."

Even though she wasn't looking at him, she could hear the pain in his voice, and she could feel the anger in the tight muscles of his body, just inches from hers. She knew her memory lapse was driving him crazy, and she suspected patience was not his strong suit, but she had to give him credit for hanging in there.

"You also knew Mrs. Murphy was hurt before you ran up the coast. Maybe she's part of the fear that's keeping your memory away," he added.

"I'm trying to face the fear, Jake," she said, looking back at him. "I keep telling myself that whatever it is, I just need to remember so I can find Caitlyn and protect her. I really wish this had worked."

"Well, it was worth a shot. I suspect there must be a police report on the break-in. Maybe I'll give Deputy Manning a call, see if he can find out what happened from the local cops."

She put a hand on his arm. "I don't think we should involve the police."

"Sarah, this is too big for us to figure out. We need some help, and we need to get you protection."

"Not the police," she said, sudden terror running through her veins. "They can't protect me. If you call them, I will find a way to run again. That's a promise."

His eyes narrowed. "I won't let you do that."

"You can't watch me twenty-four hours a day."

"Sarah—"

"No, Jake. No cops. You're going to have to trust me on this."

"That's asking a lot, after what you did to me."

"I'm still asking."

She saw the indecision flicker in his eyes, but finally he nodded. "All right. We'll play it your way for the time being."

"Thank you. I guess we can go." She took a step closer to the bed and covered the older woman's hand with her own. "Get better, Mrs. Murphy. I need you to be alive." It was an odd thing to say, she thought, but deep in her heart she knew that this woman was important to her.

"We need to find a mall or a computer store," Jake said as they left the hospital. "I want to buy a cheap laptop with Internet access. Then we can do some groundwork. We have more information now, and clues to follow, including Amanda and your other friends."

"What do you want to find out about Amanda?"

"I don't know, but like you I don't have a good feeling about her. It could be that she's just a cagey ex–foster kid like you and plays her cards close to her chest, or maybe there's still something she's not telling us."

"You don't think she has Caitlyn somewhere?"

"No, I don't, but I want to make sure she's the good friend and neighbor you thought she was, and not someone working for the bad guys."

"Whoever they are," Sarah said.

"Whoever they are," he echoed.

Chapter Seventeen

After picking up a laptop at the computer store, they found a small motel and checked into a room on the second floor. Their front door opened onto an exterior hallway with a view of the parking lot. They wouldn't be caught in another ambush if anyone tried to set fire to this place. Although Sarah sincerely hoped that no one knew where they were. They were miles away from her apartment in a different city, and Jake had taken a circuitous route, making sure that no one was following them. Hopefully they were safe for the moment.

The room had two queen-size beds and the basic hotel furnishings. Sarah set her duffel bag on one of the beds, suddenly very aware of the fact that she and Jake would be spending the night together. They'd done the same last night, but she'd been in a hospital bed with a guard outside. Now it was just the two of them. She knew why Jake hadn't requested two rooms. It was safer for them to stick together. Safer in one way anyway . . . But the night loomed long in front of her.

When they were running she didn't have to think about their relationship. There was noise and chaos and clues to distract her. Now there was only silence.

"What can I do to help?" she asked.

Jake set the computer box on the table. "Nothing yet. I need to set this up."

"Maybe I'll just stretch out for a minute then."

"Yeah, take a rest."

She sat down on the bed and kicked off her shoes, then leaned back against the pillows. It felt good to let the tension out of her tight muscles. She closed her eyes, almost afraid to sleep, because her dreams were as scary as her reality, but she had to face her fears. She couldn't keep running. She simply had to stop and let the terror catch up to her. Then she would deal with it. She would beat it, she told herself firmly. She was a survivor, a scrapper. She knew more about herself now, and while her time in foster care was still hazy and vague, she remembered the nights of loneliness, the uncertainty of the next day, the bad people who wanted to do bad things, and the knowledge that she was taking care of herself from here on out, because there was no one else to do it for her.

But Jake had wanted to take care of her. He'd told her that he'd asked her to marry him. He was building a house for her. And she had screwed it all up.

Maybe she was destined to live a rootless, homeless existence. But what about her child? Why had she dragged Caitlyn along with her?

She knew the answer to that question, and it didn't come from her head but from her heart—because she couldn't bear to leave her child behind. Growing up alone, without any family, she'd finally had someone who shared her blood, who was part of her. She couldn't give her baby up, not even to Caitlyn's father.

Restless, Sarah turned over on her side, putting her hands under her face, trying to stop thinking so much. But with the thought of Jake came a singing rush of blood through her veins. With every passing second she had become more acutely aware of him. She'd seen every side of his personality, from anger and bitterness to kindness and caring. He hated her, but he'd saved her life. Maybe he'd done it for Caitlyn, but he'd done it all the same. He was a good man—a man who claimed to have loved her.

She wanted to open her eyes, to call him over, to replay that explosive kiss they'd shared earlier. She couldn't lie to herself: She wanted Jake. She didn't know if her feelings came from the past or the present, but with each passing minute she became more acutely aware of every little thing about him: the tenor of his voice, the lingering scent of his aftershave, the strength of his hands when he held her.

She had to bite back a sigh. She couldn't let Jake get any closer. They were skating along the edge of a cliff, and the last thing she needed to do was make another mistake. So she squeezed her eyes shut and wrapped her fingers in the pillowcase. Sleep, that was all she was going to do.

Jake was relieved to see that Sarah had fallen asleep. Maybe he could concentrate better now. Since they'd walked into the motel room, his body had gone on high alert. They hadn't checked into the motel to have sex, and that was definitely the last thing he wanted to do with Sarah ... well, maybe not the last thing, but it certainly wouldn't be the smartest thing. They simply needed a place to spend the night. And there were two beds, thank God. He wouldn't have to worry about her rubbing her body against his the way she'd done every night of the two years they'd been together. He wouldn't have to be afraid that he'd wake up with her head on his chest, her arm around his waist, her hair tickling his nose, her scent teasing him into hardness, her legs wrapped around his.

Dammit. He ran a hand through his hair. He shouldn't be remembering the good times, the way she couldn't keep her hands off of him while she slept, as if she had a desperate need to keep him close to her.

Remember the bad times. Remember the night you came home and Sarah and Caitlyn were gone. Remember the lonely, desperate days when you thought you would never see them again. Remember how much you hate her now.

Only he didn't hate her. He didn't want to admit it, even in his own head, but it was the truth. He cast another quick look at Sarah stretched out on the bed, knowing he'd just made another mistake, because he couldn't look away now. His senses were fully engaged in the sight of her face, the gorgeous hair that he remembered wrapping around his fingers as he moved inside her body, those breasts, soft, full, begging to be touched. She had curves in all the right places, and he wanted to sink into those curves until he made everything right again. But that wasn't going to happen, and his desire for her was crazy.

He was lusting after a woman who had treated him like shit. What the hell was wrong with him? He could get another woman. He could get lots of other women who were nowhere near as complicated and confusing as Sarah.

Forcing himself to look away, he rolled his neck around on his shoulders. Then he tried to distract himself by setting up the computer. But as each program slowly installed, his thoughts drifted relentlessly back to the woman on the bed.

He'd told Sarah that he could never forgive her. He'd told her he could never forget what she'd done to him—that their relationship was over, done, finished. And that was the way it should be, the way he wanted it to be. Some actions were inexcusable. What kind of man would he be if he gave her another chance to hurt him?

His gaze drifted back to her, and he sighed. In sleep her face was even softer and sweeter. She wasn't a cold, hard woman, a ruthless, manipulative bitch. She just wasn't. And the truth was that until the day she'd run away, she'd always given him everything he'd wanted.

But she had lied, he reminded himself. She'd made up stories about her parents and grandparents. She'd never told him she'd grown up in foster care, that she'd been abandoned, which now appeared to be her true story. Was it shame that had kept her quiet? Was it fear that he wouldn't want her if he knew the truth? Was that why she'd turned herself into the woman he wanted her to be—because she'd needed to fit in, to be accepted?

She'd always worried about what his friends thought. The first time he'd taken her to dinner to meet some of his buddies, she'd been so nervous her hands had been shaking. He'd thought it was incredibly sexy at the time that she would care so much about making a good impression. He should have asked her why it was so important. Not that she would have told him the truth.

If her past in foster care was her true reality, then she'd grown up alone, lonely. The lack of stability in her life had no doubt created her inner core of insecurity, of which he'd had a few glimpses.

After Caitlyn was born, Sarah had told him that having a real family again was a dream come true. Yet she hadn't married him. She'd put him off every time he asked—why? Had she been afraid the danger would come back?

He should probably be happy that she hadn't married him. It would be one more legal tie to dissolve when this was all over. Not that a piece of paper made a difference. Having a child bound them together forever.

As he considered the time they'd been together, he had to believe there were days, weeks, months, even, when she'd felt safe enough just to be with him. She'd laughed. She'd smiled. There had been times of pure joy. It hadn't always been serious. However, there had also been guarded moments. Something must have changed. At some point something had occurred to upset the life they had. Sarah had no longer felt safe enough to be in their home, together. If he could put a name or names to the people who wanted to hurt Sarah now, maybe what she had done in the past would all make sense.

Then what? Should he take her back?

Could they find Caitlyn and pick up where they left off? How could he do that? It would be impossible to forget what had happened before. How could he ever trust her? How could he ever feel secure in the fact that she wouldn't run again?

One thing was for sure: The last thing he needed to do was complicate the situation even further—which meant he had to keep his distance from Sarah. He had to stop looking at her, stop wanting her.

She wasn't the woman he'd loved. He needed to refocus on the deception, the betrayal, the anger, the emotions that had gotten him through the past months.

But he had barely finished that thought when Sarah began to whimper and squirm on the bed. She was dreaming—bad dreams.

Her movements grew more agitated. Her fingers gripped the bedspread as she kicked out her feet at some unknown assailant. Was she remembering the past again? He didn't know whether to wake her or not. At some point she had to face the demons that her brain wanted to hide from her. Was that point now? Should he let her battle it out?

"No," she cried. "Please, no."

The desperation and fear in Sarah's voice touched a chord deep within him. He could no more look away or stand by without doing anything to help her than he could stop breathing.

Within seconds he was on his feet, heading toward the bed—knowing that every step was taking him closer to an action he shouldn't take. He told himself he would just wake her up, put a hand on her shoulder, help her out of the nightmare. Then he would back away. He would return to the computer. It would be but a moment.

"Sarah." He placed his hand on her shoulder.

She knocked it away, as if he were trying to hurt her.

"Wake up," he ordered.

Her eyes flew open. She looked terrified, hunted, and she wasn't seeing him, but someone else. "Don't hurt me," she pleaded.

His heart stopped at the pure terror in her voice. He had to bring her back. This wasn't the way to get her memories to return.

"It's Jake, Sarah. You're dreaming. It's all right. You're safe with me." He sat down on the bed next to her. He gently pushed the sweaty strands of hair off her forehead. She'd really worked herself up.

Her breath came quick and fast as recognition returned slowly to her eyes. "Jake," she whispered, her soft lips gently parted.

He stared at her mouth for a long time, unable to drag his gaze away. She ran her tongue along the edge of her lips. His body tightened with desire.

"Jake," she said again.

He lifted his gaze to hers. She knew him now—didn't she? Wasn't that awareness glittering in her eyes? Or was it something more—was it desire? She licked her lips again.

"Don't," he said, his control slipping even further.

She put up her hand and touched his cheek. The heat from her fingers flooded through his body. He caught her hand and meant to pull it away, but he suddenly couldn't let go. His fingers entwined with hers, and he pressed her hand against his racing heart.

"I hate you," he muttered. "I really hate you."

"I know," she said, meeting his gaze.

Her words released the last bit of his restraint. He crushed her mouth against his. He wanted to punish her for everything she'd put him through. But one taste, one soft yielding of her mouth, and he wanted far more than revenge. He wanted to have her the way he'd had her before. He wanted to touch every inch of her body. He wanted her to feel the heat of their passion as he slid into her body, and he wanted to take back what he'd lost. Most of all, he wanted her to remember him, dammit!

He wanted her to feel him again, so that when she did remember, she would know what she was losing. She would understand what she'd destroyed. She would know how good it had been. He'd have one more night—on his terms.

But as Sarah opened her mouth to his tongue, as his hands roamed across her breasts, his thumbs teasing her nipples into hard points, he stopped thinking entirely and let his body take over.

Kicking off his shoes, he stretched out on the bed next to her, his mouth leaving hers to trail across her face, her jawline, down the curve of her neck. She closed her eyes. He wanted them open.

"Look at me," he commanded. "I want you to know me."

Her eyes flew open, blue and blazing with a desire that she couldn't hide. She wanted him, even if she didn't know why. She wasn't hiding from him now. Her hands were on his shoulders, and she wasn't pushing him away. This was actually happening. She wasn't fighting him. In fact, her hands were sliding around his head as she pulled him back down, as she sought another kiss.

"If you want to stop," he said, giving her one last chance, "do it now."

She didn't even hesitate. "I don't want to stop." She ran her fingers through his hair and smiled. Then she sat up and in one quick, reckless movement pulled her shirt over her head.

Her bra was a lacy cream color, her full breasts swelling over the cups. Her nipples were tight. Her chest rose up and down with the quickening of her breath. Jake ran his finger along the edge of her bra, dropping down into her cleavage in a teasing gesture that elicited a small groan of pleasure from Sarah. He replaced his finger with his mouth, sliding his tongue along the same tantalizing path. Finally he flicked open the front clasp of her bra, pulling it apart and placed his mouth on her breast.

He'd almost forgotten how sweet she tasted, how he loved the way her nipples puckered for him, the way her body grew restless with his attention, the way her hips rubbed against his with an impatience that matched his own. He loved the soft cries she let out as he laved one breast and then the other. She was his—all his—and she would know him before the night was through.

He lifted his head, trailing his mouth down her abdomen, feeling her stomach muscles clench as he circled her belly button with his tongue, as his hands played with the waistband of her jeans. Finally he undid the snap, pulling down the zipper, sliding his hands into the hot vee between her legs. She was so wet—it drove him wild. All thoughts of going slow, of torturing her, were replaced by the desperate need to get inside all that heat.

In an abrupt movement he lifted his head and sat back. He took off her jeans and underwear with impatient hands. Then he removed his own shirt and pants, wanting to feel nothing but skin between them. The sight of her soft body under his fueled his raging desire. As he touched her intimately, he went in for another kiss.

Sarah sucked on his tongue, her hands roaming his back, cupping his ass as he settled between her legs. She was as ready for him as he was for her. "Say my name," he ordered, lifting his head just long enough to look at her.

There was no cloud of confusion now in her bright blue eyes.

"Jake." She pulled him down, wrapping her arms and her legs around him as he thrust into her.

She was tight and hot, and he'd been abstinent too long. He wanted to make it go on forever. He wanted her to feel him deep within her. He wanted to touch the core of her, open the floodgates to her memory, make her know him. And she seemed to want the same thing.

There was a reckless, urgent passion burning within her that he didn't recognize, but certainly liked. Sarah wouldn't let him slow down, urging him on, harder and deeper until they finally came together in an explosive climax.

After he caught his breath, he rolled over onto his back, pulling her up next to him, his arm around her body. He wasn't letting her go yet. The physical and emotional distance that had been between them was gone. He had her back. He could feel it.

Please, God, let her remember me, he prayed silently, knowing that deep down in his gut he wasn't at all sure that he had her back.

* * *

Sarah could hear Jake's heart beating beneath her cheek. His skin was still hot to her touch, his breath ragged and rough. Her own body felt deliciously tired and used, her nerves still tingling from every taste, every touch. The mix of anger and passion had made their lovemaking so strong, so powerful. She'd felt Jake's desire to take her back in every kiss. He was fighting for her and for them and for what had once been perfect. And she was fighting for some memory of it all.

Closing her eyes, she strained to see some other moment when she and Jake had been in bed together. There must have been hundreds of times when they'd made love during the two years they shared a home. Hadn't she slept just like this, her leg flung over his, her arm across his waist, her head pillowed by his strong chest?

Her brain stubbornly refused to go back in time. Why would her mind give her back some memories and not others? But that wasn't the most important question.

What was she going to tell Jake when he asked? And he would ask.

He'd done everything he could to shake the memories loose, to remind her of how good it had been between them. Well, he'd shaken her up, all right, but not in the way he'd intended. Her senses were singing. And her heart was beating in sync with his. She might not remember the actual times they'd been together in the past, but she could feel the love they'd shared, much the same way she felt the love between herself and Caitlyn. The three of them were connected, a bond that couldn't be broken, even if it couldn't be remembered.

But he wouldn't understand. He would hate her again. And she didn't want to go back to that place. She needed Jake to be on her side despite everything she'd done to him. It was a lot to ask of the man, probably too much.

Jake's arm tightened around her, his fingers slipping into her hair, rubbing the now tightening muscles in her neck. "I can hear you thinking," he murmured. "And your thoughts are making you tense." He paused, waiting for her to say something. When she didn't, he said, "Sarah?"

She'd expected the questioning note, but she still wasn't ready for it. "Was it always this good?" she asked. Her words had barely left her mouth when she felt him stiffen and knew she'd already revealed too much. There were a million things she could have said besides that.

"You don't remember." He didn't make it a question, just a statement of fact and frustration. His hand fell from her neck.

She lifted her head and gazed into his eyes. "I'm sorry, Jake."

"The memories aren't there. I don't know why I thought they would be."

She hated causing him more pain. "It was still great."

"It was sex."

"It was more than that. You know it was."

"I don't know anything." Moving abruptly, Jake rolled her out of his arms and stood up. He dragged on his jeans and his shirt, seemingly determined to put as much physical space between them as possible. His regret over what had just happened was evident in every tight line in his face.

"I wanted to remember," she said quietly, despair overwhelming her as she watched him withdraw from her.

"Is that why you said yes?" he challenged. "Was it some kind of experiment?"

She met his gaze and turned the question around. "Is that why you decided to make love to me—as some kind of experiment?"

Hands on his hips, he stared at her for a long moment and then shrugged. "Maybe," he admitted. "Actually, that's not true, and I'm not going to lie about it. There have been too many lies between us already."

"Then what is true?" she asked, wrapping the bedspread around her naked body.

"I wanted you, Sarah. I've always wanted you. I can't seem to get you out of my system. You treated me like shit, and I still want you. How ridiculous is that?"

"I wanted you, too, in this moment, in the present, regardless of what happened before."

"It's easy to say the past doesn't matter when you don't remember it. But the memories of you and me together are burned into my brain."

"Jake—"

"Don't say anything. There's nothing you can say. I've got to get out of here." He grabbed his keys off the table.

"Where are you going?" she asked in alarm. She wrapped the bedspread around her body as she sat up.

"I need some air. I need to get out of here. I need to get the hell away from you, Sarah."

"Jake, this isn't the time to walk away from me."

"Do you realize we didn't use any protection?" He paused by the door. "I could have just made you pregnant again. Unless you're on the pill?"

She stared at him, shocked by his words. What a fool she was. She'd been so caught up in the moment, in the desperate need to remember Jake, that she hadn't even considered protection.

"Yeah, I didn't think so," he said, not giving her a chance to answer. "Don't worry, Sarah; I'll be back. You and I aren't done yet. Although I wish to God we were."

Chapter Eighteen

"What are you doing here?" Shane Hollis couldn't believe Victor Pennington and Rick Adams were standing in his motel room, wearing their Armani suits and Ferragamo shoes and sporting their two-hundred-dollar haircuts. They were supposed to be in Chicago, waiting for his call. Their presence could mean only one thing: They were unhappy with his performance. He'd always been the weak link in their group, the scholarship student, the one who didn't really belong, the one they wouldn't tolerate at all if he didn't do their dirty work for them. Because he did he was still alive, but he felt a trail of sweat slip down his spine under their intense stares.

Victor was the self-proclaimed leader of their group and had been since college. The son of a Russian actress and the stepson of an American millionaire, he was a mix of raw evil and charming sophistication. Rick Adams was Victor's right-hand man, another rich kid who boasted more brawn than brain and was built like a tight end. Both men had led charmed lives for a while, graduating from Harvard, running several businesses, making huge amounts of money, and moving more than just art through their gallery. Then all hell had broken loose when the woman Victor was sleeping with betrayed them all—the woman Shane should have killed long before this.

Eight months ago Victor and Rick had been in prison. They would be there now if their rich parents hadn't convinced the parole board to let them go on good behavior. Now they wanted revenge, especially Victor.

"She's supposed to be dead," Rick said. He had an annoying habit of stating the obvious.

Shane glanced at Victor and saw the rage burning in his dark brown eyes. There was something wrong with Victor. There always had been. He loved a good kill—more than sex, more than money, more than anything. Not many people knew that about him, but Shane did, because he'd always been the one to carry out his orders.

"I'm working on it," Shane said. "I need a little more time."

"Your time is up," Victor said.

"Look, she has someone watching her all the time. It's not going to be that easy to get to her right now. We might have to back off for a while."

"I've waited eight years to see her die; that's enough," Victor said.

"A few more days, a week—she'll let her guard

down," Shane said. "You've only been out of the pen a few months—do you want to go back?"

"That won't happen," Victor said, nothing but confidence in his voice.

"The police are involved. If something happens to her it won't be that difficult to trace her back to you—not me," Shane added.

Dark storm clouds gathered in Victor's eyes. He hated when anyone questioned his actions. Shane should have kept his fucking mouth shut. But it was too late now.

"Do you think I'm stupid?" Victor asked.

"Of course not. The truth is, I don't know where she is right now," Shane said hastily, trying to defuse the situation. "They slipped away after the fire."

Victor stared back at him. "And you're not smart enough to figure out how to get her out in the open?"

Before he could answer, Rick said, "The kid, dude, that's the ticket."

"I don't know where the kid is."

"You didn't know there was a kid," Victor said angrily. "You should have been more thorough."

Shane should have known about the kid. He'd traced her to the apartment, but he'd never thought she was living with anyone but herself. "She doesn't know where the kid is. She has amnesia." The last thing Shane wanted to do was take out a baby. He'd fallen a long way from the kind of man he thought he'd be, but that was just too damn far. His life was not supposed to go down this way.

"There are only two people who could have the

child," Victor said. "I now know where both of them live."

"Do you want to tell me?"

"Actually, I don't," Victor said. "You're of no use to me anymore. You've become a liability. You can't get the job done, and you know too much."

Before Shane could move, Rick pulled out his gun.

"Whoa, what are you doing?" Shane asked, putting up his hands. "We're friends. We've been together a long time; I've done everything you wanted."

"Until now," Victor said.

"Let me try again," Shane said, acutely aware of the barrel of the gun facing him. "We're partners. We're fucking partners. Just give me one more chance." But even as he said the words, he knew it was too late.

While Jake was gone, Sarah got dressed again and straightened the bed. She suspected that any reminder of what had happened between them would not be a good idea. Once that was done, she went to the window and peeked through the curtain. It was dark, but she could see rain streaming down in the glare of the parking lot lights. Another storm. For some reason the rain set her nerves on edge. The last time it had rained she'd almost lost her life.

Letting the curtain drop back into place, she paced around the small room, restless, frustrated, confused, and worried. She shouldn't have let Jake go. She should have found a way to make him stay. If only she hadn't spoken so quickly. Maybe she could have prolonged the inevitable truth, but in the end it would have come out, and she couldn't change the facts: She couldn't remember their history together. That fact brought Jake pain each and every time. And the last thing she wanted to do was keep hurting him.

Wrapping her arms around her waist, she felt chilled. An hour ago she and Jake had been so close she hadn't known where she ended and he began, but now they were as far apart as they'd ever been, not just physically but emotionally as well. Why couldn't she remember him? If it had been as good between them as he'd said, why was her brain trying to protect her from those memories? Her mind had already released a bit of her childhood. Why couldn't she get to the rest of it? What was she afraid of?

Weary of asking herself questions she couldn't answer, she sat down on the bed, knowing she wouldn't be able to relax until Jake returned safe and sound. She couldn't bear to think of something happening to him. He'd already dodged death at her apartment building. He could have been shot through the heart when he'd stepped in front of her. But he hadn't been thinking about himself. His first thought had been to protect her. According to him, keeping her alive was the key to finding Caitlyn, but she'd spent enough time with Jake in the past few days to know that his caring instincts also extended to her. Although she couldn't see how she deserved his care or his protection.

Reaching over the side of the bed, she grabbed the duffel bag and pulled out Caitlyn's baby blanket and bear. She ran the satin edges of the blanket through her fingers and closed her eyes. She imagined the crib and pictured Caitlyn's sweet face. The image brought her warmth and made her smile.

But then something changed.

The room was different. There was pink wallpaper with big A-B-C letters. Lacy white curtains fluttered at the windows. Someone came into the room. She turned and saw Jake. He was wearing a suit and tie. On the floor in the doorway was his suitcase.

He walked over and kissed her, a sweet, tender kiss on the lips.

"I can't believe I have to leave my girls for two weeks," he said. *"How will I live without you both?"*

"It will be hard for all of us," she said, her gaze lingering on his face. *For some reason she wanted to memorize his features. She felt as if it were desperately important to do so. People always disappeared from her life. Things changed in an instant, and the good never lasted. She didn't want to forget him. Not ever.*

"You'll marry me when I come back," Jake said decisively. *"It's way past time for us to become an official family. No more excuses. Say yes."*

He made it sound so easy, when saying "yes" was anything but. "When you come back we'll make plans." But as he walked out the room, she wondered if she could really go through with it. There was so much he didn't know.

Sarah's eyes flew open as she realized that she'd

finally seen Jake in her mind in the time when they'd been together. It must have been the day Jake had left for his business trip, perhaps the last time she'd seen him before she ran away. He'd left town believing she would marry him when he got back.

Her heart thumped against her chest. How her departure must have hurt him. When he'd returned home with high hopes for their future together, he'd found an empty apartment stripped of all trace of Caitlyn and herself, and no explanation. Even after all this time she still couldn't give him a reason.

She wanted to scream in frustration.

How could she have ruined such a terrific relationship?

She lifted the baby blanket to her face and inhaled deeply. Caitlyn's sweet scent still clung to the fabric, a mix of baby powder and baby. She would make everything right. She would find Caitlyn. She would get her memory back, and she would tell Jake why she'd left him, why she'd betrayed him.

Then what? Would he forgive her? Would they all live happily ever after?

Somehow she didn't think so. She'd never believed in fairy tales.

Dylan stretched his arms over his head as he waited for his latest search screen to pop up. He'd been on the Internet for hours, but he was still no closer to locating Andy Hart. He suspected that if Andy were a computer genius, as Catherine had stated earlier, then he'd probably found ways to protect his personal information from appearing on the Internet. As for Teresa Meyers, he'd found a half dozen women with the name, but none of his follow-up calls had produced a likely candidate in terms of the right age or background.

Catherine hadn't offered much help, although she'd made him a delicious vegetarian pasta dish that he was sure had quadrupled his vegetable intake for the week, maybe the month. Since then she'd been puttering around the house, cleaning the kitchen, looking through the artwork done by her students, talking to her cats and her bird. Fortunately the bird didn't seem inclined to talk back. He'd always thought talking birds were a little creepy. One woman he'd dated had a talking parrot who'd called him shithead every time he walked in the room. It hadn't exactly set the mood.

A flash of lightning lit up the room, followed shortly thereafter by a crack of thunder that rocked the house. The storm was loud, rain pounding the back deck, gale-force winds shaking the windows, waves crashing on the beach. The wild night did nothing to ease the mounting tension in his body. It frustrated the hell out of him to be stuck here while Jake and Sarah were running for their lives, but if he could find Andy Hart, then they'd be one step closer to locating Caitlyn.

Glancing away from the window, he saw Catherine watching him from the kitchen. He was struck again by how pretty she was in a natural way. She didn't have a speck of makeup on her face, but her features were beautifully set in her face, and long lashes framed her mysterious dark blue eyes. He wondered what her story was—how she'd come to live in this remote location with only her pets for company. She had a story to tell. As a journalist he had a nose for stories, and he had a feeling hers would be very interesting, but this wasn't the time to get into her life. Right now it was Sarah's secrets he needed to reveal.

"You're staring at me," Catherine said.

"You're staring at me," he echoed with a smile.

"You're very intense when you work, focused, determined, relentless. You usually get what you want, don't you?"

"Usually. Unfortunately my intensity is not bringing me any luck tonight. I've struck out on both Andy Hart and Teresa Meyers. Any ideas? I've tried all the usual methods, but I've come up with nothing. Maybe there's something you know about Andy that could help me find him. You said you lived together when you were kids?"

Catherine set down her dishtowel, picked up two steaming mugs of tea, and joined him at the table. She pushed one of the mugs in his direction. "You'll like this. It's good for concentration."

"I'm more of a coffee guy."

"This is better for you."

He rolled his eyes. "I hate it when people tell me what's good for me."

She gave him a smile. "I'm sure you do, but you will like the tea if you give it a chance."

"Fine. I'll drink the tea. Now you give me something in return."

Catherine thought for a moment. "Andy lived with us for about a year. Then he was moved because he got into trouble in high school. He hacked into the computer system to change one of his grades. He was too smart for school; he didn't pay attention when he was bored."

"So he was into computers. What else?"

"Video games, movies, comic books, graphic novels, Dungeons and Dragons. He was very creative, very competitive, a big game player."

"That's good. Maybe there's a clue there. What about the fake IDs? When did he get into that?"

"High school. He made a lot of money providing underage kids with fake IDs."

"Did you have one?"

"Of course." Catherine's gaze was completely unapologetic. "We didn't grow up in a pretty world, Dylan. It was every man for himself. We did what we had to do to survive, and Andy was no better or worse than the rest of us."

"You're saying that you and Jessica also cut corners?"

Her eyes narrowed. "I know you're looking for more dirt on Jessica, but I'm not going to give it to you."

"I'm just trying to get an idea of her background," he said.

"Bullshit. You don't care about Jessica. You just want to get her child back for your brother. But I intend to protect my friend, regardless of what you think of her. You have no idea what it's like to grow up alone, to have to protect and defend yourself from all manner of danger when you're just a child," Catherine continued, passion filling her voice. "You learn early on that no one is going to stand up for you. No one is going to protect you if someone raises their hand to you or does something worse. People look the other way. They don't want to see the ugly side of life. They want to pretend it isn't there—"

"I show people the ugly side of life every day in my job," he interrupted. "That's what I do. I shine a light on things people would rather keep hidden. So don't think I ever look the other way, because I don't."

A flush of red spread across her cheeks, and he could see a spark of anger in her eyes. Her breasts were moving up and down with the pace of her breathing, and he found himself wanting to undo the buttons on her paint-spattered shirt and see if her nipples were the same glorious pink as her cheeks. *Damn.* He'd thought she was pretty before, but now, in a passion, she was something else. And he was letting himself get sidetracked.

"It's different to report what's wrong in the world than to live it," she said, her words fortunately drawing his attention away from her breasts.

He cleared his throat, trying to remember what they were even talking about. Catherine was turning out to be a bigger distraction than he would have ever anticipated.

"I'll give you that," he conceded. "Tell me more about the way you and Jessica grew up. I promise not to judge."

"I doubt that's possible," she snapped. "How do you ever keep your objectivity when you're reporting? You seem to have very strong opinions."

"My opinions are the strongest when they involve the people I care about—like my brother."

"Well, Jessica is a sister to me, so keep that in mind."

"Okay, please go on."

Catherine drew in a couple of breaths and then continued. "In foster care it's all about fitting in. Not making waves so you won't get kicked out of the home you're in, won't have to change schools again, won't have to make new friends, start over. Not that all of the homes are good. Some are horrific. Some you have to run away from. And sometimes the only people you can trust are the other kids who are fighting for their lives. That's why, when you find a couple of friends you think you can trust, you hang on for dear life."

Catherine had painted a vivid and sad picture, and Dylan had to admit he felt some compassion for what Catherine and Jessica had gone through. His family life had not been good, but at least he'd always had Jake to try to run interference for him, to look out for him. Jake had been his savior on more than one occasion, and it would take him a lifetime to pay his brother back.

"Jessica was pretty soft in the beginning," Catherine continued. "Because her parents died, she'd had a good childhood to start, so she knew what she was missing when things went bad. Some of the rest of us had never lived that other life, so in some ways it was easier to just accept what was. But Jessica kept thinking that her grandparents were going to come and rescue her. It took her a long time to give up on that hope. Finally she came to realize that you have to make a family where you can find one, and that family was Andy, Teresa, and myself. We tried to watch out for one another, but we were together for only a few years. I regret that Jessica and I lost touch after we split up. I was so happy when Teresa and Jessica said they were going to drive across country to meet me in New York." Sadness filled her eyes. "If I had told them not to come, maybe none of this would have happened. But I didn't, and it did, and that's why you're here."

"What about you? How did you end up in foster care? What happened to your parents?"

She shook her head. "I don't want to talk about that."

He knew he should shut up and respect her privacy, but his curiosity got the better of him. "You had it rougher than Jessica, didn't you?"

"It's not my turn to tell my story," Catherine said. "Nor is it yours."

"I don't have a story."

"Yes, you do—maybe a story you don't even know you have."

He frowned at that cryptic statement, feeling a cold chill wash over him. There were some unanswered questions in his past, but he hadn't asked them in a long time. Someday he might. But not tonight. "You're good at distracting people. Back to Andy Hart. How are we going to find him?"

Catherine thought for a moment. "Andy loved to do animation, cartoons, comic-novel type stories on the computer. Maybe he got a job in one of those fields."

"That's an idea. I can try that angle. You said you were in LA when you were in foster care. So I assume you were all from that area. I've found a few Andy Harts, but none the right age or ethnicity in the Southern California area. And I can't help wondering if Andy Hart, the master of fake IDs, doesn't go under another name himself."

Catherine started. "Oh, lord, I didn't even think of that. Yes, you're right. Of course he did. Put in Xander with an X. Xander . . . what was that last name he used? Xander Cross. That was the superhero he created in his comics."

Dylan typed in the words and hit search. A moment later he had a half dozen hits, including one Xander Cross, owner of a video game/comics bookstore in San Francisco.

His heart stopped when he read the address. Xander's business was very close to where Jake and Sarah had lived. He should have thought of that earlier. They'd always suspected Sarah had help leaving Jake, because she hadn't taken a car. Maybe Xander Cross, her old friend from foster care, had done the job. He pulled out his cell phone and dialed the number listed. An answering machine picked up on the third ring. The store was closed and would reopen at ten o'clock the next morning.

"No one is there tonight, but I think we found him," he said.

Catherine smiled, and it almost took his breath away. He didn't know if he was more excited about finding Andy Hart, a.k.a. Xander Cross, or the fact that Catherine was looking at him like he was some kind of a god. In truth, she was the one who'd found Xander, not him.

"Maybe Andy knows where Jessica's baby is," Catherine said.

"I sure as hell hope so. I wish we could get in touch with him tonight, but I guess we'll have to wait."

"I'd like to talk to him again, see how he is," Catherine said. "He always said he would run his own business. He wasn't the type to work for anyone else. I guess he gave up his Andy Hart persona and became Xander Cross."

"Well, if I had a choice between being a foster kid or a superhero, I'd probably choose the superhero."

"I'm sure you would. So now what? Can you relax, take a breath?"

"Hardly. We still have to find Teresa and figure out who's trying to kill Jessica."

"Finish your tea first. I want to read your tea leaves."

"I don't think so. I don't want to know the future," he said.

"Are you sure? I wouldn't have taken you for a man who liked to be surprised."

"I don't know about that. I like change. It beats the same old thing every day."

"Maybe you're just afraid."

He knew she was manipulating him, but still he rose to the bait. He drank his tea down to the leaves and pushed the cup over to her. "Fine, tell me what you see. And I hope it's a gorgeous blonde with hot legs and big breasts." He laughed at her expression.

"Is that really all you look for in a woman?" she asked.

"What's wrong with hot legs and big breasts?"

"Nothing, if you're a shallow playboy who doesn't want a serious relationship."

He gave a little shrug. "What about you? What do you look for in a man?"

"Well, certainly more than a big penis," she said frankly.

He laughed at her bluntness. Catherine Hilliard was an odd mix of bright-eyed innocence and cynical weariness. He couldn't quite figure her out. "Like what?"

"Brains, personality, sense of humor, good heart," she said.

"Kind to dogs, cats, and birds," he finished.

"Absolutely."

"So I guess Prince Charming hasn't shown up yet, huh?"

A shadow crossed her face. "He came. He left," she said softly. "Now, let's take a look at your fortune."

He was actually far more interested in her last statement than his own fortune, but Catherine was ignoring him now.

A few moments later she set the cup down and said, "Never mind."

"Hey, hold on. You can't just start something and not finish it."

"You said you like surprises. I think you have a lot of fun in store for you." She stood up. "I'll make up the couch for you. It's storming too hard for you to leave."

"Wait," Dylan said, catching her by the arm. "Do the surprises have to do with Jake and Sarah?"

"No, they have to do with your past. You judge Sarah harshly for her secrets, but you have some of your own."

He frowned. "Look, I don't know what you're talking about, Catherine, and I certainly don't want to show any disrespect for your fortune-telling abilities, but I don't believe a bunch of tea leaves can predict my future."

"There are two women," she said. "One represents danger, the other salvation. But it will be difficult for you to know which is which unless you find a way to listen to your heart instead of your head. A task, I fear, that will not be easy for you. I'll see you in the morning."

"Yeah, thanks for the bedtime story," he said sarcastically.

His words did little more than make her smile. "The disbelievers always fall the hardest."

Chapter Nineteen

The door to the motel room opened, and Sarah started, letting out a breath of relief when she saw it was Jake. His hair and jacket were wet from the rain, and he didn't look any more relaxed than when he'd left. He had a damp newspaper in his hand, which he tossed down on the table along with a brown paper bag.

"What's that?" she asked.

"Stuff," he said vaguely.

"Are you okay?"

"How the hell do you think I am, Sarah?"

Since she had no good answer for him, she said nothing. She wasn't sure if she should tell him what she'd remembered about their last day together. His mood seemed dangerously volatile. Would he be happy that she'd remembered him at all? Or would it just annoy her more? Her memory had given her little new information, so perhaps she'd keep it to herself for now.

Jake sat down by his new laptop computer and began hitting the buttons. Apparently he wasn't planning to talk to her. Well, maybe it was better that way. She didn't know what to say to him either. Glancing at the clock radio by the bed, she saw that it was ten o'clock. They still had a long night ahead of them. Would Jake sleep with her or take the other bed? Would it be as awkward and uncomfortable as it was right now?

Putting a hand to her abdomen, she thought again about the fact that she could have just gotten herself pregnant. What an idiot. She might not remember her life, but she knew better than to have unprotected sex. She just hadn't been thinking—she'd been feeling. She'd let her emotions run free for what felt like the first time in forever, and it had felt great. She suspected she'd been keeping a tight rein for the last seven months, and she'd needed the release.

But it had been more than just a release of tension and simple sex. *Simple* could never describe the relationship she and Jake shared. It was complicated in every possible way. She didn't know how she felt about him or how he felt about her. They were both afraid to care too much—even though they had different reasons for that fear. She couldn't remember enough, and he remembered too much.

She flipped on the television set, desperate to bring some neutral noise into the room. She was far too aware of Jake's presence just a few feet away.

Changing the channels, she finally settled on one of the local news shows. She wasn't paying much attention until the camera panned an area that looked very familiar to her. It was Venice Beach, a location not far from her apartment building.

She sat up abruptly. "Jake," she said urgently. "Look."

He frowned, not lifting his gaze from the screen. "What? I'm concentrating here."

"The TV." She turned up the sound as the news reporter began to speak. "A body was found behind a dumpster at Venice Beach early this evening. He was shot in the head, execution style," the woman said. "The man has been identified as thirty-six-year-old Shane Hollis of Chicago. The police have no suspects and no motive, and would like the public's help in solving this crime." A phone number ran across the bottom of the screen just as a photo came up next to the reporter. It was a head shot of a man with dark hair and dark eyes.

Sarah felt like she'd been punched in the stomach. "Oh, my God!"

Jake jerked to his feet. "That's—"

"The man who tried to kill us earlier," she finished. "Someone murdered him. Why?"

Jake's gaze met hers. "Because he didn't get the job done," he said slowly. "You're still alive."

"This is . . . insane," she whispered.

"I agree. In fact, I think we're dealing with someone who is insane."

"It's possible that the man's death doesn't have anything to do with me," she said halfheartedly. "He was a thug. He could have had lots of enemies. He could have tried to hurt someone else."

"No, Sarah. He's been up and down the state the past three days trying to kill you. This has everything to do with you. At least we have one name, Shane Hollis. And he was from Chicago, which is where Catherine placed her friend Jessica when she disappeared eight years ago." Jake turned back toward his computer. "I've just about got the Internet up. We can look up Shane Hollis and start with him."

She rose from the bed and joined him at the table, taking the seat next to him. "If Shane was murdered in Venice Beach, just a few miles from here, that means whoever did it is also close by."

"Yeah," Jake agreed with a nod.

Sarah felt a shiver run down her spine. "And we don't know what he looks like. Before, we knew what Shane Hollis looked like, but now we're in the dark again. Any man we see could be the person who's after me." She stopped and thought for a moment. "Or it could be a woman."

"I don't think so. That bullet through the head looked very macho to me, deliberate, ruthless. Not that a woman couldn't do it, but my gut tells me it's a man."

The overhead light began to flicker, and her pulse jumped again. "Did you see that, Jake?"

"Yeah," he muttered, still intent on his computer search.

"What do you think it was?"

"I don't know, a power surge."

Her imagination roared into action. What if someone was playing with the circuit breakers? What if whoever had killed Shane Hollis had tracked them to this motel? He could be outside, cutting the electricity. If they didn't have lights, they wouldn't be able to see him. As her terror began to rise, she put her hand on Jake's arm.

He finally glanced over at her. His gaze narrowed. "What's wrong, Sarah?"

She swallowed hard. "What if they cut the lights?"

"There's no reason to think anyone knows where we are."

"There's no reason to think they don't. They seem to know everything, and they're always one step ahead of us."

A loud rumble of thunder made her jump to her feet, but she still kept her hand on Jake's arm. She didn't know whether to run or hide, but she felt it was imperative that she do something.

"It's the storm," Jake said. "That's why the lights flickered." He got to his feet and put his hands on her waist. "It's okay. We're all right."

"I don't want the lights to go out. Bad things happen in the dark."

"What kind of bad things?" he asked, gazing into her eyes.

She stared back at him. "I don't know."

The overhead light flickered again, as did the computer screen. Sarah held her breath, waiting for the lights to steady themselves, but then everything went black. She let out a panicked cry.

Jake hauled her tight into his arms, pressing her face against his chest. "It's just a power outage, Sarah."

"You don't know that," she mumbled. "I can't stand this. I can't be here in the dark."

"Yes, you can," he said firmly. "I'm going to open the curtains a little, let some of the outdoor light in."

She clung to his waist as he tried to move away from her. "No, don't leave me. Please don't leave me."

The words echoed over and over in her mind. Closing her eyes, she heard another voice in her head, the voice of a young girl, pleading, begging. . . .

It was so dark. Were her eyes open?

She felt like a blind person straining to see something. She couldn't hear anyone breathing except herself. There was something holding her down. A seat belt. Her fingers felt for the release. As she squinted, she saw a touch of blond hair hanging over the vague, shadowy seat in front of her. A man was slumped over the steering wheel. She was in a car. The roof was smashed in. Something big and scary was on the hood. It looked like a monster. It sounded like his claws were scraping the top of the car as he tried to get in.

She let out a scream of terror. "Mommy, Daddy. Wake up."

No one answered her. She started to cry. Why weren't they waking up? Why weren't they trying to get out of the car?

She had to get help. She reached for the door handle, but it wouldn't open. The door was crushed in on the side. She tried the other door, but something heavy was behind it. She pushed and she pushed, sweating and straining, but the doors wouldn't open. And she couldn't see anything outside of the car. She was trapped.

Her breath came short and fast. She tried pushing on the car door again. Suddenly something gave way. The car began to rock. Then it started to slide. She was moving. She screamed again as the car picked up speed.

She tried to hold on to her seat, but the car flipped over and she felt her body fly through the air. Her head hit something hard. She couldn't see at all anymore. Was she dead? Were her parents dead?

"Don't leave me," she cried. "Please don't leave me."

"Sarah, Sarah, snap out of it." Jake gave her shoulders a shake. "Look at me. You're okay. You're safe."

He'd pushed open the curtain behind her, allowing in enough light to soften the shadows.

"It's just the storm. Listen to the rain. No one cut the power to lure us outside." He rubbed his hands up and down her arms. "You're ice-cold. I can feel the chill through your sweater. Where were you just now?"

"I was in the car with my parents," she said. "There was an accident. It was a really dark night. I tried to wake them up, to get out of the car, but it started to shake and slide and then it flipped over and over. When it finally stopped, I knew they were dead." She gazed into Jake's eyes. "And I was alone in the dark."

His eyes filled with a protective tenderness. "Oh, God, Sarah! I'm sorry you had to go through that."

"We were there for hours. Nobody moved. Nobody talked. I couldn't stand it."

"You're not alone now. I'm here. I'm not leaving."

She wrapped her arms around his neck and hugged him as tightly as she could. She knew she wasn't being fair to him. He had walked away from her earlier. He had told her he wasn't going to touch her again, but she needed him now. She needed his comfort, his warmth, his embrace. And as he'd promised, Jake didn't move away. He let her cling to him. He gave her the support, the security that she craved.

Finally she eased her death grip on his neck and pulled back so she could look at him. "Thank you."

"You never told me about your parents' accident. I knew you didn't like the dark, but you never said why. Did you remember anything else?"

She'd known the question was coming. In fact, she wondered how he'd had the restraint to wait so long in asking it.

She shook her head.

He let out a sigh. "Well, at least we have one more truth."

"Do you think in the end that the truths will make up for the lies?"

"If you're asking me if I could forgive you—"

"No, I'm not asking you that," she said quickly. "Not now anyway." But as she looked at him, she wondered if one day she'd have to let him answer that question.

"Let's sit down." Jake led her over to the bed.

She perched on the edge.

"You might as well get comfortable. We might not have any lights for a while."

She stretched out on top of the covers. Jake walked around to the other side of the bed and lay down next to her. There was a good foot between them, and Jake had his arms folded over his chest. He made no attempt to touch her. He simply stared at the ceiling. But she could tell by the stiffness of his pose that he wasn't at all relaxed. The air between them grew thick and heavy and restless.

"Don't," Jake said abruptly. "We're not going there again. I can't let you back in."

"Can we just hold each other?" she asked, rolling onto her side.

He shook his head. "No. No touching. Too dangerous."

"I didn't make love to you earlier to prove something to myself or to bring my memory back. I did it because I feel a connection to you."

"We always had good chemistry. No surprise there."

"I'm not talking about physical attraction, although it definitely exists."

"Sarah, you don't know me. And I don't know you. Let's just leave it at that."

"I know that you're protective and kind and loyal."

"I'm not a damn Boy Scout," he growled.

"No, you're far too angry and intense and impatient for that. But you're a good person."

He turned his head to look at her. "Don't say any more."

"I can't stand this wall between us."

"Well, it's not coming down tonight." He swore. "Dammit."

"What?"

"Come here."

She didn't know why he'd had a change of heart, but she wasn't going to argue. She curled up into his embrace, her head back on his shoulder. This was where she belonged. This was home, she realized. Where she wanted to be. It was perfect—well, almost perfect. When they had Caitlyn, then her world would be right again.

"Just sleep," Jake ordered.

"I want to," she said. "But I'm afraid of where the dreams will take me."

"Don't be afraid. We'll go there together. Take me with you this time, Sarah. Take me into the nightmare. Let me help you find a way out."

She closed her eyes, keeping Jake's image front and center. Wherever she went, he was going with her.

When Dylan woke up the next morning, the storm had passed. After using the bathroom, he walked into the kitchen and saw a kettle on the stove as well as more tea bags. He might have to stop at a Star-

bucks on his way to LA or die of caffeine depriva-
tion.

He poured himself a cup of tea and took it out on
the back deck. Catherine was on the beach with her
dogs again, a big floppy sweater around her jeans
and T-shirt. Her feet were bare as usual. She apparently wasn't that into shoes, the first woman he'd
ever met who seemed more comfortable out of heels
than in them.

She was a lonely-looking figure, he thought, curious again as to why she'd chosen to live such a her-
mitlike existence. He also wondered what had
happened to her Prince Charming, the one who'd
come and left, as she put it. Was that guy responsible
for the angry mood of her paintings? Or did her art
come from some other dark place in her soul?

She certainly wouldn't be an easy woman to love,
not with her psychic claims and cryptic predictions.
He wasn't sure he'd want to live with a woman who
could see the future. Not that he really believed in
her fortune-telling skills. Still, despite his best efforts
to ignore her predictions about his own life, he
couldn't help wondering about the two women
she'd seen in his future, one who was supposed to be
his worst enemy and the other his salvation. Maybe
Catherine should be writing mystery novels instead
of painting. She had a knack for opening up a good
story, anyway. Not that she'd been interested in fin-
ishing it.

Turning away from the view, he reentered the
house and checked his watch. It was almost ten

o'clock. Time to give Xander Cross a call. He hoped this would be the break they desperately needed. But if not, he was going to get Catherine down to LA to meet up with Sarah face-to-ace. Maybe she could jog Sarah's memory.

Punching in Xander's number, he waited for someone to pick up. Finally a woman's voice came over the phone. "Hex-Games," she said, giving the name of the shop.

"I'd like to speak to Xander Cross," he said.

There was a long pause at the other end of the phone. "I'm sorry, but that's not possible. Can someone else help you?"

"No, it's a personal matter. Is he there?"

"No."

"Can you give me another number for him? It's very important that I speak to him as soon as possible."

"Hold on a second."

Dylan tapped his fingers on the table as he waited for her to return, but instead a man's voice came over the phone.

"This is Joe Morgan, the owner of the store. Can I help you?"

"I need to speak to Xander Cross," Dylan said. "I thought he was the owner."

"He used to be. Are you a friend?"

Dylan frowned, wondering why he was getting the runaround. "Not exactly, but we have a mutual acquaintance. A friend of mine is in trouble, and I think Mr. Cross might be able to help her."

"Mr. Cross won't be helping anyone. He died seven months ago," Joe said.

Dylan let out a breath, shocked by the news. "What . . . what happened?"

"He interrupted a robbery in progress at his home and was killed."

Seven months ago. Just when Sarah disappeared.

"Do you know the exact date?" Dylan asked.

"It was August third."

And Sarah had disappeared on August fourth. Had Xander's death sparked her run?

"Did the police catch who did it?"

"Not to my knowledge. I'm sorry, but I have to go. Is there anything else you need?"

"Did Mr. Cross leave behind any family?"

"He had an ex-wife, but I haven't seen her since the funeral."

"Do you know her name—where I might be able to contact her?"

Joe hesitated. "Well, her name is Adele Kramer—I don't have her phone number."

"Thanks for your help." Dylan ended the call, his mind reeling from what he'd just learned. Was Xander's death connected to Sarah's disappearance? Did the robbery at Xander Cross's home have something to do with Sarah? It seemed more than likely. Unfortunately, the fact that Xander was now dead did not help him find out who was chasing Sarah.

He looked up as Catherine came back into the house. Her cheeks were flushed from her run, her eyes bright and curious. "You found out something, but it's not good news, is it?"

"Xander Cross was killed seven months ago, the day before Sarah disappeared from an apartment building about three miles away from where he worked."

"Andy is dead?" Catherine murmured, her eyes turning sad. "That's tragic. He was so young—my age. I can't believe it."

"I'm sorry."

"How was he killed?"

"He interrupted a robbery at his home. Apparently he left behind an ex-wife by the name of Adele Kramer."

"Adele Kramer?" she echoed in surprise. "I know Adele Kramer. She was married to Andy?"

"Don't tell me Adele was another foster kid."

"No, but Adele went to high school with us. She was Andy's high school girlfriend the year we all lived together. She was a nice girl from a good family who risked her cheerleader reputation to date the oddball geek. I always liked her. Jessica did, too."

"So she knew Jessica," Dylan said thoughtfully. "That's good. That gives Jessica—or Sarah—a friend in San Francisco, a friend who could have helped her disappear. Maybe even a friend who knows where Caitlyn is." He started up his computer again. "Time for another search."

"You don't have to do that," Catherine said. "I know how to find Adele."

"How? You didn't know how to find Andy or Xander or whatever his name was."

"Well, I know how to find Adele. She's an art lover. She works in a museum in San Francisco, and she writes a column for an art magazine. I had no idea she'd married Andy. She certainly never used his last name or talked about him in her column. I thought of writing her a few times, but I didn't." Catherine grabbed a magazine off the bookshelf. "I think her e-mail is listed at the end of her article. Yes, here it is."

Dylan pushed the computer in Catherine's direction. "You write her. Tell her you need to find Jessica, and you think Andy might have spoken to her before she disappeared. Ask her if she knows anything about Jessica or Sarah or the baby, Caitlyn."

Catherine typed slowly and deliberately. When she was finished, she hit the send key.

Dylan hoped it wouldn't take long for Adele to reply, but it was Saturday. She might not check her e-mail until Monday. And that could be too late. He picked up the phone and called Information, but there was no listing for her. They would have to wait. But which was more important, keeping the computer connection open or hitting the road to LA?

He could also call his friends at the San Francisco Police Department. They might be able to tell him more about Xander's death. He knew Sarah's departure was connected to it. He was getting closer to finding out exactly what had happened to make her run.

The computer beeped as an e-mail was received. He clicked the button, excited to see a quick reply from Adele Kramer. The message was short. *If you're really Catherine, then why does your e-mail say Dylan Sanders?*

Dylan typed in, B*ecause I'm using his computer. But it's really me. I remember you from high school. You were Andy's girlfriend.* He paused, glancing over at Catherine. "What else can I tell her to make her believe me?"

"Tell her that I still remember the ugly orange corsage Andy gave her for the prom."

Dylan did as Catherine suggested and hit send. They sat in silence, waiting for a reply. It came in less than a minute.

Give me your phone number. I'll call you."

Catherine recited her phone number for him as he typed. He let out a breath when the message was sent. He hoped Adele would call. She was being very careful, and why not? Her ex-husband had been killed. She was smart to be cautious.

Within minutes the phone rang. Catherine drew in a breath and then picked it up. "Hello?" She held the receiver away from her ear so Dylan could hear.

"Catherine—this is Adele," she said in a brisk, no-nonsense voice.

"Thanks for calling me," Catherine said. "I just recently learned about Andy's death. I'm so sorry."

"It was terrible. I was always afraid something like that would happen to him. I warned him that he was playing with danger, but that's the way he liked

to live, you know. I certainly couldn't change him."
Her voice was edged with bitterness. "I don't know
why I thought I could."

"I remember how stubborn he was," Catherine
murmured.

"Yes. Now, you said something about Jessica in
your e-mail?"

"I also recently learned that Jessica was living in
San Francisco near Andy, and . . . well, she disappeared the day after he died. I'm trying to find her. I
wonder if you know where she is now."

There was a long pause on the other end of the
phone. "I know this much, Catherine: Jessica was in
a lot of trouble. She asked Andy to make her some
fake IDs for her and her baby. Two days later Andy
was dead."

"I'm so sorry, Adele."

"Me, too. I don't know what happened to Jessica
after that. I always liked her, but not as much as
Andy did. He had a soft spot for her. I know he
helped her over the years, not just a few months ago.
Several years ago she actually stayed with us for a
couple of nights. She was using a different name
then—Sarah, I think it was. She said she'd gotten
into some bad trouble, and she couldn't trust anyone. She looked horrible at the time, terrified of her
own shadow. I think Andy helped set her up with a
job, and then I didn't see her again. To be honest,
Andy and I were fighting, and I didn't really care
what he was doing. I just wanted to get on with my
life. I wasted too many years trying to turn him into

a law-abiding citizen. I couldn't do it anymore." Her voice caught. "But I miss him. I still miss him."

"You loved him. I loved him, too."

"Well, life goes on. That's what Andy always used to tell me when I had a problem. Is that all you wanted?"

"Can you think of anyone else Jessica might have run to after Andy died—if she still needed help?" Catherine asked.

"I don't know what was up with the man she had the baby with. Aside from him, I would have thought you, maybe. She talked about you sometimes, but she said she was afraid to bring trouble in her wake. I guess she thought Andy with his superhero talents could fend off any danger. But she was wrong. He wasn't a superhero; he was just a nut." Adele paused and then added, "Oh, wait—Andy kept in touch sometimes with Teresa. She became a female boxer, even opened her own gym somewhere. Andy was quite impressed. I remember that he told her he was going to draw a female superhero character after her."

"Do you know where the gym is?"

"I can't remember. I think it was somewhere in LA. I have to go, Catherine. I don't mean to be rude, but I don't really want to get involved in anything having to do with Jessica or any of the rest of you."

"I understand," Catherine said. "Thanks for calling me back." Catherine hung up the phone and let out a sigh. "I guess Teresa is our next best bet."

"Can't be too many female boxers with the name

Teresa," Dylan said, excited about the new lead. But he could see by the expression on Catherine's face that she wasn't feeling nearly so good. "Are you all right?" Her cheeks were pale and her eyes were bleak.

"I'm sad for Andy and worried about Jessica. And I have to admit it kind of stung to have Adele tell me not to call her again, to stay out of her life. I don't know why it bothers me, though. It's not the first time I've heard those words." She forced a false smile. "Adele called Jessica Sarah, so I guess that's her name now. They're the same person."

"Are you ready to go to LA?"

"You don't even stop to take a breath, do you? I'm still reeling from finding out Andy is dead."

"I know, Catherine, and I'm sorry if I'm rushing you, but we need to find Sarah before what happened to Andy happens to her."

Chapter Twenty

Sarah awoke disoriented and alone. She sat up abruptly, then blew out a breath of relief when she saw Jake tapping the computer keys, a stream of sunlight coming through the window.

"I made coffee," he said, without looking up from what he was doing.

"Thanks," she mumbled. Since Jake had obviously taken a shower and changed his clothes, she decided to do the same. She stumbled out of bed, grabbed her duffel bag, and headed toward the bathroom. She had a bad case of morning breath, and she suspected her hair looked like a family of birds had made a nest in it. She couldn't remember her dreams. Maybe Jake's presence had chased the nightmares away.

The hot water from the shower felt good on her head and shoulders, and she stayed under the spray for long, luxurious minutes, almost dreading the moment when she would have to confront another day of uncertainty. But as Caitlyn's sweet face appeared in her mind, Sarah knew there was a very good reason for getting on with things. She did not want to spend another night without her daughter back in her arms.

Twenty minutes later she was dressed and ready to get down to business. She moved over to the table, where Jake seemed absorbed by whatever he was reading on the screen.

"What's up?" she asked.

"I found some information on Shane Hollis."

"Who is he?" Sarah asked, sitting down next to Jake.

There was new energy in his voice this morning, as well as an eager light in his eyes. Whatever he'd discovered had certainly gotten him charged up.

"He's a Harvard graduate, for one."

"No," she said in disbelief. "The guy in the beanie who tried to kill me several times went to Harvard?"

"On scholarship. He was part of a grade-school class sponsored by a wealthy businessman who promised to put them all through college at his alma mater."

"Are you sure you're talking about the right Shane Hollis?"

"Listen to this and then tell me what you think." Jake flipped to a new screen and started to read. " 'A group of students thought to belong to one of Harvard's most secret societies, the Eye of the Tiger, were questioned today regarding the recent suicide of one of their members, Daniel Haggarty, under suspicion that there was some type of hazing involved. Shane Hollis and Timothy Fontaine, the grandson of Harold Fontaine, the state senator from Connecticut, were the first to discover their friend's body. After lengthy questioning and a review of Daniel Haggarty's psychological records, no charges were filed in the case."

"Eye of the Tiger," she repeated, the name echoing through her head.

"Exactly. That would explain the tiger tattoo you saw in your dream."

Sarah pushed back her chair and stood up, feeling unsettled, but she didn't know why. "What else?" she asked.

Jake flipped to another screen. "Once I found the tiger connection, I started researching the group. There were at least five to six guys involved, as far as I can tell. All, with the exception of Shane Hollis, were rich, well-connected, privileged young men who, according to other students, were arrogant, cocky, and felt they were better than everyone else. Their activities were shrouded in secrecy, most involving college-type pranks, until Haggarty's suicide."

"Okay, but what's the connection between Shane Hollis and me?" Sarah asked.

"That's what we have to figure out. But here's at least a small link: After college, two of the men opened an art gallery in Chicago."

"Go on."

"The gallery quickly became a huge success. Apparently the men's Harvard connections were happy to invest in the art that they sold. They were also good-looking guys, playboys, who had no trouble finding beautiful women to come to their parties. They quickly became the toast of the town."

Sarah's pulse began to speed up as something teased at the back of her brain. "What was the name of the gallery?"

"White Tiger. They were apparently hooked on the tiger theme. What gets even more interesting is that it turns out the gallery was a front for black-market art and drug smuggling. One of the boys was half Russian and apparently had some contacts back in Russia who had gotten their hands on some stolen art secreted away since World War Two. But they weren't satisfied with just selling priceless paintings on the black market. They also got involved with smuggling heroin within the frames. The DEA got wind of the deals, and two of our Harvard boys went to prison."

Sarah swallowed hard, a thick knot growing in her throat. She wanted to tell Jake to stop talking. He was going too fast. It was too much. And yet it wasn't enough. There were a million questions hovering at the back of her mind, but she couldn't get the words out.

"That was eight years ago," Jake added, looking her in the eye. "The same time you disappeared from Chicago. I'm guessing you were connected in some way to what happened at the gallery." He paused. "And I found a photo taken of the three of them. It's kind of grainy, but I think you'll be able to recognize Shane." He turned the laptop computer screen so that it was facing her.

Sarah stared at the photo of the three men, especially the man in the middle. Her chest tightened and she felt light-headed, dizzy. She put a hand on Jake's arm to steady herself.

His eyes narrowed in concern. "Sarah, what's wrong?"

His voice seemed very far away. Her vision began to blur. "I . . . I can't breathe," she said, her fingers gripping his arm like a lifeline.

"Yes, you can. Just take one breath, then another, slowly," Jake advised.

She shook her head, biting down on her lips as a flood of anxiety and adrenaline surged through her bloodstream. "I . . . I can't do this."

"Why not? What did you see? What did you remember?"

The images of the men flashed through her head. She knew those faces. How did she know them? She'd never gone to Harvard. She was a foster kid. She didn't move in the circles of the young and privileged. But she had lived in Chicago. And eight years ago they'd gone to prison.

The faces flashed in front of her again, one of them with a mocking smile. It was someone she knew, someone she'd touched, someone she'd kissed, someone she'd loved.

"Oh, God," she said, her brain spinning out of control. The blackness came at her like a freight train, and she welcomed it with blessed relief. She didn't want to remember. She couldn't go back there. She just couldn't.

"Shit!" Jake swore as Sarah collapsed on the floor in a crumpled heap. He gathered her in his arms and carried her over to the bed, laying her down on her back. Her face was completely white, drained of any hint of color. The bruises still lingering from her accident stood out in vivid relief, giving her a fragile appearance. Had the information been too much for her? Had he driven her further inside of herself by telling her too much too fast?

Fear raced through him. What if she didn't wake up this time? What if he'd pushed her into some deep comatose state where she could continue to hide from her painful memories? What if he never found Caitlyn?

He shook her shoulders. "Sarah, wake up," he demanded.

When she didn't move, he sat back, wondering what to do next. Would he hurt her more if he tried to wake her up? Did she need to do that in her own time? But how long could he wait?

Walking into the bathroom, he soaked a washcloth with cool water and took it back to the bed. He placed it on Sarah's forehead, gently stroking her cheek with his fingers. She didn't stir at all. He put a hand on her heart, reassured to feel the steady beat beneath his fingers. She was still breathing. She just needed a few minutes, he told himself, and then she'd wake up. She'd tell him what she'd remembered and they'd be able to find Caitlyn.

But as seconds turned to minutes, he wondered if that was going to happen at all, or if this time he'd lost Sarah forever.

She'd never been to such an elite party. Everyone who was anyone in Chicago was there. And so was she. She felt like pinching herself. Was this her life now? Fabulous parties, rich friends, families with blood ties dating back to the Mayflower? It hardly seemed possible. She'd spent so many years on her own, on the edge of—if not in—a state of homelessness. But one chance meeting with a sexy, sophisticated man and her entire life had changed.

Victor Pennington was her Prince Charming, her darkhaired, dark-eyed, half-Russian prince, and she was Cinderella at the ball, only her dress wasn't going to turn to rags, nor would the stretch limo change into a pumpkin. This was real. Victor loved her. He said she was his lucky charm, and she'd never been anyone's charm, lucky or otherwise.

He probably wouldn't think she was lucky if he knew who she really was. She shouldn't have lied to him, but whenever she had the chance to be someone else, she usually took it. She and Teresa had pretended to be lots of different people during their trip across the country. It was fun, a lark. She'd been a struggling country-western singer in Nashville. Teresa had been a supermodel on the rise in Denver. They'd both been flight attendants on layover in Dallas. Only those games hadn't lasted long, just a day or two. She'd never anticipated when she'd met Victor

and his Harvard friends that they would still be seeing
each other a few weeks later.

Now it was too late to change her story. A wave of fear
rushed through her. She told herself it would be all right.
Victor didn't have to know the truth. She could be who-
ever he wanted her to be. She'd spent her life learning how
to fit in. Fake it until you make it, *Teresa always said.*

The party scene faded in front of her eyes, replaced with
the shadows of the back room, the clatter of the heavy or-
nate frames being opened, the sound of soft yet harsh
whispers in the night, the late-night calls, the hours alone
waiting, wondering, and then she saw the faces of the men
who'd tracked her down, who'd blackmailed her, who'd
forced her to see what was really happening, who'd taken
her fairy-tale life and turned it into a never-ending night-
mare from which she couldn't escape.

"Sarah."

The sound of Jake's voice warmed her heart. She
loved Jake. He was the real prince, but she couldn't
tell him her dark secrets. She couldn't bring him into
the madness of her life. Victor would kill anyone
who tried to protect her or to help her. He'd already
done it several times—the guards in the safe house,
Andy—even Mrs. Murphy had almost lost her life
because of Sarah.

"Sarah, come back to me. We need to find Caitlyn.
I can't do it without you."

Jake's pleading, desperate words warred with her
desire to remain in a safe, quiet place, to just let the
worst happen, because she was so tired. But her
daughter needed her. Jake needed her. She'd put

them in danger, and she had to get them out. She had to fight. She couldn't quit now.

Slowly she opened her eyes, blinking at the sight of Jake's anxious expression. His face was white, and the worry lines across his forehead and around his mouth were deep and tight.

"Thank God," he breathed. His hand stroked her cheek. "Are you all right?"

Her brain felt thick and slow. It had been empty for so long. Now it was crowded with memories from her childhood, from Victor, from Jake—so many conflicting thoughts hit her, she didn't know what to say, what to do. She glanced around the room, trying to focus on the present, on simple facts. They were in a motel room in Santa Monica. They were on the run. They were looking for Caitlyn.

Suddenly everything clicked into place.

"Jake," she whispered, his name rocketing through her body in a series of sharp, tingling sparks of memory. It was all coming back. Finally.

She closed her eyes again, feeling a deep sense of relief that she had to savor—if only for a moment. She knew who she was. Her past was in line with her present. Her head and her heart had made the last connection.

"Sarah, I know you've remembered something. Can you talk to me now? I don't want to rush you, but we don't have a lot of time."

She opened her eyes and looked at him, really looked at him, noting all the wonderful details of his face, his beautiful green eyes, his strong jaw, his passionate mouth. There had been a time in her life when she'd thought she would never see him again. The memories flooded back through her head like images from a video collage: the first meeting at the café, their first kiss in the moonlight under the Golden Gate Bridge, the first time they'd made love in his apartment, the day Caitlyn had been born, Jake cutting the umbilical cord, laying their baby across her breast, the nights the three of them had spent in bed together like a real family.

Her heart broke at what they'd had, what they'd lost. Just because she remembered what had happened didn't mean she could change it. She'd made mistakes, decisions that she couldn't take back, and now she would have to explain them. Some of them were indefensible.

A tear dripped down her cheek. Jake wiped it away. "Not now, Sarah," he said, his voice husky and raw.

He was right. It was time to face the music. It was time to talk to Jake with total and complete knowledge of who she was to him, and who she'd been to other people in her life.

"I remember everything," she said slowly. "Every last detail of my life, where I was born, who my parents are, where I lived, Chicago, Victor, Shane Hollis, everything."

Excitement flared in his eyes. "I want to hear it, but let's start with the most important piece of information. Where is Caitlyn? Do you know?"

Her daughter's name pierced another hole through

her heart, and she bit down on her lip as she nodded. "Yes, I know where she is."

"Thank God! Where?"

"With Teresa—in Santa Barbara."

Jake shook his head in confusion. "Santa Barbara? That doesn't make sense. If Teresa's in Santa Barbara, she would have seen the news broadcast, your picture in the local paper. Why didn't she come forward? Why didn't she come to the hospital?"

"I told her not to tell anyone she had Caitlyn, no matter what happened to me. I made her promise that she would keep Caitlyn safe. She grew up like I did, Jake, with no one to trust. She didn't ask me questions I didn't want to answer. She just said she would guard Caitlyn with her life until I came back."

Jake stared at her "If you stopped there right before your accident and someone was following you, then they already know where Caitlyn is."

"I didn't take Caitlyn there myself," she said quickly, seeing his mind racing to a horrible conclusion. "I sent her with Amanda. We were closer friends than Amanda said when we saw her yesterday. She'd grown up like me. She was a street kid. We had a lot in common. She knew how to survive, too. When she heard I was in trouble when that guy tried to grab me in the elevator, she offered to help."

"Amanda," he echoed in bemusement. "I suppose she made you the same promise of silence, and that's why she kept the secret when we saw her yesterday."

"Yes. It's my fault, Jake. I didn't tell them who I

was running from. I thought too much information would put them in more danger. I guess when Amanda saw you with me she just couldn't trust that you were the good guy. And since I couldn't remember, she—"

He cut off her explanation with a wave of his hand. "Whatever. We know where Caitlyn is; let's go." He jumped to his feet. "I don't want to lose another minute. You can tell me the rest on the way there. It's almost a two-hour drive."

She grabbed her bag and packed up her clothes while Jake closed up the computer and grabbed his own things. Within ten minutes they were in the car and on their way to get Caitlyn. She felt better now that she knew who she was, but she wouldn't feel completely right until she had her daughter in her arms.

Halfway down the street Jake pulled out his phone again and pushed in a number. "Dylan," he said a moment later. "Sarah has her memory back. Caitlyn is with someone named Teresa in Santa Barbara. What's the address?" he said, turning to Sarah.

"Eleven-oh-one Mirada Drive," she replied.

Jake repeated the address to his brother. When he'd finished the call, he turned to Sarah. "Dylan and Catherine will meet us in Santa Barbara. I told him to give us a head start. I don't want him to spook Teresa if she sees a stranger at the door."

She nodded, knowing that there was a lot to be said, but where to start? That was the big question. First she needed to call Teresa. "Let me use your phone. I'll give Teresa the heads-up that we're coming."

"I don't want her to run with our child. If she thinks someone has a gun to your head, she might do just that." He shot her a dark look. "Believe me, I'd like nothing more than to have you get her on the phone and confirm that Caitlyn is safe, but at this point I'd rather not do anything that's going to send Teresa into hiding."

She thought about what he was saying and then put down the phone. "I'll wait until we get closer then." It was hard not to make the call when she desperately wanted to hear Caitlyn's voice, but she had to think about what was best. "We have to make sure we're not being followed. We can't lead anyone to Caitlyn."

"I'm well aware of that," Jake snapped. "Give me a little credit, Sarah. I'm not a complete fool."

"I never thought you were."

"Obviously you did, or you would have brought Caitlyn to me."

"Do you want to get into all that now?" she asked warily.

"No." He shot her an indefinable look. "Because I can't have that discussion and drive. We're going to leave it alone until we get Caitlyn back."

Jake's voice was tight. She knew he wanted to have it out with her, to get the answers to all the questions he had about why and how she'd left him, but he was right: They couldn't have this discussion while racing through LA traffic.

"One thing I do want to know," he said. "Who exactly is trying to kill you? I assume it's one of the Harvard guys."

"Victor Pennington. Do you want me to tell you what happened in Chicago?" She figured that part of the story would be less personally upsetting to him, and he needed to know the danger they were up against.

"Go on," he said, his gaze on the road.

It was easier when he wasn't looking at her. "You already know some of it. My real name is Jessica Holt. When I was twenty years old, Teresa and I decided to drive across country one summer. We were headed to New York to meet up with Catherine, but our car broke down in Chicago. We didn't have any money to fix it, but we were young and had no roots, no families to worry about us, so we got jobs and lived in a shelter for a couple of weeks until we had enough money to get an apartment. It was a dump, but it was something. I got a temp job working in a law office. Victor Pennington was one of their clients. He came into the office one day and he invited everyone, all the secretaries and clerks and attorneys, to a party at his art gallery. I thought I was Cinderella, and I'd just gotten an invitation to the best ball in town."

She paused for breath. When Jake didn't comment, she continued. "Victor and his friends were handsome, smart, rich blue bloods, everything I wasn't. They'd all gone to Harvard. One of their grandfathers was a state senator. Another was a billionaire. When Victor asked me out, I couldn't believe my luck. I thought he lived in this beautiful world, a world I'd never thought I could belong to. For a while it was great. He wined and dined me; he swept me off my feet. He told me I was beautiful and desirable and that he'd never met anyone like me." She'd been so stupid, so easy to manipulate.

"Teresa didn't like Chicago and decided to go home. After that it was just Victor and me and this fairy-tale romance I thought we were having." She inhaled, knowing she had to confess another sin. "I told Victor a story about myself that wasn't true. Teresa and I played this game on our trip that whenever we hit a new city we'd be someone different. I know it probably sounds crazy, but our childhood lives were filled with a lot of crap, and playing 'let's pretend to be someone else' always made us feel better. With Victor I was the disowned granddaughter of a rich Texas oil man. That's why I was working in the law office. I said it was just a temporary thing. My grandfather wanted me to learn to appreciate the money that I'd be coming into with my trust fund."

Jake's eyebrow shot up in disbelief, and he gave her another amazed look. "You lied to him, too. Do you ever tell the truth?"

"The truth is hard to live with sometimes. You wouldn't understand, Jake. You didn't grow up like I did."

"That's an excuse?"

"No, but when I met Victor I was barely out of my

teens. I knew if I told him who I really was, he'd walk away. In the beginning it was just a way to be Cinderella for a night. But once I started the lies I couldn't stop them, and then I didn't really want to stop, because I was falling in love. Victor seemed to feel the same way. He called me all the time. He bought me pretty clothes and paid for me to get my hair cut and have manicures and pedicures and days at the spa. I'd never had anyone care so much about me. I thought for sure I'd wake up any second. Then the unthinkable happened. Victor asked me to marry him. He gave me a huge diamond ring. He took me to the bridal salon to pick out my dress."

"That was the memory you had earlier," Jake said. "Did you marry him?"

"No. A few days after that I found him in bed with another woman. My little fairy tale came to an abrupt end. I tried to break things off, but he begged me to reconsider. He told me that it was a mistake and he'd been drunk and it meant nothing. He still wanted me." She stared down at her fingers, remembering how beautiful and yet how wrong the ring had looked on her finger. She'd known she was living a lie, but she hadn't been able to stop. "Growing up without a family, I wanted to be wanted. In the beginning, when I'd go to a foster home I'd try to be perfect, so they would want to adopt me. But no one wanted to make me a permanent part of their lives. I was just a temporary guest. Victor was the first one who wanted a legal contract."

"A legal contract based on a lie. Didn't he ever ask to meet your family?"

"I put him off. Victor had so much pride and money that he thought it would be fine to get married and tell them afterward. He said he wanted to pay for the wedding anyway; he wanted it to be the highlight of the Chicago wedding season."

"So you took him back."

She nodded. "Stupidly, yes. I didn't realize that Victor was more than just a cheater. He was also dealing in stolen art. I thought he was a reputable businessman. I knew he had some family contacts in Russia, but I didn't realize they were fencing stolen art from the war. Apparently it brought in millions of dollars. But that money wasn't enough for him. Victor and his friends wanted more. So they began smuggling heroin inside the frames of the art that came into the gallery. I didn't know it at the time. That is the truth. And I certainly didn't imagine that men who were born into such a wonderful life would want to risk what they had to break the law, to smuggle drugs."

She'd thought she was street-smart, but she'd been naive when it came to how the other half of the world lived. "I grew up with kids who had nothing—who had to steal to survive. But Victor and his Harvard buddies had everything they'd ever wanted. In retrospect, I realized that they didn't care about money, because they'd never had to earn it. I thought Victor was my ticket to a good life, the life I'd always wanted to lead, and not just because of his money, but his respectability, his family connections. I didn't understand that evil could wear an expensive suit and have an Ivy League education. That was a shock to me."

Sarah glanced out the window as a dozen emotions ran through her. It felt good to let it all out. She'd never told anyone the whole story of her foolish affair with one of the most dangerous men in the world, a man who now wanted her dead. Not even Andy had known everything. He'd known just enough to get him killed. She couldn't let the same thing happen to Jake. He had to know exactly the kind of people they were up against.

"So what happened?" Jake asked. "How did you find out what was going on? How did you end up on Victor's hit list?"

She turned to face him. "Two agents from the DEA approached me and told me that Victor was smuggling drugs. They presented the facts to me in such a way that they convinced me I could either be charged as an accessory and go to prison for a very long time, or I could help them set up a sting operation. They scared the hell out of me. They made it sound as if I had no choice. It was jail or turning on Victor. They said Victor was going down either way, but their way I could protect myself by helping them, and in return they would put me into the Witness Protection Program. They would give me a new identity, and I would be safe from any repercussions."

She thought about those terrible moments of

shock and fear when she'd learned the truth about Victor. "I wasn't going to do it at first. I told them I didn't know anything. That I couldn't help. But they kept pushing me. They showed me a photo of a woman who'd been strangled. It was the woman I'd seen in bed with Victor. The agents told me that Victor had killed her when she found out too much. I didn't know if they were lying or not, but I couldn't get the image of her dead body out of my mind, and I knew they'd been together."

Her voice caught, but she cleared her throat and kept going. "I had a date with Victor that night. I was earlier than I was supposed to be. I overheard Victor on the phone making a deal. Suddenly all the mysterious phone conversations, the people who came to the door in the middle of the night, the odd times when Victor would have to go down to the gallery to check out a shipment began to make sense. I knew deep in my heart that I'd been so caught up in my fairy tale that I'd denied what I'd seen with my own eyes. I was so afraid that night that I was going to make a mistake and Victor would know that I was considering turning against him. I thought I might just run away, not work with anyone, but then I remembered the woman and figured she'd probably tried to run, too.

"So the next day I went back to the agents and I agreed to help. I still wasn't sure that what I was doing was right or smart, and the next two days were really tense as I waited for them to set up the sting. They wanted to raid the art gallery just after a shipment was received. In the end they arrested Victor and his partner, Rick Adams, for drug smuggling and murder. After Victor was arrested, the U.S. Marshals whisked me away, keeping me in a safe house until I could testify. They convinced me that since Victor was in jail, I would be safe. After the trial I would be given a new identity and moved to a new location."

"But something went wrong. Didn't it?"

She nodded, meeting his gaze. "Victor had a lot of connections. He was very rich. He found out where I was. Somebody leaked the information. The man I saw in my dream with the tiger tattoo on his wrist was Shane Hollis. He shot one of the guards. But there was another guard in the back room. He got into a fight with Shane, and while they were battling it out, I ran like hell. I climbed out the bedroom window and I never looked back. I knew I was on my own from then on. I couldn't trust the police or the government or anyone. I later read in the paper that both agents had been killed. Shane had gotten away."

"You didn't go back to testify?" Jake asked, glancing over at her. "You didn't tell them what you'd seen at the safe house?"

"No," she said, shaking her head. "I was too scared to go near anyone in a uniform. In the end they didn't need my testimony. They had enough evidence without me. Another one of Victor's Harvard buddies, Timothy Fontaine, pled out to a lesser charge in exchange for his testimony against Victor and Rick. In case you were wondering, Timothy Fontaine ended up dead six months after the trial. Apparently he wasn't safe in Witness Protection either. I knew that Victor would keep trying to get me. I had betrayed him. And he would get his revenge. So I lived on the run, moving from town to town, state to state, changing my name, my hair color, my background. Sometimes I lost track of who I really was."

"But you got some help."

"From Andy Hart. He was the only one I confided in. He swore that he would never tell anyone, and I trusted him."

"What about your other friends, Catherine and Teresa? Catherine said you never contacted her after you disappeared from Chicago."

"I sent her a note. I didn't want her to worry, but I guess she still did. I didn't contact Teresa at all. It was bad enough that Andy knew where I was. I couldn't risk any leaks, and I couldn't put anyone else in danger. After a while, as the years passed, I started to relax. Victor was sentenced to twenty-five years in prison. Nothing bad had happened in a long time. I thought maybe they'd given up on me. I was lonely and tired of running, so after about five years I went to San Francisco. Andy was there, and I thought it would be nice to live near someone I knew. That's when I met you."

"And lied to me, too," Jake said grimly. "It was just another game, wasn't it?"

"No, it was never a game," she denied. "I was a lot

older when I met you. I had suffered for the lies I told Victor. I didn't lie to you on a lark. I was just used to being someone else."

"You should have told me after we moved in together, after we had a baby together."

"I couldn't. You were so great. I didn't want to lose you."

"Stop right there," he said sharply. "I don't want to talk about us."

"We have to get it out."

"Not now."

"Okay," she said warily. "What else do you want to know then?"

"When did Victor get out of jail?"

"Eight months ago, he got out on parole. I had no idea it could happen that fast or that he would have to serve only a third of his sentence. I'm sure his family was responsible for getting him released so quickly. At first I tried to tell myself that he wouldn't come after me, that it had been too long. I went to see Andy. I confided to him my fears. He told me I should be ready to leave town just in case. He made up some fake birth certificates for Caitlyn to match my IDs. Three days later, Andy was dead. His house had been ransacked. Andy was the only one who knew where I lived."

"So you ran."

"Yes. I wiped our apartment clean, because I didn't want anyone to put you and me together. I didn't think Andy would have left any clues in his house, but I couldn't be sure. You were out of the country. There was no one to leave Caitlyn with, so I grabbed her and I ran. I took a bus to San Mateo, another to San Jose, a third to Santa Cruz. I hid out in a motel there, thinking I would buy myself some time until you came back from your trip."

Jake started shaking his head. "That's enough, Sarah."

"But, Jake, you have to know that I tried to contact—"

"I don't want to hear any more," he interrupted. "I don't know whether you're lying or not. But I can't drive and listen to this, and right now we need to get to Caitlyn. So just shut the hell up."

Sarah sat back in her seat and stared out the window, knowing what she'd known all along: that Jake would never forgive her.

Jake's stomach was churning, his heart racing, his mind spinning with a million questions, but he couldn't ask them now. There was a ton of midmorning traffic on the maze of LA freeways, and he needed to concentrate on getting out of town as fast as possible. He forced a lid down on the anger bubbling through his veins. He couldn't afford to lose his cool. There was too much at stake. And while part of him did not want Sarah to utter one more word, another part of him knew he still needed more information.

"How do you think Victor figured out that you and Andy were friends?" he asked. "You said you didn't tell Victor about your past."

"I didn't, but he did have my real name, Jessica Holt. After I disappeared he must have figured out who I really was. I thought Andy was safe, because he actually lived under another name, too—Xander Cross. But Victor's had eight years to make the connections, and I'm sure he was extremely motivated."

"Which means Victor probably knows where Teresa is, too."

"I hope not," Sarah said. "Teresa goes under the name Tracy Hutchinson."

"Good God! Does no one live under their real name?"

"Actually, Tracy was her real name; she just liked Teresa better, and she got married for a few years, hence the Hutchinson. Andy didn't even know where Teresa was. Mrs. Murphy found her for me."

"The same Mrs. Murphy who was beaten up," Jake said, his pulse roaring again.

"She didn't have it written down anywhere," Sarah protested, but he could see the uncertainty flicker in her eyes.

"Do you know that for sure?"

"Yes, I do. I had told her I was interested in finding Teresa, and she said she'd ask around discreetly. She gave me Teresa's address a week before she was attacked."

"Shane obviously traced Mrs. Murphy to you. That's how he showed up at your apartment."

"But he couldn't have seen Amanda take Caitlyn to Teresa's house, because if he had Caitlyn, he would have used her to get to me. Victor would have used Caitlyn. She's safe. She has to be."

"I hope you're right."

"I didn't have a lot of choices after I saw Shane in LA. Maybe it was wrong to have Amanda take Caitlyn to Teresa, but I knew Shane was going to come after me again, and if I left Caitlyn behind, he'd find her. I didn't have anyone else to turn to."

"Except me," he couldn't help pointing out.

"You were too far away. San Francisco was a seven-hour drive. I didn't think I could get that far without a better plan."

He wanted to argue that she could have found a way to make contact with him. She could have gone through one of his friends, called him at work. Lord knew she was creative at the lies. She could have reached him if she wanted to. But it was pointless to rehash what hadn't happened.

"Okay, so where were you going when Shane chased you up the coast?" he asked. "Were you heading to Catherine's house?"

"No. I thought Catherine would be too easy to find. She hadn't changed her name or anything."

"Imagine that," he said sarcastically.

Sarah ignored him. "I was just looking for a new safe place to hide. And I thought if Shane were still after me, at least I'd get him away from Caitlyn. I told Teresa if anything happened to me, if I died, that she should take the baby back to you."

Jake wanted to believe that, but how could he? "Sure you did."

"It's true."

She gazed at him with her heart in her beautiful blue eyes, and he forced himself to look away from her, to concentrate on the road back to his daughter.

"I don't know what I would have done if you'd been in town when Andy died," she murmured. "But in some ways I was glad that you weren't, because I didn't want you to get hurt. I didn't want you to die, Jake. And make no mistake, Shane would have killed all three of us if he'd had the chance."

"Don't tell me you disappeared to protect me. What kind of man do you think I am—that I would want to hide behind you and my daughter?" he demanded.

"I had to make a quick decision, and you weren't there. I had to protect Caitlyn."

"You could have gone to the police."

"I was in the custody of the U.S. Marshals when Shane tried to kill me. I didn't believe I could trust anyone. Maybe it was the wrong decision," she admitted. "But everything happened so fast, and I was terrified."

"It was the wrong decision," he said sharply. "And I told you I don't want to talk about this right now."

"You brought it back up."

"Fine, then I'm putting it away again. I just hope to God you didn't make another wrong decision when you left Caitlyn with Teresa."

* * *

Sarah hoped so, too. Every mile between LA and Santa Barbara seemed to take an eternity. When they were a few minutes away she tried calling Teresa on Jake's cell phone, but there was no answer. It could be that Teresa was simply out of the house, maybe at the park with Caitlyn or on some other innocent outing. Even if Victor found them both, he wouldn't necessarily know that Caitlyn was Sarah's child. She'd colored Caitlyn's hair before she'd taken her to Teresa's house, turning her daughter's blond locks an ordinary brown. And since Teresa was also a brunette, Caitlyn could easily pass for her daughter.

"I dyed Caitlyn's hair," she told Jake. "It's brown now. I wanted us to match. Just so you know."

"I'd recognize her no matter what her hair color is."

"What are we going to do after we get Caitlyn?"

"Find a way out of this. I won't have my daughter growing up in fear."

"You have such confidence that you can change things. I lost mine a long time ago. I got it back for a while when I was with you. I thought I could have a normal life, a good life, but I screwed that up, too." She stared out the window, half hoping Jake would say they could have that life again, but he didn't.

For the next ten minutes they drove in silence. Finally they neared the town of Santa Barbara. Sarah's tension increased as they exited the freeway. Teresa lived in a modest neighborhood of Spanish-style houses with red tile roofs and neat lawns. Her two-story house was set in the middle of the block.

Everything appeared quiet. There were no strange cars in the driveway. Why hadn't Teresa answered her phone when her Toyota hybrid was parked in front of her house?

Jake parked the car but put a hand on her arm as she started to get out. "Just wait a second."

She looked around. Everything appeared normal. Getting out of the car, they walked quickly up to the front of the house. Sarah knocked on the door and was surprised to realize it wasn't all the way closed. She pushed it open and said, "Teresa?"

There was no answer from her friend, but at the sound of Sarah's voice, Caitlyn let out a shrill, piercing scream.

They ran for the stairs. Jake beat her to the top, pushing open the door to one of the bedrooms. Sarah was right on his heels.

A second too late she realized their mistake. Her ex-lover, her worst enemy, the man she had been running from for eight long years was here in this house, and he was holding Caitlyn under one arm. In his other hand was a gun pointed straight at her sweet daughter's head.

"Hello, Jessica. It's about time you got here," Victor Pennington said. "You and I have some unfinished business."

Chapter Twenty-one

"Put down my daughter," Sarah ordered, her heart in her throat as Caitlyn screamed in fury, her tiny face turning red as tears streamed down her cheeks. "You're hurting her. Let her go."

"I don't think so." Victor tightened his grip on Caitlyn. "Stop right there."

"It's me you want. Just put her down. I'll do whatever you say."

"Mama!" Caitlyn screamed, her little arms reaching out for Sarah.

Sarah's heart broke at the sight of her daughter's fear and fury. "It's okay, baby. Please, Victor, leave my child alone."

He gave her an evil smile. "The way you left me alone? You betrayed me, Jessica. You turned on me. You became my enemy, and my enemies do not survive."

"I had no choice. The agents blackmailed me.

They said I'd go to prison if I didn't work with them."

"So instead you sent me to prison." His wild eyes glittered with anger. "Does your friend here know we were lovers? Or shall I tell him in exact detail what we did in bed together?"

Sarah licked her lips. She didn't dare look at Jake, but she could feel the tension emanating from his body. So far he'd said nothing, but she knew he was trying to think of some way to take Victor down. He wouldn't let Victor kill Caitlyn, not without a fight—which scared her even more. If they weren't careful, they could all end up dead.

"This is between you and me," she said to Victor.

"You're not going to be able to kill all of us," Jake added.

Victor's thick lips tightened as he glared at Jake. "All I have to do is kill you first. Do you think Jessica can stop me from taking her life—or your daughter's? Quite a little family you've made for yourself, Jessica, while I was rotting in prison. Did you think about me? Did you really believe I was going to let you live after what you did to me?"

"You did it to yourself. You smuggled the drugs. You fenced the art. The feds had other witnesses besides me, including Timothy."

"Timothy paid for his betrayal, and so will you."

"Where's Teresa?" she asked, trying to keep him talking.

"Your friend can't help you. This time you aren't going to escape. Shane is dead. Timothy is dead.

And soon you'll be dead, too. It's much sweeter this way. I thought it would be enough to know you had taken your last breath, but it will be much more satisfying for me to pull the trigger. But first your friend, I think." He pointed his gun at Jake.

"Don't!" Sarah cried.

Her loud yell made Caitlyn scream. Her tiny fists swung in the air, her feet kicking wildly as she fought to get away.

Victor had one arm around the baby, and Sarah could see that Caitlyn's squirming was distracting Victor. Like any good toddler, Caitlyn knew instinctively how to go boneless and limp, how to use her weight to flop around like a rag doll.

"Dammit," Victor swore at Caitlyn. "Shut the fuck up."

Caitlyn screamed again as Victor tried to get a better grip on her. Sarah took a step forward, unable to bear the sight of her daughter's struggles.

"Don't move," Victor said. "Or I'll kill the baby first."

Sarah stopped abruptly. Victor made another attempt to get a better grip on Caitlyn, but in one wild flurry of arms and legs, her daughter knocked the gun right out of Victor's hand.

Sarah watched in shock as the weapon flew across the room and landed on the hardwood floor, sliding on a straight path toward the bed.

For a moment everyone froze. Then they all moved at once.

Victor let go of Caitlyn to grab for the gun.

As Caitlyn fell to the floor, Sarah ran to her, sweeping her up in her arms.

Jake kicked the gun farther away from Victor and tackled him. But Victor had at least forty pounds on Jake.

Sarah wanted to help, but she needed to protect Caitlyn first. Jake would want her to run. And that was what she would do. She turned toward the door, then gasped in horror when she realized the door was blocked.

There was another man facing her now—another gun pointing straight at her head. And on the man's wrist was the tattoo of a tiger. Rick, another Harvard boy gone bad.

Casting a quick look over her shoulder, Sarah saw Victor shove Jake against the far wall. Jake's head bounced against it so hard a picture frame came crashing down. Jake fell to the floor while Victor staggered to his feet, blood dripping from his mouth and nose, fury in his eyes.

Jake looked like he'd blacked out, Sarah thought as she saw his eyes flutter closed. It was over. There was no way she could escape now. They were going to die.

"Should I shoot her?" Rick asked.

"No, I want the pleasure," Victor answered, wiping the blood from his mouth with the back of his hand. There was an evil light in his eyes as he looked at her. "First your baby, then you."

"You just got out of prison," she argued desperately. "You have your life back. If you kill me they'll track you down. You'll go back to jail."

Victor shook his head. "No one will ever know it was me. They'll think it was him. Everyone knows you were running from someone—who better than your ex-lover? Time to say good-bye, Jessica."

Sarah couldn't say a word. Fear paralyzed her throat. There was not a damn thing she could do to stop him. Or was there?

She pressed Caitlyn's tiny head against her breast. "She's just a child. She's innocent. Let me put her down, and then you can kill me. Please, Victor. I'll do anything you want. Just don't kill my baby." She knew her pleas were falling on deaf ears, but she had to try. If Victor had one ounce of humanity in him, he'd let Caitlyn go. But as she looked into his eyes, she knew that whatever humanity he'd had was long gone.

"She has your blood, the blood of my enemy." Victor bent down to pick up the gun that had slid halfway under the bed.

She turned back toward Rick, hoping to find some compassion in his eyes, but they were ice-cold. The man had no heart, no soul. He'd spent just as many years in prison as Victor had. There was no way he would let her go. He would have killed her already if Victor hadn't said he wanted to do it himself. "She's just a baby," she said helplessly.

Caitlyn began to cry again, obviously sensing Sarah's growing panic.

And then the unthinkable happened. Dylan came out of nowhere, ramming Rick from behind, sending the large man sprawling across the room, colliding with Victor. The two men got tangled up together.

The gun skittered out of Rick's hand, hitting Jake in the side of the leg.

Jake's eyes flew open, and he scrambled to his feet.

As Dylan went after Rick, Jake rushed Victor again.

With the doorway free and clear, Sarah ran from the room. She had to get Caitlyn to safety. To her shock Catherine was running up the stairs, determination in her eyes, a baseball bat in her hands.

"Take Caitlyn. Give me the bat," Sarah said.

"No way. She needs you, Jessica. You're her mother. Now get the hell out of here."

Catherine charged into the bedroom like a female warrior.

Sarah heard a thud, then a boom as a gun went off.

God, she prayed the bullet hadn't hit Jake or Dylan or Catherine. She covered Caitlyn's ear with her hand and raced toward the stairs. As much as she wanted to help, her first priority had to be Caitlyn. She had just reached the bottom of the stairs when her name was called.

"Sarah."

Her heart came to a thudding stop.

Jake stood at the top of the stairs. His face was bloodied and bruised, but his eyes were triumphant. "Victor is dead."

"What about—"

"Knocked out," Dylan said, dragging Catherine toward the stairs. "Thanks to our leadoff hitter here. Someone call nine-one-one. I want to make sure that guy doesn't wake up." Dylan headed back toward the bedroom as Catherine dashed down the stairs past Sarah, heading for the phone in the living room.

Jake walked down the stairs, his gaze never leaving his daughter. Caitlyn was still crying, her face buried against Sarah's breast.

Jake looked like there were a million things he wanted to say, but no words crossed his lips. His hand came to rest gently on Caitlyn's back. He closed his eyes as if he couldn't believe he was touching his child again.

Sarah felt her eyes fill with tears. She was sure Jake wanted to rip Caitlyn out of her arms and take her into his own protective embrace. But he wouldn't do that to his child. He wouldn't scare or hurt Caitlyn by taking her away from her mother—the woman who had also betrayed him.

Instead, in a move that reminded her exactly why she had loved him so much, Jake put his arms around both of them, pulling Sarah close, keeping Caitlyn between them. His forehead touched hers. She closed her eyes at the tender gesture. They were safe. They were back together—at least for the moment.

"Look who I found," Catherine said, leading a dazed Teresa into the living room. "She was tied up in the kitchen."

"Oh, my God!" Sarah whispered. Teresa had always been a short, scrappy brunette, but she looked even tougher now with a black eye and a bump the size of a golf ball on her forehead. "What did they do to you?"

"I would have gotten away if they hadn't double-teamed me," Teresa complained. "At least I got a few punches in. I'm sorry, Sarah. I went outside to the garbage early this morning and they came up behind me. They told me they were only letting me live so I could keep the baby alive until you got here. That's when I took a swing at one of them. I guess he hit me harder than he intended, because when I woke up, I was alone and tied up in the kitchen. I heard Caitlyn screaming upstairs. It scared the shit out of me. But Catherine says they're dead—or at least one of them is."

"Victor is dead. The other one Catherine took out with a baseball bat. I didn't do anything except grab Caitlyn." Sarah realized that she had always felt so alone, but today her friends had risked their lives to save her and her daughter.

"Hey, I saw you," Jake said abruptly, his gaze on Teresa. He pointed a finger at her. "You were in the hospital outside of Sarah's room a couple of days ago. I thought you were waiting for someone, but you were watching me."

"You were there?" Sarah asked in amazement.

Teresa nodded. "I saw the report of the accident on the news, and I came to see how you were. I left Caitlyn with my neighbor just for an hour. When I got to the hospital and realized you had amnesia, I wasn't sure what to do. You never told me who was after you except that it was a guy, and when I saw him," she said, tipping her head toward Jake, "I didn't know who he was. I decided it was safer to just keep Caitlyn with me until you got your memory back. You told me not to tell anyone no matter what happened. But maybe I should have."

Sarah shook her head. "You did the right thing. I didn't get my memory back until this morning, when Jake found Victor's picture on the Internet. I'm really sorry you got hurt, Teresa. I knew I was putting you in danger. I shouldn't have done it."

"Don't say that. You were forced off the side of a cliff. If you'd had Caitlyn with you, who knows what would have happened? It was my fault they got in here today. I should have been more careful."

As Teresa finished speaking, Sarah heard sirens in the distance.

"The police," Jake muttered. "Take Caitlyn into the living room." He gave Sarah a gentle push.

She hesitated. "Jake—did you kill Victor? Or did Dylan?"

"I did," he said calmly. "We were fighting for the gun and it went off. The bullet hit him in the heart— if he even had a heart."

"I can't believe he's dead. Are you sure?"

"Positive. You can take a look at him when the coroner brings him out, but right now you need to stay with Caitlyn."

"I don't want you to go to jail. This was my fight.

Victor was my enemy. You're the one who needs to take Caitlyn. I'll say I killed Victor in self-defense. I'll put the gun in my hand, cover your fingerprints with mine." Her mind raced with what else should be done to protect Jake.

Jake's gaze searched hers in amazement. "You want to lie for me?"

"Well, you know I'm pretty good at it," she said, trying to make a joke, but she choked on a sob.

"Don't tell any more lies, Sarah. It's time for the truth."

"Not at your expense."

"It's going to be all right. It was self-defense."

She shook her head at his naïveté. He didn't know what he was talking about. He'd never been on the wrong side of the law. She had. "You believe the system will work, that justice will be served, but that doesn't always happen, Jake. Sometimes the bad guys win."

He cupped her chin with his hand. "And sometimes the good guys do. Trust me. For once in your life, Sarah, trust me."

"I do, but—"

Before she could finish they heard heavy footsteps on the porch. The police and paramedics had arrived. It was time to officially end her life on the run.

Chapter Twenty-two

"Hell of a day," Dylan said as he joined Jake on the back deck of Teresa's house just before nine o'clock that night. "Are you all right?"

Jake glanced down at his daughter in his arms and smiled. "Better than ever."

The past ten hours had been filled with grueling questions from both the local police and the feds, but he had finally been released. He'd come straight back to Teresa's house, and now he was right where he wanted to be. Caitlyn had one hand on his shoulder and the other hand on the bottle of milk she was sucking down. She stared up at him with complete trust and love. He didn't know if she remembered him or if she was just happy with her bottle, but whatever the reason for her joy, he was thrilled. His daughter was safe, and he had her in his arms, where she belonged.

"I picked up some food," Dylan said. "If you're hungry. It's inside."

"Maybe later. Is Sarah back yet?"

"No. She's still down at the station."

Jake was sorry to hear that. He wondered why they were keeping her so long. She hadn't even been in the room when he'd shot Victor. He hoped to God that Sarah wasn't right about the justice system not always being just. "I wish they'd release her," he said aloud.

"There was a time when you would have wanted them to lock her up and throw away the key."

"It's more complicated now," he muttered.

"I know. The feds want Sarah to retrace her steps since she disappeared out of Witness Protection eight years ago," Dylan replied. "I'm sure they also want her to help them link Victor to some of the other deaths in his circle of friends." Dylan sat down in the chair across from Jake. "I think Sarah is going to get some unexpected help in that regard."

"What do you mean?"

"I just checked on the condition of Victor's buddy, Rick Adams. He has a concussion, but he's awake. Apparently when he learned that Victor was dead, he was eager to talk about how Victor had killed off a bunch of people, including that guy you tangled with earlier, Shane Hollis. That should back up your self-defense argument." Dylan paused, frowning at him. "By the way, you should have let me tell them I killed Victor. No one else would have known. We were the only ones in the room—well, except for Catherine, but she wouldn't have told."

"I would have known," Jake snapped back. "For God's sake, I'm not going to let you go to prison for me. What the hell kind of brother do you think I am?"

"You have a kid to take care of. I don't have anyone. You have a lot more to lose than me."

"I don't lie. I don't shirk my responsibility. I wouldn't let Sarah take the fall for me, and I certainly wouldn't let you."

Dylan appeared surprised by his statement. "Sarah offered to take the fall for you?"

"Yeah, before the police got there."

"That seems out of character, but I guess neither one of us really knows who she is, do we?"

Jake was about to agree, but the words wouldn't come. He'd learned a lot about Sarah in the past few days, more than he'd learned in the entire two years that they were together. And now that he knew about her past, her behavior made a lot more sense. Still, he wasn't quite ready to talk about Sarah with Dylan. He decided to change the subject. "I don't think I said thank-you for saving my ass."

"Sure you have—about a dozen times. And you saved your own ass. I was just your wingman."

"If you hadn't come in when you did, we'd all be dead."

"Finally, my timing was right." Dylan's gaze moved to Caitlyn, then back to Jake. "You look good doing that. Like a dad."

"I'm not sure I know how to be a father. We certainly didn't have a good example."

"You'll figure it out. You have a heart. Our own father didn't. You actually love your kid."

"More than I ever imagined. I wasn't sure I'd ever see her again. I hope to God she never remembers being held or taunted by that bastard. When I saw him with his gun at her head, I wanted to kill him."

"He had the gun at her head?" Dylan echoed.

Jake nodded grimly, still remembering that moment when he'd run into the bedroom and seen his daughter's life in jeopardy. "But this little angel here, she knocked the gun out of his hand and started screaming. I tackled him, but his buddy showed up and distracted me, and the next thing I knew I was halfway to unconscious. Then you came in. I hope Caitlyn doesn't remember what she went through."

"She won't. She's forgotten already. Look at her. She's happy as can be."

"I think the bottle might have more to do with her good mood than me."

"Her hair is darker than I remember," Dylan commented.

"Sarah colored it so it would match her own hair and they would look like mother and daughter."

"That woman is always thinking. I'll give her that."

Jake didn't reply. His feelings were too conflicted, too confused, and he already knew Dylan's opinion on the subject of Sarah. He just wanted to savor this time with Caitlyn. Sooner rather than later he'd have to think about what was going to happen next, but not at this moment.

"How are Catherine and Teresa?" he asked, changing the subject. He was thankful the cops had let the women watch Caitlyn at the house while the rest of them had gone down to the station. Neither Catherine nor Teresa had seen Sarah in years, and yet when she'd needed them, they'd come through. Sarah had probably never expected that to happen.

"Teresa has a mild concussion," Dylan said. "She apparently isn't the type of woman to let that get her down. She's a female boxer, you know."

"No kidding? She's not that big."

"That's what I said, but she told me that she's very quick and crafty," Dylan added with a grin. "She's a pistol, that girl. They have very different personalities, the three of them."

"Catherine doesn't seem to be short on courage either. She did quite a job with that bat. She took Rick Adams out with one swing."

"She shocked the hell out of me," Dylan admitted. "I can't quite figure her out. She's a vegetarian psychic with a menagerie of pets. She is innocent and wise, hard and soft all at the same time."

Jake caught something in his brother's voice he hadn't heard in a while—interest. "You got a thing for Catherine?" he asked in surprise.

Dylan snorted. "I don't think so. She actually claims to have had a vision about my future, something that involves two women."

Jake laughed. "That sounds right up your alley."

"Yeah, well, Catherine didn't make it sound fun,

more like ominous. She has this dark side to her. You should see the stuff she paints—abstracts of evil, the essence of nightmares. It's crazy."

"I think I'll pass. I've had enough nightmares to last me a lifetime."

Dylan leaned forward, resting his arms on his knees. "I know I was hard on Sarah. I guess there are two and sometimes three sides to every story. Something I should have learned a long time ago, considering I'm supposed to be an objective journalist."

Jake raised an eyebrow. "You sound like you've changed your mind."

"I wouldn't go that far. Maybe I understand her a little better. What she did to you—I still think it was wrong." He paused, giving Jake a thoughtful look. "But my opinion isn't important. What do you think now that you know everything?"

Jake shook his head. "I'm done thinking for the night. I just want to enjoy being with my daughter." He pulled Caitlyn's blanket more tightly around her. The heat lamp on the deck provided warmth, but it was getting a little chilly. He could take her inside now. He'd wanted to keep her away from the cleanup and the chaos inside the house, but things had quieted down.

"I'm tired, too. I'm going to turn in." Dylan got to his feet. "Teresa generously offered me the couch in her office. She also moved the crib into the master bedroom for you or Sarah or both of you." He cleared his throat. "Look, whatever you decide to do about Sarah, I'm behind you—one hundred percent."

"Thanks. The truth is, I don't know what to do. Sarah lied to me so many times, I don't know if I can forgive her. I don't know if I can trust her. But I also don't know if I can stay away from her," he confessed. "She's got her hooks in me. I'm not even sure I want her to let go. And then there's Caitlyn—how can I deprive her of her mother? When Mom left it almost killed us. How can I do that to my own child?"

Dylan stared back at him. "I think there's another story as to why Mom left—why she stayed away and never once tried to see us. I've thought so for a long time." He gazed down at the ground for a moment, then back up at Jake. "Catherine told me that I investigate other people's lives so I don't have to look too closely at my own past. That might be more perceptive than psychic, but it's still right on the money. I'm thinking about tracking down Mom. I've been thinking about it for a while."

"Really?" Jake asked, not too happy about the thought. "I don't think that's a good idea."

"Why not? I'm getting good at finding people."

"You might not want to find her. She left a long time ago, twenty-three years. She could have returned at any moment. She didn't. Aside from a few Christmas cards and random birthday presents, she didn't want us in her life. How could finding her now possibly make things better for any of us?"

Dylan shrugged. "Yeah, you're probably right. I'll think about it later. Tomorrow I need to get home and go back to work before I lose my job." He stretched his arms over his head and let out a yawn. "Anything else I can do for you tonight?"

"No, you've done more than enough," Jake said. "The rest I have to do on my own."

Sarah peeked into the master bedroom on the second floor just before ten o'clock Saturday night. She couldn't believe the police had finally let her go. She'd been afraid they would keep her overnight, and that by the time they released her Jake and Caitlyn would be gone. But here they were—the two people she loved more than life. She blew out a breath of relief.

Jake was stretched out on the bed on his side. Caitlyn was cuddled up next to him in the middle of the bed, her thumb in her mouth, her blanket in her hand. She was fast asleep. Jake stroked her forehead and whispered to her as he watched her breathe in and out.

The tender sight broke what was left of Sarah's heart. Jake had his daughter back, and he would never let her go. He was a good man. He was a great father. And he deserved to be with his child. Where did that leave her?

Jake saw her standing in the doorway. He waved to her to come in. She moved across the room, stopping by the side of the bed across from him.

"She called me Da-da," Jake said, a smile on his lips. "She remembered me."

Sarah smiled back at him, her eyes blurring with tears. She wouldn't tell him that Caitlyn called every man she saw Da-da. She wouldn't take this moment away from him.

"Of course she remembered you," Sarah said instead. "How could she forget her father?" She had spent the last few hours worrying about whether Caitlyn was at home screaming for her, but it was clear Caitlyn was happy with her dad.

"She's grown up so much," Jake said. "She's like a little person now."

Sarah sat down on the corner of the bed and gazed at her daughter's face. In sleep Caitlyn truly looked like an angel sent from heaven. Or maybe she'd been sent to save Sarah from herself. "Giving birth to Caitlyn is the greatest thing I've ever done in my life. She's the best part of me."

"And me," Jake murmured.

"I never believed I'd have a family after what happened with Victor. Once I was on the run, living my life in disguise, I thought it would be impossible to have anything close to a normal life again. I didn't think I could trust another man, or that I could risk bringing a baby into my life. But you changed all that. The two years I spent with you were wonderful. You brought me back to life. You made me feel hope again."

Caitlyn squirmed a little in her sleep. Sarah crawled onto the bed, stretching out on the other side of her daughter. She put her hand on Caitlyn's forehead as her baby frowned and sucked on her thumb again. "I hope she isn't having a nightmare. She's been through so much today."

"With any luck she won't remember it."

Sarah gazed over at Jake. "I should have brought her back to you. I don't regret taking her when I did, because you weren't in town, and there was no one I could trust. I had to make that decision."

"Maybe at that moment. But in seven months, Sarah, there had to have been a time, an opportunity for you to find a way to reach me."

"I was too busy trying to survive on my own. I thought about calling you a million times, but I kept remembering how they killed Andy. I was afraid for you, and I loved Caitlyn so much. I knew what it was like to grow up without a mother."

"So did I," Jake said. "Did you think I could let Caitlyn grow up without a father? You were selfish, Sarah, and you put our child in danger."

"It wasn't fair to you," she agreed. "I was just in too deep. I didn't know how to get out of the mess I was in. I kept thinking that something would change and I'd find a way to get back to you, that it would just be temporary."

"That sounds like another lie you told yourself."

"More like a wish. I loved you, Jake." He looked away from her, but not before she saw something flare in his eyes. "When I met you, I was a lot older and a lot wiser than when I was with Victor. I wasn't looking for a fairy-tale prince anymore, but the truth is, I found one. You and I had great chemistry right from the start, but there was also an emotional connection between us. I loved that you were strong and protective when it came to your family, to your brother, to your grandmother. You cared about your work and your friends. You threw your mind and body into building a dream house for us. You had values, a sense of right and wrong. You understood responsibility. I knew that I couldn't let you get away. And that old optimistic part of myself that refuses to die told me to hang on to you as tightly as I could. I didn't believe that I could tell you the truth and keep you. I thought you would walk away. I honestly believed that."

Jake lifted his gaze to hers, but his expression was completely unreadable when he said, "We'll never know, will we?"

"No, we won't. But while I lied to you about my past, I never lied about my feelings. I was happy with you, the happiest I've ever been in my life. And I didn't want it to end, but it did. Because nothing good lasts forever."

"Nothing good built on a lie lasts forever," Jake corrected. "If you don't have a strong foundation, your house falls down. That's what happened to us. And I have to take some of the blame, because I never called you on any of the lies you told me. I never made you answer my questions. I'm a detail person in my work, but in my personal life I saw only the big picture. But you're free now, Sarah. Victor is dead. Just about everyone else in his group is dead. You don't have to be afraid anymore. You don't have to lie. You can be yourself."

"I'm not sure who I am anymore," she confessed. "I've been so many people and answered to so many names. I don't feel like Jessica or Samantha. I feel more like Sarah, but I made up that name, too."

"If you want to be Sarah, be Sarah. It's not your name that's important. It's who you are. It's living a life of truth. A life without fear."

She wondered if that was possible. "I've been scared for so long," she said. "I can't imagine going to bed at night and not having to worry about whether or not Victor is going to come after me. It's hard to believe he's dead."

"You looked at him. You saw him."

"I had to be sure, see him with my own eyes. It was still difficult to grasp."

"Now you can go on with your life."

"How?" she whispered. "How do I do that without you—without Caitlyn—because that's the way you want it to be, isn't it?"

Jake didn't answer for a long time. There was an expression in his eyes she couldn't decipher. "I don't know yet, Sarah."

Her heart sank. "I can't give up my child, Jake."

"I need some time to think about the future."

"How much time?"

"As much time as it takes," he said shortly. "You made your choices, Sarah, and I had to live with them. Now it's my turn. Right now I'd like to be alone with Caitlyn."

Sarah hesitated and then leaned over and kissed her daughter on the forehead. She rose from the bed and walked out of the room. After what she'd put Jake through, she owed him this night—but the rest would be a battle.

Chapter Twenty-three

Sarah paused in the doorway to the living room where Catherine and Teresa were eating pizza and catching up on their lives. As usual their conversation jumped back and forth between topics, Teresa eager to express each and every opinion in her head and Catherine trying to get a word in edgewise.

Listening to them took Sarah back to the past, when they'd gathered on Catherine's bed late at night and talked about what they were going to do when they grew up. Teresa had wanted to be an astronaut. Catherine had always wanted to be a painter. And when Sarah had seen her own future, she'd always pictured herself with a bunch of kids. The other girls had teased her about having no ambition, but creating a family had always been her dream. Neither Teresa nor Catherine had ever been part of a real family, at least not for any length of time. Teresa had been taken away from her single mother when she was two and didn't remember anyone. Catherine had never told them when or why she'd been taken from her parents, but Sarah had always known that something bad had happened. There was a dark sadness to Catherine that she couldn't quite hide, but she'd always refused to talk about her past.

Since Sarah had spent most of her life hiding her own history, she could hardly quarrel with Catherine's decision just to keep moving forward. Sometimes there was no point to looking back. Her big mistake had been to lie. She shouldn't have tried to be someone else. She should have had more confidence in herself.

"There you are," Teresa said, spotting her in the doorway. "Get in here, for God's sake. Are you all right? What did the cops say?"

Sarah moved into the room and sat down on the couch next to Catherine. "I have to go back in the morning to talk to some more people, but the bottom line is that I don't think any of us are going to be charged in Victor's death. The police seem to believe it was self-defense, and Rick has been talking about the other murders that Victor was involved in, so my fingers are crossed that it will be all right. I hope so, anyway. I certainly don't want to see Jake arrested for murder when all he did was try to protect me, nor do I want to go to jail. But I would rather it be me than anyone else." She paused. "How do you feel, Teresa?" She watched Teresa take the ice pack off her head with a grimace.

"Like a big Russian guy knocked me out with the butt of his gun," Teresa said dryly.

Sarah smiled. Teresa was a tough-talking, no-nonsense brunette who made up for her lack of height with a generous amount of bravado. She'd missed talking to Teresa—having her in her life. She should have left Chicago when Teresa wanted to go, but instead she'd chosen Victor—another bad mistake. She'd certainly made a lot of them.

"How are *you*?" Teresa asked.

"Not bad."

"Did you make things right with Jake?"

"I'm not sure I can."

"But you want to."

"I really do." She shook her head. "I don't know that he can forgive me for what I did."

"He sure as hell should forgive you. You were running for your life."

"With his child under my arm. He doesn't see it in quite the same light as me, and I can't blame him. I did put Caitlyn in danger. I can't deny that."

"She would have been in danger if you'd left her with Jake," Teresa said firmly. "Victor is the one to blame, not you. You did what you had to do."

"Okay, my turn," Catherine interrupted. "I want to know why you never got in touch with me, Jessica. I looked for you in Chicago. I stayed there for two weeks, searching the streets, talking to your friends."

"I sent you a note as soon as I could," Sarah said, knowing that what she'd done wasn't nearly enough. But at that point she truly had been running for her life.

"A cryptic note that you could have been forced to write at gunpoint."

"I was afraid to make contact with you again. And for a while I couldn't physically do it even if I wanted to. I was in Witness Protection. Then Victor sent Shane to kill me in the safe house. If he'd found me there, he could find me anywhere. I had to run. I had to stay in the shadows. I was afraid one wrong move would bring him straight to me, or to someone else I cared about."

"You told Andy. What did you think—that his comic-book superhero could protect you?" Catherine asked.

Sarah saw the pain in Catherine's eyes. So many of her decisions had hurt the people she loved. "I needed a new identity. Andy was the only one who could do that for me. But he died for it."

"He died because of Victor," Teresa put in again.

"He died because he helped me," Sarah said, "and because Victor thought Andy knew where I was. So many people have been hurt because of me, including the guards in the safe house who were supposed to protect me. And .then poor Mrs. Murphy got beaten up and Amanda got burned out of her apartment. I'm like a hurricane, bringing trouble in my wake."

"You could have brought it my way," Catherine repeated. "I would have helped you."

"You finally had what you wanted, the art school

scholarship, the glamorous life in New York. I didn't want to take that away from you. After a while, when things settled down, I thought about calling you, but I figured by then the damage had been done and nothing could be gained. You had your life, and I had mine, such as it was."

"She didn't call me either," Teresa interjected. "Which also pisses me off. You waited eight years to get back in touch, Jessica. Way too long."

"You were my family. And you were safe away from me. I wanted to keep it that way."

"But you let Jake into your life," Catherine pointed out. "You had to know it was a risk."

"I did know it. In the beginning I told myself it was a fling, a temporary thing, but he was too great to let go," she said with a helpless shrug. "I was being selfish hanging on to him. When I got pregnant—oh, my God, I was terrified. It was a complete accident. I had never intended to get that involved with any-one. But I couldn't get rid of my baby. I couldn't walk away from Jake. That's when I started telling myself lies—like, It's been five years and Victor has probably forgotten about you. And my other favorite—Victor is in jail; he can't hurt you now. I was an idiot. I never even considered that he could get out on parole after serving a third of his sentence." She let out a sigh. "I don't expect either of you to understand or for-give me."

"I'm not judging you," Catherine said. "I just wish I could have helped you, Jessica. I always thought of you like my little sister. And I never stopped worrying about you. I saw you in my dreams. For months I could hear your voice calling out to me. I could see you running down this street late at night, and all I could think about was how much you hated the dark."

"That was after I ran away from the safe house," Sarah said slowly. She'd forgotten about Catherine's visions. She had had no idea that Catherine would have spent so much time worrying about her. They hadn't seen each other in over a year when she'd disappeared from Chicago. She'd just assumed that Catherine would go on with her life.

"I knew you were in danger. I felt terrible that I couldn't help," Catherine added.

"Well, you helped me today. If you hadn't hit Rick over the head with that bat, we could all be dead now. Where did you get it, anyway?"

"Teresa's hall closet. I was going for an umbrella, but I found something better. Dylan had told me to stay put, to call the cops, but I knew he was walking into a volatile situation. I couldn't stand by and do nothing."

"I never thought you had that in you," Teresa said, amazement in her voice. "You, Catherine, were always such a pacifist, peace, love, joy, harmony. What happened to that?"

"I'm not a pacifist when it comes to people I care about. By the way, what's with going back to your old name, Tracy?" she asked, turning her attention to Teresa. "You hated that name."

"I've been trying it out, but I think I'm going to stick with Teresa."

"You two always thought that changing your names, or pretending to be someone else, would make a difference," Catherine said. "It was a stupid game you played. You can't hide from yourself. Don't you get that?"

Sarah glanced over at Teresa and saw the same sheepish expression in her eyes. "We get it," Sarah said. "It just took us a while."

"A long while," Teresa agreed. "So what am I going to call you now?"

She thought for a moment. "Sarah. I'm going to be Sarah, because that's who I am to Caitlyn and to Jake, and with any luck I can keep them both in my life."

"You will," Teresa said with confidence.

"And you're keeping us, too," Catherine said firmly. "We're family. And now that we're back together it's going to stay that way. Besides, someone needs to keep you two out of trouble." Catherine stood up and opened her arms, sending them both an expectant look.

Teresa groaned. "We are not doing a group hug."

"Yes, we are," Catherine insisted. She went over to Teresa and threw her arms around her. Teresa squealed in protest.

Sarah moved to join them. For the first time in a long time, everything was right in her world. She wondered how long it would last.

* * *

Sarah's optimism faltered with the dawn of a new day. She'd received a call earlier that morning from a police detective in Los Angeles who wanted to talk to her in regard to Shane Hollis's murder and the fire at her apartment building. He'd insisted that she come down to Los Angeles for an interview. She'd had no choice but to agree. The more crimes she could pin on Victor, the easier it would be to keep the police from being interested in prosecuting Jake for Victor's murder. So far Jake seemed to be in the clear—so much in the clear that the local cops had said he could return to San Francisco. And, of course, Jake wanted to take Caitlyn with him.

He hadn't asked her permission. He'd just started making a list of what he would need to take care of Caitlyn once he got home. Then he'd headed out to the store to pick up supplies. Those supplies were now packed in his car, and he was waiting on the sidewalk for Sarah to bring Caitlyn to him.

Everything was changing. One chapter of her life was over and another was beginning. She'd done this before, started over, but she hated having to do it again. This time she really had no choice. She wasn't the only one making the decisions.

She moved slowly down the porch steps, dread and worry weighting each step. She knew she had to let Jake take Caitlyn home. He deserved time alone with his daughter, and Caitlyn needed to be somewhere settled and safe. Sarah also knew she had to go to LA and finish cleaning up the mess she'd made eight years ago. Those were the facts. The facts sucked.

How on earth could she let Caitlyn go?

Aside from the past few days, they'd never been apart. And having been apart had only made Sarah want to keep her daughter at her side for every second of the rest of her life.

Caitlyn played with Sarah's hair as she walked down the path to the sidewalk. She liked to twist her fingers in the curls, a happy little game that always made her smile.

Sarah paused by the car and turned back around so Caitlyn could see Teresa and Catherine on the porch. "Say bye-bye," she told Caitlyn.

"Bye-bye," Caitlyn said with a cheery smile, mimicking her mother's wave.

Sarah would have liked to play the moment out, but Jake was waiting. As she turned to him, he held out his arms.

"I'll take her now." His tone was quiet and determined, as if he were afraid she was going to make a scene.

She hesitated for a long moment, her arms instinctively tightening around Caitlyn's small body. For seven months it had been her and Caitlyn against the world. But for those same months Jake had sweated out the nights alone in fear and worry.

She had to let him take Caitlyn. He was a good man. He was a good father.

She was the one who had screwed up. She was the

one who had brought danger to their lives. She'd made one mistake after another. And now it was time to do the right thing—the only thing. Still, she stalled. "She likes to sleep with her blanket at night, and if she's fussy, you can read her a story. She likes the butterfly book or the book with the pink bears on the front."

"I got it."

"Oh, and if she gets really cranky, she likes the sound of the vacuum cleaner."

Jake nodded. "Vacuum cleaner, right."

"Applesauce. That's her favorite after-dinner snack."

"You wrote it all down, Sarah."

Sarah kissed Caitlyn on the cheek, tears welling in her eyes and streaming down her face as she said, "I love you, baby. But you need to go with your daddy."

Caitlyn's tiny hands cupped Sarah's face. Her daughter had no idea what was happening.

"Mama cry," Caitlyn said, wiping her hand across Sarah's wet face. "Mama sad."

"I'm okay. I'll see you soon, baby," Sarah said, her heart breaking in two. With one last tight squeeze, she handed Caitlyn over to Jake.

Caitlyn, God bless her, gave Jake a happy, trusting smile, not realizing that he was about to take her away from her mother.

Jake stroked Caitlyn's curls as he looked at Sarah. The pulse in his neck was beating fast. "You'll see her tomorrow, you know. I'm not going to keep you out of her life. I wouldn't do that to you."

"I know. It's just difficult. We still haven't talked about how we're going to take care of her in the future. There's so much we haven't discussed. This is happening so fast. I'm not ready."

"We'll talk when you get to San Francisco." Jake cleared his throat. "It's going to be all right. We'll work it out."

"Drive carefully," she said.

"I will." Jake put Caitlyn into her seat and strapped her in. When he got out of the car he gave Sarah a reassuring look. "Don't worry, Sarah. She'll be safe with me."

"I know that. I trust you. I do."

Jake started to say something and then changed his mind. He walked around the car and got in. He started the engine and pulled away quickly, giving her no chance to beg him to stay.

Catherine and Teresa came down the path. Sarah saw the questions in their eyes. They didn't understand her actions, but they would support her anyway. "I have to give him this time. I owe him."

"You're so strong now," Catherine commented. "The little girl who used to crawl into my bed at night is all grown-up and braver than I could ever be."

"I'm not brave. I'm really not." But Sarah waited until Jake's car had turned the corner before she sank into Catherine's loving arms and cried her heart out.

"It will be all right," Catherine said soothingly.

"You'll figure out a way to make it all work. Jake seems like a good guy," Teresa put in. "And if he tries to take sole custody from you, we'll kick his butt."

"He is a good guy," Sarah said, sniffing as she tried to pull herself together. "He's the best. I ruined everything. I had the perfect family."

"Oh, sweetie," Catherine said with a sad smile. "Don't you know yet that perfect doesn't exist?"

"I still want it to."

"Cinderella and the prince—your favorite fairy tale," Teresa said. "How about we get some breakfast before I drive you to LA?"

"Are you sure you want to do that? I can rent a car."

"Do you actually have an ID?" Teresa asked.

"Come to think of it, no, but I do have cash." And now she remembered where she'd gotten the cash. She'd never put any of her paychecks into the bank. She'd cashed them and kept the money in the heater vent with her IDs. She wondered what it would be like to live her life above ground again, to be able to walk freely down the street, not be concerned whether anyone was following her. She couldn't even imagine it.

"I'll drive you," Teresa said. "It will be fun. A road trip."

"I'm coming, too," Catherine said.

"I don't know why you're both being so nice to me." Sarah shook her head. "I don't deserve it."

"Yes, you do. You're a good person," Catherine stated firmly. "Don't forget that. Every decision you made, you made out of love."

Before Sarah could reply a car came around the corner, a very familiar car. She straightened in alarm.

Jake pulled up in front of them and jumped out of the driver's seat. He dashed across the sidewalk.

"What's wrong?" Sarah asked as he jogged toward her. "Did you forget something?"

"Yes, dammit. You. I forgot you." He grabbed her by the arms and kissed her long and hard on the lips. "I can't leave you behind. I can't do it."

She couldn't believe what she was hearing. "You still want me?"

"With every breath I take." His eyes burned with desire and need. "You are connected to me, Sarah. I can't let you go. I don't know how I thought I could."

"Oh, Jake," she whispered. "How can you forgive me?"

"Because I can. Because I want to. Because you're the woman I love."

"Still? After everything?"

"The truth is that I never stopped loving you," he said, gazing into her eyes. "Even when I hated you, I loved you. You got under my skin. You haunted my dreams."

She put her hands on his face and let all of her emotions show. There was no more need to be guarded, to try to protect her heart. She'd already given it to him. "I love you, too, Jake. I always did. I never lied about that. If you'll give me a second chance, I'll do better."

"So will I." He pulled her up against his chest. "It wasn't all you, Sarah. I have to share some of the blame for not wanting to rock the boat. But we can start over. We can get it right. We know who we are now. The last few days I fell in love with the real you, the one who couldn't hide from me. There are no more lies between us. And that's the way it's going to stay."

"I can't believe you still want me."

"I do. Forever."

She kissed him lovingly on the mouth, tasting the truth on his lips, and nothing had ever tasted sweeter.

"I have to go to LA," she said, breaking away. "Damn, I can't believe I have to go to LA now."

"Caitlyn and I will go with you, and when you're done there we'll go home together. We'll finish building our house. And when we both know the time is right, we'll get married."

"That plan sounds perfect," she said as he kissed her again and again and again. Finally, laughing and breathless, she pulled away. "Caitlyn," she started to say.

"I've got her," Teresa said, holding Caitlyn in her arms. "Although, if this is going to get X-rated, you might want to take it inside."

Sarah smiled as tears of pure joy now filled her eyes. She took Caitlyn from Teresa, and she and Jake wrapped their arms around their daughter. They were going to be a family after all.

"Well, Sarah," Catherine said, "I think you finally got your happily ever after."

"I think I did," she said, meeting Jake for another kiss, another promise for the future.

Epilogue

Two months later

Jake and Sarah said their wedding vows just before sunset in the garden of a beautiful mountain lodge overlooking Lake Tahoe. Teresa stood up for Sarah, while Dylan offered his services as best man. Catherine held a squirmy, giggling Caitlyn on her lap while the minister blessed the union between Caitlyn's parents. It was a damn Hallmark card moment, Dylan thought, as he watched his brother and Sarah share their first kiss as husband and wife.

He followed them down the aisle and was the first to offer his big brother a hug and congratulations in the receiving line. Then he kissed Sarah on the cheek. "You got yourself a good guy. Treat him right."

"I know it," she said, a loving smile on her lips as she glanced back at Jake. "He's the best."

"So are you," Jake replied.

"You two are sickeningly happy," Dylan said. "I'm going to get a drink—a strong one."

"Your turn next," Jake said with a grin.

"Dream on, brother. Not everyone wants to have a ball and chain strapped around his ankle. No offense, Sarah."

She laughed, as Dylan had known she would. In the past couple of months he'd come to know his new sister-in-law a lot better, and she had an amazingly good sense of humor, especially about herself. She'd stripped the murky brown color from both her hair and Caitlyn's, returning them to their natural blond beauty. She had also decided to keep the name Sarah and, in fact, had legally changed her name to Sarah Jessica Sanders, combining her present, her past, and her future. Since Jake had forgiven her for putting him through seven months of torture, Dylan had forced himself to let go of any lingering resentment. As long as Jake was happy, that was really all that mattered.

"Thanks for being my best man," Jake said.

As he left the receiving line, Dylan wandered over to the bar, grabbed a seat, and ordered a shot of Jack Daniels. He enjoyed the burn as the liquor slid down his throat. After draining the glass, he immediately ordered another. He didn't like weddings, and usually avoided them at all costs, but this one he hadn't been able to miss. He wa thankful that he'd finished his formal duties as best man. He just had to get through the next hour before he could call it a night.

Glancing across the room, he watched Jake and Sarah share their first dance on the back deck of the Woodlake Mountain Lodge. In the glow of candlelight and the backdrop of the purple-blue twilight sky, they looked exceedingly happy, as if the past year hadn't tested their love in every possible way. But they'd come through the bad times. From here on out, it would be nothing but smooth sailing—at least Dylan hoped so. He smiled as Teresa brought Caitlyn to the dance floor. Jake's eighteen-month-old blond angel was the hit of the wedding, and as usual Caitlyn wanted to be part of the action. Jake swung his baby daughter into his arms, and the three of them danced together like the family they were.

Dylan tossed another shot down his throat, pushing back the ridiculous thought that he was jealous of their happiness. While he loved his brother, he did not yearn for marriage and a family of his own. Having grown up in a broken home, he didn't intend to repeat the experience. Although he hoped Jake and Sarah would make it, and that they would beat the odds of divorce.

A cool evening breeze blew through the open patio doors, drawing goose bumps down his arms. However, it wasn't the wind that put his nerves on edge; it was the woman who slid onto the bar stool next to his.

"Are you drinking to your brother's happiness or to the demise of yet another bachelor?" Catherine Hilliard asked.

He ordered another shot as he considered the woman next to him. Catherine had cleaned up pretty well since their first meeting. There were no paint spatters on her clothes today, and instead of bare feet, she had on a pair of very high heels. She wore a gorgeous, sexy black dress with a low-cut halter top that showed off her beautiful breasts. He loved the way the freckles danced across her chest. He had the sudden urge to see whether she had freckles all over her body.

He tugged on his tie, feeling tightness in his chest at the very bad ideas flooding through his brain. Catherine was an old friend of Sarah's and, as far as he was concerned, off-limits, not to mention the fact that she was a little on the crazy side. He was grateful for her help in getting Sarah and Jake back together, but he didn't intend to have any kind of personal relationship with her.

"Hello," Catherine said pointedly. "You're staring."

"You're stunning," he replied, unable to stop the words from crossing his lips.

She gave him a quick smile. "That's a good start to the conversation. The wedding was lovely, didn't you think? Jake and Sarah make a good match. I think they have a chance."

"A chance, huh? That's an enthusiastic endorsement," he said dryly, hearing the same note of cynicism that echoed through his own head.

Catherine shrugged. "I haven't seen a lot of happy marriages in my time."

"Neither have I. So, how have you been? Painting a lot?"

"Every night. I even painted you."

He raised an eyebrow. "No kidding? Do I want to see it?"

Her smiled widened. "Maybe I'll show you sometime."

"I don't get down the coast much."

Catherine accepted a glass of champagne from the bartender. "I brought the painting with me. I wanted to work on it some more. I'm staying here at the lodge for a few days. The mountains are beautiful. The air is clear and fresh, and everywhere I look the view is dazzling. It's not the ocean, but the lake has a peacefulness about it, a depth and a secrecy that appeal to me."

Dylan didn't see the lake the way she did, but he had always enjoyed Tahoe. For years he and Jake had come here with friends or family members to escape the overbearing presence of their father, who luckily for them never left the city. Dylan wasn't surprised Jake had wanted to get married here. It was a good start to his new life, although Jake and Sarah wouldn't be staying in Tahoe long. They were taking a late-night flight to Hawaii, where they would spend the week with Caitlyn, as well as Teresa, who'd offered to babysit. Dylan thought having a baby and a babysitter along on a honeymoon would cramp his style, but neither Sarah nor Jake had wanted to be away from Caitlyn for even a day.

"What about you?" Catherine asked, interrupting his thoughts. "Are you staying past the weekend?"

"I leave in the morning."

"Are you sure?"

His gaze narrowed. "What does that mean?"

Her dark blue eyes grew mysterious. "Do you remember what I told you about the two women entering your life? It starts here."

"What starts here?" he began, and then quickly backtracked. "You know what? I don't want to know. I don't believe in your psychic visions. I'm sorry. That's just the way it is."

"I understand," she said, raising her glass to her lips.

He didn't like the look in her eyes. He told himself to forget what she'd said. She was just trying to yank his chain.

Someone took the seat on the other side of him. A waft of familiar perfume made his head turn. The brunette gave him a big smile. Damn, he was in trouble.

Catherine leaned over and whispered in his ear, "Be careful, Dylan. She's one of them."

"Who's the other one?" he asked as she walked away. Catherine didn't reply. It didn't matter. He had a feeling he already knew the answer. But he was not going to let Catherine's words get him going. He'd just finished solving one mystery. He had no intention of starting another one.

One woman will bring about his
downfall. . . . Another will save him.
Catherine Hilliard's vision for
Dylan Sanders comes true in
Barbara Freethy's next exciting novel
of romantic suspense

SILENT FALL

Available from Onyx in April 2008

An excerpt follows. . . .

Golden Gate Park, San Francisco

She was going to die. The terrifying thought made her stumble, her spiked heel catching in a crack in the pavement. She fell forward, breaking her fall with her hands. Tiny pebbles of cement burned into her palms and her knees. For a moment she was tempted to quit. She was so cold and so tired, but if she stopped, he'd catch her, and there would be no tomorrow, no second chance.

Forcing herself back to her feet, she pulled off her broken shoes and headed deeper into the park. The grass was wet beneath her feet, the midnight fingers of fog covering everything within reach with a damp mist. Her hair curled around her face as the wet spray mixed with the tears streaming down her cheeks.

She'd never been a crier, but this was too much. She'd never felt so alone or in such mortal danger.

Everywhere she turned, he followed. She couldn't seem to get away. How did he keep finding her?

Even now she could hear the footsteps behind her, the crack of twigs, the sound of a distant car. Was it him?

She probably should have stayed on the city streets, but she'd thought the tall trees and the thick bushes of the park would offer her protection, a place to hide. Now she realized how desolate the area was at night. There were no phone booths, no people, no businesses to run into. She was completely on her own.

She gasped and stopped abruptly as a shadowy figure came out of the undergrowth. Her heart thudded against her chest. The man walked toward her, one hand outstretched. His clothes were old and torn, and his face was covered with a heavy beard. He wore a baseball cap, and a backpack was slung over one shoulder. He was probably one of the homeless people who set up camp in the park at night. Or maybe not . . .

"Hey baby, give me a kiss," he said in a drunken slur.

"Leave me alone." She put up a hand to ward him off, but he kept moving forward.

"I'm just being friendly. Come on now, sweetheart."

Turning, she ran as fast as she could in the other direction, hearing him call after her. She didn't know whether he was following her, and she was too terrified to look, so she left the sidewalk and moved deeper into the park, looking for a little corner in which to hide. Her side was cramping and her feet were soaked. She desperately needed to find some sanctuary. Branches scraped her bare arms and face, but she kept going. It was so dark in the heavy brush that she could barely see a foot in front of her. Tall trees and fog had completely obliterated the moonlight.

Fortunately, she had her hand out ahead of her when she ran into a cement wall that rose several stories in the air. She must have hit the side of one of the park buildings. Pausing, she caught her breath and listened. She could hear nothing but her own ragged breathing. Maybe she was safe, at least for the moment.

Leaning back against the cold cement, she pondered her next move, but she didn't know what to do, how to escape. She was out of options.

How had she come to this—running for her life, all alone? This was not how it was supposed to go. This was Dylan's fault. He'd put her in this situation, and dammit, where the hell was he?

But she couldn't count on him to rescue her. She had to find a way out on her own. She couldn't let things end like this. She'd fought for her life before, and she'd won. She would do it again.

Her heart stopped as a nearby branch snapped in two. A confident male whistle pierced the silent night. Whoever was coming didn't care whether she heard him or not. The bushes in front of her slowly parted. Terror ran through her body. There was nowhere left to run.

AVAILABLE NEXT MONTH

From *USA Today*
BESTSELLING AUTHOR
BARBARA FREETHY

Double the Romance...
Double the Suspense...

SILENT FALL

Dylan Saunders is attending a wedding in
the mountains when a former lover
appears out of nowhere, luring him into
the woods, then leaving him there,
drugged and disoriented. When he wakes,
the woman has disappeared and Dylan is
accused of her murder. Now he must rely
on the help of a beautiful psychic haunted
by her own dark past—and find the killer
before the killer finds them.

Available wherever books are sold or at penguin.com

From the *USA Today* bestselling author
of *Taken*

PLAYED

Barbara Freethy

Charmingly diabolical con man
Evan Chadwick is back in another blockbuster
romantic suspense novel.

FBI Agent J.T. McIntyre is determined to catch
the thief who conned his father and destroyed
his family. He wants revenge as much as
justice, and he won't let anyone stand in his
way—not even beautiful art historian
Christina Alberti, whose secrets make him
wonder just which side she's on...

**Available wherever books are sold or
at penguin.com**

From *USA Today* bestselling author
Barbara Freethy

TAKEN

TAKEN BY A PROMISE...

Kayla Sheridan has longed for love, marriage, and a family.
Now, miraculously, after a whirlwind courtship with the man
of her dreams, she is his wife. But on their wedding night he
vanishes, leaving Kayla with the bitter realization that her
desire has made her an easy mark for deception.

TAKEN BY SURPRISE...

Nick Granville has an ingrained sense of honor and an intense
desire to succeed in building the world's most challenging
high-tech bridges. But when he crosses paths with a ruthless
con man, he's robbed of everything he values, including his
identity. With nothing left to lose, he'll risk any danger to
clear his name and reclaim his life.

TAKING BACK THEIR LIVES...

Thrown together by fate, and endangering their hearts, Kayla
and Nick embark on a desperate journey toward the truth—
to uncover the mysterious motives of an ingenious and
seductive stranger who boasts he can't be caught...and to
reveal the shocking secrets of their own shattered pasts.

**Available wherever books are sold or
at penguin.com**